Praise for Hot Mess

'I'd need the fingers and toes of all the Tinder dates that Ellie Knight goes on in *Hot Mess* – and then some – to count the times I laughed out loud while reading this bawdy broad of a book. More lifestyle-affirming than *Bridget Jones*, I loved it!' Sarah Knight, author of *The Life Changing Magic of Not Giving a F*ck*

'The most relatable book I've read in years – funny, real, filthy, if you liked *Fleabag* and *Broad City*, you'll love this' *Heat*

'*Hot Mess* is one of the funniest, warmest books I've ever read. Heroine Ellie is a loveable, likeable everywoman and I laughed and sighed with recognition as I turned every page. A truly lovely and lively debut'
Daisy Buchanan, author of *How to Be a Grown-Up*

'Lucy Vine is always hilarious and with *Hot Mess* she's channelling her unique pithy tone into shining a light on the daily toils of being single and millennial. I'd swipe right for *Hot Mess*' *Grazia*

'The funniest thing I have read in a very, very long time. Ellie Knight is your new single soul sister and the perfect antidote to nosy relatives constantly asking when you're going to meet someone "nice"' *Cosmopolitan*

Lucy Vine is a freelance journalist based in London, who regularly writes and edits for the likes of *Grazia*, *Heat*, *Cosmo*, *Stylist* and *Marie Claire*. She also writes a weekly newsy column for *Grazia Daily*. Fed up with seeing the happily-ever-afters in films, she decided to write her own and her debut, *Hot Mess*, is the result.

Follow her on Twitter @Lecv

hot mess

LUCY VINE

First published in Great Britain in 2017 by Orion Books,
an imprint of The Orion Publishing Group Ltd
Carmelite House, 50 Victoria Embankment,
London EC4Y 0DZ

An Hachette UK company

3 5 7 9 10 8 6 4

A CIP catalogue record for this book is
available from the British Library.

ISBN 978 1 4091 7220 8

Typeset by Input Data Services Ltd, Somerset

Printed and bound by CPI Group (UK) Ltd, Croydon, CR0 4YY

www.orionbooks.co.uk

hot mess

As you know, I've been seeing a "therapist" lately and I wanted to let you know it's going very well. She is very nice and has a lot of framed "certificates" on her wall. I've "attached" some pictures of them for you. As part of our conversations, she suggested I start writing a "diary", and I've been enjoying it so much, I decided I am now going to write a "novel". I started last night and it's going very well. I am very proud of both of you and love you equally and thought you might like to read the "novel" as I go along. Here is the first "chapter", which I wrote last night. I stayed up until 10.30 p.m.!!!!!!!!!! Do not tell your Aunt Susie or Psychic Sharon because they said could they come over for tea and I said I was having an early night.

Love you both and I'm very proud of you both.

Best wishes,
Dad

---

75 HUES OF TONY
A novel, by Alan Bernard Knight

Once you've seen Tony Braxton, you can never forget his face. He has intense eyes that are like liquid coffee with no milk in it and an erotic nose. His mouth is that of a man who knows all the words in the whole dictionary but also knows to stay silent when his wife is having one of her difficult moods which she does actually have quite a lot even though Tony handles it really well. He may be almost sixty, but his physique is that of a much younger man who doesn't worry about the gym very much but can hold some weight in his stomach area without looking like he's let himself go even when his grown-up children say he's let himself go. To sum up: he is very handsome and gets a lot of compliments on his calves. He uses the step machine in his living room while he's watching the telly almost every day.

Tony has been going through a difficult stage in his life recently. His wife, Anita, has been extra moody and has even talked about leaving him which is clearly a strange idea – just look at his calves! He's been incredibly sensitive with Anita's moods and has had two separate and very lengthy – at least fifteen minutes each – conversations with her last Wednesday and Friday during the advert breaks of *The Chase* to discuss why she would do such a thing. But alas, he has not been successful. Tony arrives home that Friday evening after a long day at work, ready for nut roast and chicken night to find Anita's bags gone and a letter with *Tony* written on the front waiting for him by the landline telephone, which he still uses because he used to work for BT and he doesn't want landlines to die out altogether.

The letter from next to the landline is devastating. Anita wants a divorce and while she appreciates that he is the best man she could ever meet and he has always been very helpful around the house, unfortunately she no longer feels she deserves him and feels she should look for a lesser and probably much older man without an erotic nose to cook nut roast for. Tony is very, very upset. He is secure enough in his masculinity to have a little cry but first he remembers that he's really quite hungry so he goes to look around the kitchen for food.

Inside of the kitchen that he went into, he is surprised to find his neighbour, Wanda, waiting for him in a very casual way leaning on the kitchen counter. She is wearing a very fetching jumper that Tony recognises from the Boden catalogue that he recently read on the toilet. Wanda says hello and looks immediately down to Tony's calves, which are on display because he's wearing shorts because it's been quite sunny even though it's only February. He can tell she is impressed and he knows that either a compliment is coming now or else Wanda is about to tell him why she's here.

'You have such shapely calves, Tony,' says Wanda. 'And let me now tell you why I'm here.'

He was right.

'Anita told me she was leaving you, which is a strange idea, just look at your calves and your liquid coffee eyes. I thought "poor Tony" and rushed straight over to cook dinner for you. What would you like?' Tony thinks about it for a good five minutes while Wanda makes it clear that she admires his very attractive thinking face. At last Tony makes his decision and tells Wanda his decision and it is that he would like nut roast and chicken for dinner. Luckily for them both, they have all the ingredients for this dinner because it is nut roast and chicken night, so Wanda immediately springs into action, moving around the kitchen like a beautiful Nigella Lawson, who Tony has often admired basting her chicken. Tony is hoping Wanda will also be like Mary Berry because Tony usually likes cheesecake to follow his nut roast on a Friday evening. Anyway, when it is finally ready, Tony and Wanda sit down to eat dinner together in front of the telly, and then Wanda says something that is set to change Tony's life FOREVER even though he doesn't yet know that.

'Tony,' says Wanda. 'Would you like to come to my book club tomorrow?'

Their eyes meet and Tony senses that his life is set to change FOREVER.

END SCENE

2

10.10 a.m. Monday, 17 February
Location: My actually-quite-nice office at design firm The Hales. It's big and airy with glass walls. At one end of the open plan office there's a big TV screen and sofas for, y'know, totes casual coffee breaks. There's also a table football that literally no one has ever used but it helps gives the place a real media-twat vibe.

I've been staring at an InDesign document on my computer screen for the last forty minutes, achieving new levels of nothingness. Every time I try to focus on work, I feel another awful, hot flush of humiliation about Friday night creep up my neck. When I woke up late on Saturday, still fully dressed, with eyes glued together from congealed make-up, I had a grand total of eight missed calls from Jennifer and four furious voicemails, all reminding me in very specific terms that I am a pathetic loser who ruins – quote – everything. My hangover was next level, and as I crawled to the loo to be sick, pieces of the night before came flooding back. The flashbacks kept coming throughout the day as Jen tried to ring me several more times and I kept ignoring her.

I didn't need to hear her tell me I had failed again. That I'm stupid. That I'll be alone forever. That Martin is a perfectly good name.

And I really didn't need anyone else's help with the looming self-hated.

*

Oh fuck, Jackie's coming over to my desk. Jackie is the office manager and sees herself as my 'work mother'. She's always telling people this, but the only real evidence of this familial relationship is our constant bickering, the way she tells me what to do even though she has nothing to do with my department, and the fact that we basically hate each other. Other than that, she's a pretty standard human being: married, two teenage boys, thinks I'm broken because I'm single. Standard. She's that co-worker everyone hates because she won't stop looking at your computer screen when she's near your desk. Reading your emails, scanning whatever you're working on (for me that means Instagram stalking ex-boyfriends). You know those people, they're dreadful.

Right now, her excuse is to ask me something about how to enter a key code as if I know how – as if anyone does – and she's scanning the document I've done nothing to. When I first started here three years ago, I found it so infuriating, I would actually try to awkwardly cover my screen or distract her by waving one hand as I talked. I tried leaving my desk, pointedly minimising all my open windows but nothing worked. So now we're in a stand-off, where she keeps looking, and I find new and inventive ways to piss her off. Until recently, that mostly involved Google-imaging 'funny looking cocks' whenever I saw her approaching, but last week I stepped up my game and just wrote 'Fuck off Jackie' in a word doc in bright red, positioning it centre screen. She did not like that.

I would say it's weird I haven't been sacked yet, but my boss is a very nice man. Very, very nice. And therefore, completely terrible at his job. He cannot stand any kind of confrontation, which I find very entertaining. After FuckOffJackie-Gate, he eventually called me into his office where he was sweating like I have never seen a person sweat. 'How are you doing just a catch up, just a catch up,' he said, dabbing at his face with his sleeve.

'Yep, all fantastic, as ever, Derek,' I replied, ducking the flying droplets.

'Great great. Er . . . so . . . you're happy with everything? Happy with how your work is going?'

'Yes, Derek, very happy. Are you happy with my work?'

'Oh goodness, yes! The clients love you and that last project you did was . . . very happy very happy, I mean . . . good. Um . . .'

We sat there for a few minutes, silently, and I felt a little sorry for him – his neck was pooling and his shirt was gradually changing colour as the sweat spread across his chest – but I couldn't bring myself to help him.

'Anything else you need today, Derek?'

'Um, no no . . . well . . . no no.' I got up to leave and he panicked. 'It's just . . . er, Jackie . . . Jackie Jackie Jackie . . .'

'Yes?'

'Jackie wasn't sure if she . . . how are you getting on with Jackie?' he tried so desperately.

I gave him a thumbs up. 'She's in my top five people in this place, Derek.'

'Oh! Good! Good! That's . . . good. I'll tell her we had this chat. It's just . . . did you . . . you . . . Jackie said . . . Jackie Jackie Jackie.'

I sighed. 'Is this about the Word doc that said fuck off Jackie?'

'Yes!' His relief was palpable.

I smiled. 'I didn't do it,' I said sweetly, eyes wide and daring him to challenge me. Of course he didn't, he just stared at me helplessly until I offered to return to my desk. He just nodded sadly, aware of his own failings. Poor guy.

But that was a couple of weeks ago and Jackie, clearly past it, is standing over me at my desk.

'How was your weekend?' she asks, all innocent-eyed.

Aha, now I see. The key code question was an excuse. We'll get to the real reason for her hovering now.

'It was great,' I say, cautiously. 'Thank you for asking, Jackie. How was yours?'

'Oh, Colin took me for dinner to a wonderful restaurant on Valentine's Day, but five minutes in, he had an allergic reaction to the salmon, so we ended up on the floor with an epi-pen, and then in A&E for the next seven hours. When we eventually got home it turned out the boys had wrecked the place so I spent the rest of the weekend cleaning and ordering new plant pots from Argos.' She pauses dramatically. 'But at least I wasn't on my *own* on a day like Valentine's. It must've been much, much worse for you. I can't imagine having to be all *alone*, with *no one* – like you are. I'm so sorry, Eleanor.' Her smile is syrupy. She is drunk with delight and faux sympathy, awkwardly apologising like someone has died. And certainly, my dignity is on its last legs.

I breathe carefully, screaming inside as I return her smile and say casually, 'Actually, Jackie, I had a really great weekend. I had so much sex, with so many different gigantic cocks, that I now have cystitis. Excuse me, won't you? I have to go drink some cranberry juice and then piss more blood.'

I skip away as she scowls, muttering something about telling Derek.

I'd love to see him try and have *that* conversation with me.

In the office bathrooms – picture your primary school loo – I stare at my reflection. Even three days on, I am yellow with post-binge-drinking jaundice, and my dark eye bags are threatening to become dark whole-face bags. Sighing, I pull out my phone to check for messages. I don't want to go back to my desk and I consider trying to do a poo just to kill an extra five minutes. But I know it won't work. The only time my bowels are cooperative is during my period, when I will poop seventeen times a day. Sophie and I keep each other updated on our poo tally during periods. It gets pretty competitive but I always come out on top. It's the one area of my life I get to win, even if it's only once a month.

The bathroom door slams open and Maddie is shrieking my name. 'Did you tell Ursula that you had sex this weekend? Is it true – was it that date? – or were you just trying to upset her?'

We call Jackie 'Ursula', after the evil sea witch with killer lipstick (it is a good shade, I'll give her that) from *The Little Mermaid*. It's because Ursula has so many tentacles in everything and is basically trying to rule the ocean/The Hales and King Triton/Derek is afraid of her. Plus, she wears these long, floaty black dresses and is obsessed with her garden. We haven't yet found any evidence that she makes deals with mermaids and then turns them into shrivelled up brown, bug-eyed things, but WE ARE WORKING ON THAT.

'Just trying to start an office war,' I say, giving her a long hug. 'And I can't talk about the Friday date yet – it's too humiliating. I'm in the denial stage.'

'Oh, shame. I was excited to hear about it,' says a crestfallen and slightly squeezed-too-hard Maddie. She loves hearing about my dating life. She's been with her boyfriend, Ben, for thirteen years – literally since they were fifteen years-old – and is constantly afraid he's going to propose. It's got to the point now where she's started refusing to go on holiday with him because she thinks he might get down on one knee on a beach somewhere. And once a week she rifles through his sock drawer to check for hidden rings that she insists she would throw away. She loves him – of course she does – but she's also gripped by this fear of having met her 'one' so young. What if she's missed out on other, sexier ones? Other possibilities, other romances, other penises. So ours is a friendship based totally on Maddie's desperate need for single-people stories. She's fairly explicit about the vicarious nature of this, and occasionally asks me would I mind please please please having sex with Aaron from the postroom so she can pretend she did it. 'Let me know when you're ready to tell me about it?' she says pleadingly, and then pauses, before asking me for what must be the seven-millionth-no-exaggeration time. 'Are you still definitely going next Friday?'

Maddie doesn't get out much for things like parties. She and Ben bought a dog, Alfred, six months ago who they treat like a needy desperate baby. *Worse* than a needy desperate baby. They read multiple parenting books in preparation and slept in shifts for months so Alfred the dog wouldn't have to be alone. It's been a very difficult period because apparently Ben's into 'attachment parenting', while Maddie says that the dog should have a regular bedtime and sleep in his own room. Yes, the dog has his own room. It's caused some tension, and Maddie keeps trying to tell me how damaging helicopter parenting can be for a dogchild. And I keep trying to tell her how damaging this conversation is for our friendship.

I laugh. 'Of course I am,' I reply, squeezing her hand reassuringly. 'Even if you weren't making me, it's pretty much a three-line whip, isn't it? It's the first time I've ever seen Derek put his foot down about anything.'

The Friday in question is a work event (I say 'event' because I refuse to use the word 'party' after 'work'). It's the official launch of a national art competition and The Hales is one of about fifty sponsors. Which means there will be a hundred guests who think they're being 'fun' because they're not wearing a tie, and will pretend to be drunk so they've got an excuse to dance and flirt with each other. That's despite the 'drinks table' – which will consist of seven bottles of Jacob's Creek white wine – totally running out of alcohol by 7.02 p.m., at which point we will all drink from jugs of Robinson's Summer Fruits squash and pretend we're having the best night ever.

I'm looking forward to it.

Maddie and I stroll back to our desks together, and she tells me about Alfred's latest behavioural problems and how his therapist is at his wit's end. I nod supportively and slump back down at my desk. As Maddie wanders off, I sigh loudly and other sighs echo back at me from around the room. Everyone's feeling the pressure over a new project we've been pitching for. Derek wants some sketch concepts outlined ASAP, but I seriously cannot be fucked. I want to shout that across the room but then I remember that they do technically pay me to be here. The Hales is a design company that produces children's literature; books, magazines, posters, educational pamphlets, that kind of thing. The office is mostly made up of men over fifty – which you're thinking seems creepy, but that's just sexism and ageism. In reality, it's creepy because they're all creepy people.

My job here is as an illustrator. In theory. But there rarely seems to be any illustrating involved. It's all just meetings with clients to pretend I'm impressed by their terrible ideas ('What about if this character is a pig?' 'Could we make this character's nose look more like a pig's nose?' 'Did you know pigs are smarter than humans?? I read it somewhere.' I blame Peppa Pig for this bullshit).

It's mostly fine, but it's not exactly my dream gig. I did an art degree – which *is* a real degree OK GRANDMA GLADYS? – and for years I thought about becoming an actual, real life artist. I did a lot of painting at home – big, colourful profiles on huge canvases – before I moved into The Shithole, where my box room barely fits the squeaky single bed. But I won't be stuck there for much longer. Once the old place is sold, I can find somewhere just for me. Maybe I'll even have my own studio flat and I can paint the walls bright colours that everyone will complain hurt their eyes. I smile at the thought and then remind myself it's unlikely to happen any time soon.

I think again about asking Dad if I can move back in, and suddenly my phone rings – it's him. If you're thinking that's a coincidence, it's not really. It is coming up to eleven a.m., so *of course* this is the obvious time for a person to ring another person who they know works regular office hours.

Dad retired early a year ago and it's like he immediately forgot how work, y'know, works. He's always baffled – BAFFLED – that I'm not able to chat at 3.40 p.m.on a Thursday afternoon about who's trying to murder whom on *Coronation Street* this week. Usually I let it go to voicemail and ring him back at lunch but all this cock talk has got me in the mood to speak to my dad (that is a disgusting joke – don't worry, I feel ashamed). I press answer and wander casually into reception, making eye contact with Ursula across the room, daring her to tell on me.

'Hello Dad,' I say warmly.

'Lenny? Is that you? It's Dad.'

'Yes, it is the daughter whose mobile phone you rang. I see you're calling on the landline, good for you. Last one left I'd say.'

'How do you know that?'

He sounds amazed. He does use a mobile too, so it's always entertaining that he's so confused by their various abilities. But then, he's confused by most things about the modern world. My dad is the cutest thing. He's short and round, with huge, bushy grey hair – mostly sprouting from his eyebrows – and looks quite a lot like a middle-aged woman from the back. And, indeed, the front. He gets called 'madam' by strangers quite a lot, and last week a man wouldn't let him into the gents at his local pub. He kept pointing him towards the ladies and they had this awkward stand off until Dad gave up and wandered off.

I ignore his question.

'How are you, Dad?'

'Oh, I'm fine, love. Just fancied a chat.'

'OK well that's very nice, but I am at work . . .'

'ARE you? But it's ... (I know he's checking the wall clock) (yes, he's also the last person in the world to own a wall clock) ... it's 11 a.m., Lenny?'

I'm not totally sure what his point is.

I clear my throat. 'Maybe I could call you back at lunchtime?' I offer.

'That would be nice. But not when I'm watching my soaps, if that's OK, Lenny.'

Hey, do you remember when *Neighbours* and *Home and Away* were on twice a day? Once at lunchtime, and once around tea? Dad liked watching it with his lunch, so now he records it (ON VHS, I SHIT YOU NOT) and watches it during its old time slot.

He pauses. 'Although I could watch them later on if need be?'

This is extra kind of him. I know he likes his routine.

'No, that's fine,' I say and then pause. 'Dad, are you sure you're OK?'

'Yes! Yes. Actually I do quite want to talk to you if possible. It's something my therapist has encouraged me to speak to you and Jenny about. Don't worry about ringing, but would you be able to pop round this weekend?'

If this is coming from his therapist, it could literally be anything – maybe his tomato plant isn't coming along as well as it usually does.

'Saturday? Of course I will, Dad.'

Honestly, I go over pretty much every Saturday anyway, he doesn't have to act like I've abandoned him.

'Lovely! Candice says she's going to make a cake for you. You'll like it.'

She recently put tomatoes in a fruitcake – I won't like it.

'What a treat,' I say enthusiastically. 'Right, I better get back to my desk now, Dad. I'll see you on Saturday, love you.'

'Love you, Lenny.'

I return to my desk to continue not working.

3

6.54 p.m. Friday, 21 February
Location: Outside my best friend Sophie Ellis' beautiful red brick house, hidden away from the main road by a row of huge old trees. The house is in the middle of getting a major basement excavation for a 'games room', so it's currently covered in scaffolding, because – dahling – everyone in Surrey has a games room in the basement. But trust me, underneath all the ladders and men showing their bumcracks, it's a really nice house.

Sophie opens the door looking pristine. Her long hair is neatly tied to one side and flowing over her shoulder like she's Princess Jasmine, and her pressed white shirt is actually white. I mean, unlike every white item that I own, which are all more yellow-y grey. On her bottom half are what I think might be chinos but I don't really know what chinos are. Whatever is happening, it's working. God, my best friend is fabulous. Sometimes I just show strangers pictures of her so they can marvel at the perfection.

Sophie swishes her hair and shrieks hello, pulling me in for a hug, and for a second I wish I'd spent some of that half hour train ride applying make-up. To be fair to me, I was pressed into someone's nipple for most of the trip and I don't think nipple guy would've liked a ring of lipgloss to take home to his wife/husband/interfering mother. I've come here straight from work, always thrilled at the prospect of seeing Sophie. And, of course, Thomas, who has just appeared from the living-room, laughing and pushing past Sophie for a bear hug. He picks me up and fireman lifts me inside, as Sophie sings 'Here comes the bride', and I joyfully kick my legs and add solemnly, 'All fat and wide!'

Thomas White is in love with me. Definitely. Everyone says so. I think it's mostly a fancying of convenience because we've been friends for so long, and everyone else is coupled up, but I will take any crushing I can get. We've never talked about the situation, and I think again now, as he puts me down in the kitchen and pats me on the head, that I hope we never do. I adore Thomas, totally and completely, but I'm pretty sure that's all there is to it. And I don't really want to be forced to analyse it too closely. Plus, it's a dumb cliché, but it would ruin the friendship trio, and I'd never forgive myself for that.

Sophie shouts that she'll fetch me a drink and orders me to say hello to her daughter, Ciara, who is aged somewhere between a couple of months and a couple of years (I checked my phone calendar – apparently she's twenty months old, who knew?), and sitting quietly in the living-room. I wave in the direction of *Frozen*, duty done, and return to the alcohol Sophie's pouring. We cheers to the prosecco and to being in the suburbs where it's all anyone drinks, and for the next few minutes we shout over each other in that way old friends do. Complaining about work, scrutinising the weather, and asking after Sophie's new people – Ciara, and Ciara's dad, Ryan – who are only really 'new' compared to us.

Sophie and I have been best friends since we were thirteen, when her Russian-Latvian-African heritage proved too much for a group of unevolved fifteen-year-old boys to cope with.

I'd seen her around the playground, as one does, but we met properly when I found her crying one day in the biographies section of the school library. So obviously I started crying too.

'Is this about Ryan Atwood?' I asked her after a few minutes of quiet sobbing, thinking about the dramatic cliff-hanger on the previous night's episode of *The OC*.

Of course it wasn't about Ryan Atwood, she explained, it was about some first-class playground racism. I don't remember what I said, but I know I checked she was an *OC* fan before I offered any comfort re: the racism. We cried a bit more together, and then we decided, there on the floor, that we should be best friends. I promised to protect her from the boys with the help of my recent arrivals – hey, overnight boobs! – and their powers of distraction, and she promised to help me locate Adam Brody in real life and seduce him, again, probably with the help of my overnight boobs. The problem though was my fairly strict onc-in-one-out policy when it came to friendship, so Sophie and I went to visit Thomas over by the maths block. Thomas and I had lived next door to each other as kids and been best friends ever since, but he wasn't really into *The OC*, which was starting to be a deal-breaker for me. I explained the situation and he was pretty fine about no longer hanging out, but then Sophie suggested maybe we could all be best friends? She said we could be a trio and she had all three costumes for the Powerpuff Girls at home that we could wear to fight crime! But Thomas didn't like that idea and said friends was enough. And so we became a three, and even though we didn't have Powerpuff magic, we did have the combined super power of my thirty-two double Ds and Thomas' popular-boy position as striker on the football team. The racists – along with the rest of the school's population – pretty much let us be after that.

Sixteen years later and we're still mostly only into each other. Sophie's husband, New Ryan (not Atwood), turned up a few years ago, but he knows he's not really in the club. He's really lovely – Thomas and I thoroughly approve of him, or, obviously, there would've been no marriage – but he understandably feels left out when we're around, so he tends to clear out on a Friday night to make way for us. You can't blame him. Who wouldn't feel out of the loop listening to three adults heading down a school-related rabbit hole, discussing the sexual inappropriateness of Mr Trump the science teacher, who once tried it on with all three of us aged sixteen, when we met him in a pub on a Friday night in town. (Sophie was up for it but we talked her out of it) (he was at least fifty) (and his wife was literally at the bar) (he also had a neck beard) (but, like, no other facial hair?) (It was so weird, like he forgot to shave his neck when doing his face. So weird right?). Ryan also doesn't get it when we call him New Ryan, and gets even more confused when we explain about Ryan Atwood. He wasn't really into telly when he was younger, so cultural references are lost on him. He's dead smart – an accountant for, like, billionaires – but he has these weird holes in his general knowledge. We call it the 'genius gap' and whenever he is here, we sit around asking him about stuff he hasn't discovered about the world we live in. Last week we added *Friends* and crumpets to the list of basic things he's missed.

Sophie's cooked us a salmon stir-fry and over dinner talk turns, as it generally does, to my life as a single person. Sophie's already heard the excruciating detail of last week's non-date, but Thomas listens, fascinated, to my woeful failure. He doesn't say anything when I tell him about Cassie shouting 'shithead' into the voicemail of a man who was trying to have dinner with his grandparents, and he nods solemnly when I tell him how Jen shouted at me for eighteen solid minutes when she eventually got me on the phone. It was a new record and she awarded me a week long 'sibling penalty'. Jen gives penalties to people who piss her off, it's her thing. It's a bit like being in adult detention or getting grounded, but in this case I'm not allowed to call or text her for a week. If I do, that time period will be extended to a month. I finish up explaining and pause, waiting for lovely, lovely Thomas to comfort me, or offer some wise and reassuring words.

He leans in seriously and, after another beat, says, 'Can I have the barmaid's number? She sounds great.' I growl and flick food at him. Sophie tuts at me like I'm a badly behaved child, but we all know Ciara would never behave so childishly (although, if someone was feeding me meals with an aeroplane-spoon maybe I wouldn't make such a mess either).

Sophie pats my hand affectionately. 'Try not to worry about it, these things happen. At least you never have to see him again. And Jen will forgive you eventually.' Then Sophie's face lights up. 'What about Tinder?!' she says excitedly, like she is the first person to think of such a thing and not, in fact, the six-hundred-millionth this month.

I shrug. I tried a bunch of dating apps after my break-up with Tim, and found the process really fun and then horribly, horribly depressing within the space of eight minutes. Or weeks. Not sure. Time blurs inside the Tinder vortex.

Unfortunately my shrug has been taken as consent (it's

like a drunk campus party in here), and Sophie has already snatched my phone. Thomas shuffles over next to her and the pair of them start giggling about photos and location ranges. Since I clearly don't have a role to play in any of this, I go stare at Ciara in the other room. *Frozen* has finished and she's now giggling over a copy of *The Hungry Caterpillar* that she can't even read. I gave her this copy (I'm such a thoughtful godparent). But one day I hope she'll like it because it was one of my favourites when I was little. I loved the bright colours and the delicious-sounding food. I remember making Mum read it to me over and over again. Ciara giggles again as she sticks her chubby little finger into the holes.

'I think that's funny too,' I tell her, crouching down and poking one of the other holes. She looks up at me and beams, reaching out her fat little fists for my face.

Isn't it funny when your friends have babies? You have this tight knit group – people you've carefully selected over the course of your lifetime, who you like and want to spend your time with – and then one of them has a baby and you no longer have that choice. This tiny new person is an automatic part of your gang and you better hope they're cool, because even if they're not, they're one of you now.

It's a good job Ciara is so nice. She fits in very well, partly, I think, because she leaves us to it and Soph doesn't change her nappies in front of me. I pick her up and sniff her head. People talk about how babies smell, don't they? Especially if you're a girl – you're told that sniffing a baby will make your womb throb and throb, until you can't help but Google local sperm banks.

That doesn't happen to me.

I put her down, wishing I felt more than I do. I think she's cute as anything – and I know from having met other babies, that this one is the easiest ever – but she doesn't make me want one. And I don't know what that means for me. I feel a flash of frustration with myself. I want to want one, but I just can't imagine a time when I will ever feel grown-up enough to be a parent.

When Sophie told me a couple of years ago that she was trying for a baby I was in such awe. The idea that she could see herself as responsible enough to grow another person and put that person out into the world is . . . just unfathomable. Sophie! Sophie, who texts me to boast about her poos. Sophie, who slept with three guys in one twenty-four hour period when she was twenty-two (the year of The Great Slut Race). Sophie, who once sent me a close-up picture of her nipple and tried to convince me it was a UFO. That person is now a mother to a real-life human being. And she doesn't even seem worried that Ciara could go on to become the next Hitler.

Ciara puts *The Hungry Caterpillar* on her head and waves at me, but she's not fooling anyone. 'You could be Hitler one day,' I whisper and she nods agreeably.

Ciara and I quietly watch two episodes of *Peppa Pig* (George and Peppa are sooo Ross and Monica) (OK, I have no idea what's happening on this show) cuddled up on the sofa. She starts to nod off and I wonder if sucking my thumb would be as comforting as she's making it look, but then Sophie starts shrieking at me to come back. She wants me to look at a man wearing an elephant mask. To clarify; an elephant mask that he is not wearing on his face.

'Is it wrong that I find it a bit attractive?' she asks, laughing and flicking through the rest of his porn star photos, each featuring the elephant mask in some different, imaginative way.

Thomas shakes his head, 'Uh-oh Sophie, is New Ryan not putting out much these days?'

She tuts again and I take my phone back. It seems that I've just matched with Elephant Man, along with an impressive sixty-two other prospective daters.

'We swiped yes to everyone,' Thomas explains helpfully. 'I personally swiped at least two hundred men, so don't be flattered by the number of matches, that's actually only a small percentage of interest. Especially for a Friday night. It's peak Tinder time. You already have messages too.'

Oh hey, look at that, I do. Quite a lot.

There are nine messages that just say 'Hey'.

Three comparatively convoluted, 'Hey, how are you?' messages.

Seven 'Hey how r u' messages.

Two 'Ur so hot' messages.

And one that says 'Hey babe u around later', with no punctuation but plenty of emoticons tacked on the end.

Oh, here's another one. This charmer's just sent me a Gif of a dancing monkey. Which cannot be a compliment. Surely it can't?

I sigh and flick through the rest of my matches, rolling my eyes at my good friends, who seem so pleased with themselves. Sophie and Thomas have been indiscriminate with their right swipe, but there's still an awful lot of the same-looking dude in here. Seventy per cent of the men seem to be very angry about posing with tigers, and the other thirty per cent are topless selfies taken in the gym. I give Sophie a withering look and she shouts in my face, 'Don't judge a book,' because apparently she doesn't understand how Tinder works.

'Is there no one you're interested in?' she adds, disappointed. 'What about the topless guy in the gym?'

'Which one, exactly?' I say, showing her again the pile of posers.

Just then a man with murder in his eyes pops up. He's 'super liked' me and as I scroll down, I can see that Murder Eyes – AKA 'Steve' – has only one interest: Lady Gaga. His description reads, 'I've got a big heart and I'm into tickling people. If you can't be open minded and open hearted about that then you should just swipe left right now.' Thomas reaches across me and touches the heart button. We match, and Murdery Steve immediately sends me a message that reads, 'Your tits are huge.'

I feel so special.

Thomas snorts, 'He had that line ready.'

That might be as much 'dating' as I can handle for now. I click out of the app and put my phone face down on the dining table. 'Nooo,' says Sophie, pouting. So I pout back at her.

'Why aren't we forcing Thomas to do this too?' I complain and she looks surprised. It hadn't occurred to her, because of course nobody ever thinks about force feeding online dating to hot, single men.

'I don't need it,' Thomas says, giving me a smug grin and a wink. I exaggerate a dry heave and Sophie sighs, picking up my phone again.

'I just really want you to meet someone. I want to double date with you. I want New Ryan to have someone to talk to when we're all out together. I want to see you settled down and happy.'

'I am happy.'

She gives me a hard look. She doesn't believe me.

'Just give it a go for a few weeks?' she says, offering me back my phone. 'Go on a few dates, see what happens. Try for me?'

I laugh. 'OK fine.' Anything for an easy life, and if this will stop the nagging – not just from Sophie, but from the whole world – then bring it on. She claps excitedly and disappears to the kitchen to clear up.

I get it. I get why Sophie wants me to meet someone so badly. She thinks I'm incomplete without a partner, and that a happily ever after means a husband and a baby. Just like she has. She's been indoctrinated by society's stupid fantasy message. But it's more than that. I'm aware that – amazing as her life is – we both have our own version of FOMO. She worries about losing what we had, missing out on our fun nights out, on our old life. She is Sophie the mother and wife now, someone new, and she has to work out who that is and whether I'm coming with her. And I need to work that out too. Am I being left behind? Will I be replaced by these new 'mum friends' of hers, who understand parts of her better than I could? I am a tiny bit scared because I don't know if I necessarily fit into this conventional, suburban thing she has going on with Ciara and New Ryan. And I know it would be easier for her if I met her halfway, with A Someone on my arm. So I will try, I'm willing to try. It can't be that bad, right? Maybe I'll even meet someone great.

By the time we've cleared up, it's nearly eleven and Sophie asks me if I want to stay over. I think about The Shithole waiting for me and nod my head, yes please.

I've been living in the three-bed flat, known universally as The Shithole (TS), for nine months now. It's a run-down mess on a council estate, with two other inhabitants – Josh Day and Gemma Something. I genuinely don't know her surname because I've only seen her once from the back. Josh says she's a medical supplies driver, doing night shifts, and that's why she's never around. She's awake when we're sleeping. But I'm not even totally convinced she exists. I talk myself in and out of the conspiracy theories: like, maybe Josh keeps his dead ex-girlfriends in that room, like a council estate Bluebeard. Maybe it's his secret Christian Grey sex dungeon where he stores his nipple clamps. Or maybe it's where he shoots his pornos. Honestly, that boy is capable of anything. Or maybe it's me – maybe I've *Beautiful Mind*ed 'Gemma' into being.

On the other hand, I cannot believe it's possible that Josh and I are solely responsible for the level of clogging in that shower plug hole. So she must be real. Either way, I hate her. I hate the whole place.

I'm living there temporarily. Tem. Por. Rar. Ily. I keep repeating that to myself so I don't get too depressed about the rusting broken kitchen, piled high with washing up, or the bathroom that smells like it does, however many bottles of Domestos I empty down the loo. I hate how small it is, I hate how dark it is, and I hate the tube seat-type décor and threadbare carpeting. I hate the black mould spreading across the living-room ceiling that the landlord genuinely tried to tell us was 'designer wallpaper'. I hate the damp, musty smell that follows me from room to room. I hate the way it clings to my skin and hair, like a bad shampoo. Every day I come home, put my key in the shitty lock and open the broken door, knowing it's a miracle we've survived another full day without being robbed (but when you live next door to drug dealers, thieves tend to give you a wide berth). It grinds me down, but I also know it's my own fault.

We were three weeks into living in our very own lovely, brilliant flat – one we'd somehow wrangled an actual mortgage for – when I broke up with Tim. And of course, because it was all my doing, I was the one who volunteered to move out. My dad wasn't so far away, so I stayed with him. But it only took a couple of months before I couldn't stand his daily humming of the *Neighbours* theme tune any more, and moved into the only place I could afford – The Shithole. It was the first place I spotted on SpareRoom and I know I should've looked at more places, but it was so cheap. I was broke and my hormones took over when the door opened and I saw Josh. Josh is hot – like Poldark levels of hot – so I said I'd take the room before I'd even seen past the peeling hallway. It took me a week to realise that below Josh's hotness lies a total dick. Moody, antagonistic, with a constant revolving door of hot blondes coming in and out like he's Leonardo DiCuntprio. He's a total wannabe hipster who clearly dreams of one day upgrading to the coolest parts of east London, where he will no longer have to hide his tiny fucking beard comb and can wear scarves with abandon.

But still so hot.

I hate that I fancy him.

Obviously I won't do anything about it.

I cannot be yet another girl he knows he can have.

As if he'd want to have sex with me anyway, I'm not blonde or thin.

But still.

Definitely will not have sex with him.

But he is so hot.

Gah. I just wish Gemma was around more, or literally at all, so I could sit in the living-room with him without feeling like my vagina needs handcuffing down.

Either way, this is only temporary. Tim's going to put our place on the market any day now, and with my share of the money I'll be able to get somewhere better, maybe even buy somewhere again. I just need to hold on. I need to hold on and not have sex with sexy Josh. No shitting where you eat – that's what they say, don't they? Except, honestly, shitting where I eat could only improve the sanitation levels of TS. I need to hold on another few months without making The Shithole an Awkward Shithole.

Wah.

From: Alan Knight <Alanknightinshiningarmour@BTInternet.co.uk>
To: Eleanor.knight@gmail.com, Jennifer.seevy@hotmail.com

21st February

Alan Knight
106 Castle Rise
Judfield
East Sussex
TN22 5UN

Dear Eleanor and Jennifer,

I hope you are both very well and enjoyed the start of my "novel"?

Lenny – I am looking forward to seeing you tomorrow. Thank you for your "feedback". I know you were only joking when you said I've "let myself go" all those times in real life but please remember that this is a "novel" and therefore this is "fiction".

Jenny – I hope you, Andrew and Milly are very well. I love you all very much. Thank you for your email too, but I didn't understand what "UNSUBSCRIBE" meant.

Here is the next part. I think it's getting very exciting and I hope you will agree. I went over to Candice and Peter's last night and Candice said she thought I was very "talented", which I thought was very kind of her. I also read some to my "therapist" who said she was "very pleased" with my progress. I think it is helping me feel more "positive" about life. I have decided not to mention this to Psychic Sharon or Aunt Susie because I am worried they will shout at me about not consulting them, so please do not bring it up the next time you are having your palms read.

Love you both very much and I'm very proud of you both.

Best wishes,
Dad

---

75 HUES OF TONY
A novel, by Alan Bernard Knight

When Tony arrives at the Book Club the next day after Wanda had invited him the day before he has no idea his life is about to change FOREVER. Of course, Tony is very perceptive and he had sensed that it might a little bit, but he didn't know for sure. He has come along really dressed to the nines in his most stylish but also very comfy tracksuit that really highlights his calves that everyone comments on. He was previously in a tiny bit of a bad mood because the downstairs shower at his house is currently out of action thanks to some really aggressive lime scale that Anita has abandoned him with. He is very disappointed with Anita about this and very nearly wrote her a very cross email eloquently expressing this disappointment, but then he decided to be the better man because that is who Tony is all the time. Anyway, Tony was able to have a bath instead in the downstairs bathroom and his hair is still wet, which no one could argue really, really suits Tony. His wet hair complements his deep liquid eyes because they are both liquidy. Anyway, anyone looking at him right now – and there are ALWAYS people looking at Tony – would be comparing his appearance to that scene in James Bond where James Bond comes out of the ocean with similarly wet hair. Although Tony has that extra air of gravitas about him, being older and no doubt stronger than James Bond.

As Tony walks into the village hall, he counts ten women at the Book Club, including Wanda who is also there because she was the one who actually invited him. Tony feels a little overwhelmed because all the ten women are looking at him and seem impressed. He hasn't even tried to impress them but they seem impressed anyway and are no doubt comparing Tony Braxton to James Bond or to Captain James T Kirk. The women all crowd around him asking him questions about his recent single status and also mentioning his calves a lot – unsurprisingly!

'Oh Tony,' says one of the very attractive women, 'you smell superior to every other man I've smelled before. You smell like cinnamon.'

'Thank you, madam,' says Tony seductively, 'that is Anita's Christmas hand soap you are smelling, which I used as shampoo this morning because I could not find any shampoo and I appreciate you noticing.'

Then they ask him what he thought of the book and Tony realises he has forgotten to ask Wanda what the book they're discussing is, but he's a very well-read man, if he does say so himself. They tell him that it is a Stephen King book and he explains that he knows basically all the pages off by heart. In fact he wrote a dissertation on it at university even though he didn't need to and wasn't at university at that time but he still got an A* and it is now in the dissertation library as an example of amazing dissertations.

As Tony talks really compellingly, he looks around the room, because he can definitely multitask despite what Anita always said to him. His eye is drawn over the ladies' heads – because Tony is taller than all of the ten women – to another, eleventh woman in the corner standing alone by the Victoria sponges on a table which also has lots of other cakes and pots of tea on it. She is incredibly, incredibly attractive. She looks exactly like a young Helen Mirren except she is probably the same age as Tony, so it's not inappropriate that he finds her very attractive. He and the Helen Mirren lady stare at each other and the room fills up to the ceiling with sexual tension. It is clear that they really, really fancy each other and Tony feels an unfamiliar feeling. He is nervous! Tony is never nervous about anything!!

The other ten ladies all fall silent and turn to look at the Helen Mirren lady, and they are no doubt sensing all that sexual tension that has really, really filled up the room, even though the village hall is quite spacious. There is a really long silence and then Wanda suggests they all have a little sit down to continue talking about the book. As Tony sits down, he feels a presence right behind him and a really nice sultry voice that is all gravelly but also very feminine speaks.

'Please may I sit here next to you?'

It is the lady from the corner who looks like Helen Mirren and she is asking if she can sit here next to Tony. She also has an accent and Tony thinks it is probably Russian, which he recognises because he spent many years living in Russia and everywhere else in the world. Tony is a very well-travelled man, as well as being very well-read, as previously mentioned.

'Of course,' Tony says, really gracefully jumping up to pull the chair out for her. 'May I take your coat?' he says very gallantly even though she's not wearing a coat.

'No, thank you,' she says, because she's not wearing a coat, but it is clear she thinks it is very impressive that he is being so gallant.

'I am Svetlana,' she says in her deep but very feminine voice. 'You can call me Lana.'

She then pauses and then she says in a really knowing deep feminine voice, 'I know who you are. You are Tony, I have heard all about you.'

They look at each other deeply, like her voice, for a really long time.

Then Wanda, who is no doubt a bit jealous of the sexual tension that is something akin to a big sexual fog or some other type of sexual weather inside the village hall, suggests they all start talking about the book because that is why they are here, of course. For the next few minutes Tony forgets about trying to impress Svetlana because he is so involved in the discussion and everyone is very impressed with Tony for knowing so much about the book even though he didn't even know what the book was until today.

'You are so clever' says one woman who is very attractive but is definitely no Lana.

'I am so impressed with you for knowing so much about the book even though you didn't even know what the book was until today,' says another woman who is also very attractive, but again, just to emphasise, not as attractive as Svetlana.

When Tony finishes reading the last four chapters out to the group even though no one asked him to, he suddenly remembers Lana is sitting next to him and he looks at her. She is staring at him, incredibly aroused with really dilated pupils that indicate sexual arousal which he knows from Anita, who spent their entire marriage, all twenty-four hours a day with really dilated pupils. Svetlana makes Tony very nervous and he suggests everyone has a break so all the ladies can powder their noses as he knows they like to do. He is very sensitive like that. Lucky for Tony, he is the only man there, so he is able to visit the loo with ease while all the women have to queue up to use the ladies'.

In the loo Tony cannot help but admire his undeniably attractive frame in the mirror. Tony is a very modest man but even his exceptional modesty cannot deny the alluring shape of his erotic nose. His show-stopping tracksuit is almost glowing in the loo's dim lighting and Tony nods in the mirror, acknowledging his very impressive choice of outfit. When he comes back out of the loo, renewed with vigour and confidence, there is no sign of Lana and the ten other women all gather round him like freshly powdered hens. They are all saying that they are worried about him but it sure does seem like they might actually be really jealous.

'Svetlana is dangerous!' says one of the women. 'You must stay away from Svetlana!'

Another one says, 'She will hurt you, Tony, you must not talk to her any more!'

And then another one says, 'Tony, do you want to go into the cupboard under the stairs to discuss this a bit more?' And she is winking at him. Tony is used to this and gives her a provocative wink back but also says no thank you to her offer.

Then his neighbour Wanda takes Tony to one side and offers him some of the Victoria sponge that she made, which Tony says yes to because he did go on the step machine for ten minutes this morning before his bath.

'Tony,' says Wanda, nicely, 'you mustn't listen to all of that. You are a very attractive man, Tony, and many of the women here obviously desire you. I know you are a very clever, very wise, very intuitive man, Tony, and you must make your own decisions. Everyone here can see there is a big sexual fog between you and Svetlana, but all I ask is that you just be careful. That is all I ask, Tony, just be careful.'

'Who is she?' asks Tony, who always asks really insightful questions.

'She is called Svetlana,' says Wanda, helpfully. 'I think she is from Russia.'

Tony was right.

'Other than that, she is quite mysterious,' says Wanda. 'She runs her own company and she is very, very, very rich. She owns a helicopter and also the huge mansion at the edge of this village. I think I can tell that you like her, Tony, but just please be careful. We all care about you here at the Book Club that you are now a member of, and we don't want you to get hurt.'

Tony is intrigued, and just as he picks up his second slice of Victoria sponge, which is OK because he did do an hour on his step machine this morning while watching *Bargain Hunt*, he senses a presence and feels someone breathing sexily on his neck.

It is Svetlana!

'Hello, Tony,' she says.

Tony doesn't know what to say because she has such an effect on him, so he drops his Victoria sponge and then trips over a bit because the sexual fog engulfs him.

Svetlana smiles because his clumsiness really humanises him, and she starts stroking his arm. 'Tony,' she says, and she is pouting. 'Sorry for my mysterious disappearance just now, I was having a wee and there was a long queue for the ladies' loo. Anyway I came to ask you for help. I believe you used to work for BT, no? Would you please come to my house tomorrow to help fix my landline phone? It is broken somehow, I do not know how.'

Tony is flattered that Lana knows so much about him and also would trust him with such an important job. But he is also manly enough to admit that he is a bit scared of this woman who is so ravishing. Everyone has told him to stay away from this very dangerous and very rich woman although he doesn't know why. He has amazing instincts and his instincts are saying, 'Be careful, Tony!!!' He also has a lot of inner turmoil debating whether he should say yes or not. He has only just split up with Anita, after all, and he was hoping to use this time on his own to get in even better shape with the help of his step machine, hence the two hours on it this morning, and then also really get a handle on his gardening, even though his garden has already won awards for being so well kept. After all, Tony does like a well trimmed bush!! His other worry is that Lana does not look like the type of lady to cook nut roast and chicken for him on nut roast and chicken night, which is what he thought he would want in a second wife. But he cannot deny the very, very strong feelings he is now feeling towards Lana. The feelings he felt immediately when he saw her in the corner of the village hall. She is like a giant magnet, like those ones they use at the scrap yard to pick up old bangers. Much like a car, he cannot stop himself from drawing closer to Lana as he whispers seductively in her ear, 'Yes! I'll come to your house tomorrow.' She smiles and slips her number into his pocket, before leaving. At the door of the village hall she turns back and says, 'Until tomorrow then, Tony-who-smells-like-cinnamon.'

Tony cannot help but feel that, much like a car and the magnet, which is the same metaphor he used a minute ago, he is about to be crushed into a small cube, or possibly used for spare parts.

But maybe he likes that idea . . . or maybe he doesn't . . . or MAYBE HE DOES . . .

END SCENE

Lenny and Jenny! It's Dad here again. I really hope you enjoyed this latest "chapter"?! I know I've left you on a "cliffhanger" here, but I read an "article" that said you should do that for "dramatic effect". But I didn't want you to worry because I'm ALREADY working on the next "instalment". It will be with you shortly, so don't despair! Love you both.

4

12.34 p.m. Saturday, 22 February
Location: On a bench in Warner's Park, which is a huge expanse of green, with a feeble set of swings and a roundabout that no one ever uses. We're surrounded by pigeons and pigeon faecal matter – because there is an idiot around here who feeds them, even though there are signs all over the place saying please don't. Ugh, people.

There is a bird actually standing on my foot. He does not care, he totally does not care that I am a human who is bigger and more violent than him and I could crush him with my angry human fist.

I don't do that – I squeal and run in a circle.

Dad laughs and shoos the bird away. This happens every time we come here and I complain every time, but we continue to come pretty much every week. Dad loves this place. He brings his Yorkshire terrier, Lily, most days, and they sit among the shitting pigeons and chat to his fellow retiree passers-by. All the locals love Warner's Park, and every year or so, the neighbours gather together to launch a campaign to save it. They get really into it, start a petition, hand out leaflets at the local train station and have a protest, chanting 'Save our local park' outside the council office. The campaign is always an enormous success, and the council make some kind of official announcement that they have 'decided to support the community by protecting Warner's

Park' – because they never had any interest in destroying it anyway and the mayor likes having his picture in the local paper. Either way, the neighbourhood ends up having a big celebratory party round Psychic Sharon's house and Psychic Sharon ends up drunkenly pointing at couples and predicting their divorce. And then those couples get divorced because everyone's too scared to cross Psychic Sharon.

Actually, I have my own fond memories of this place. Most of which I haven't shared with Dad. He doesn't know, for example, that this is the park I vommed in at least once a week from the ages of thirteen to seventeen. And he doesn't know that over there is the ditch that eight of us from year ten all hid in that one time, frantically trying to dispose of off-brand cider after we became convinced that 'the pigs' and/or 'the fuzz' were coming to arrest us and throw us all in jail. Dad doesn't know those are the swings where Danny Arringford tried to finger me and I told him I couldn't because I didn't have a vagina – because I genuinely didn't think I did. Our sex ed lessons at school were so explicit and detailed that I'd decided, staring up at that horrifying white board, that there was no way I had all that stuff up in me. And then when Danny was really nice about it and said he wouldn't tell anyone about my lack of vagina, I went round telling everyone he was frigid with a tiny cock. I think Danny's homeless now.

It's changed a lot over the years. Not in terms of how it looks – actually it's literally the same, down to each blade of grass, thanks to the overbearing micro-management of self-appointed 'head landscaper' Psychic Sharon – but it's changed for me. It stopped being the fun, silly destination of a not-particularly-misspent youth and started being a place to escape the difficulties of adulthood. This is where I came to think and reflect about my stupid life. Where I sought out solitude after fights with Jen. It's where I came to escape from Dad's well-intentioned but overbearing questions after I split up from Tim. It's where I came to sit and cry about my mum.

I love this park, but they're not all fond memories.

Dad's talking.

'I'm very proud of you Lenny.'

Oh my God, he's so proud of me. He's constantly telling me and Jen this, ever since he started therapy, where he learned to speak Spiritual Dickhead, a language which includes phrases like 'high nurture intentional parenting' that helps 'foster feelings of safety and connectedness'. He now starts and ends every sentence explaining how proud he is of me, even though there is so very little to be proud of. I'm his single almost thirty-year-old daughter, with a job she barely tolerates, renting a room in The Shithole across the hall from a boy she has to try every day not to drop her (greying) knickers for.

He's probably not aware of that last part, but still.

'I'm proud of you too, Dad,' I say, patting his gloved hand. It's just something to say, isn't it?

'I was hoping to talk to you about something, if it's OK?'

I pause. When people ask in advance if they can say something, my usual policy is to say no. It's always something you don't want to hear and the fact that they're asking you permission means it's your fault if you don't like it. But short of getting up and leaving, there's not much else I can do here. I reply carefully. 'It's hard to answer that without knowing what you want to talk to me about. I mean, I do have some things I would rather not talk about with you.'

Danny Arringford.

Dad nods, looking worried. I don't think this is about Danny Arringford.

'Go on, Dad, tell me. It'll be OK,' I say resigned. Surely it can't be any worse than 75 *Hues of Tony* – reading your dad's thinly veiled attempt at *Fifty Shades of Grey* is one of the most uncomfortable experiences I've had. This week, at least. He turns to me on the bench, sinking his leg into a fresh blob of pigeon poo. Bugger. I'd been so carefully avoiding it and it's all over his trousers now. They're his 'good' trousers too, poor Dad. Shall I tell him? He looks so earnest, I decide not to.

He clears his throat. 'Lenny, you know I've been lonely since your mum . . . er, since your mum . . . '

(Mum left us.)

(OK, to be fair to her, she's dead.)

'. . . since your mum passed away.' He looks at me anxiously and I stare blankly at the ground. He goes on. 'And I've been thinking a lot lately about what my future might hold. Jacquetta –' (his therapist) '– suggested I speak to you about the possibility, about the possibility of me maybe starting to, to date again.' He suddenly picks up speed; 'I just thought, maybe I could try it. Try meeting someone. Try dating. Obviously I'm not looking to replace your mum, and you wouldn't have to call her Mum or Mummy. I mean, unless you wanted to . . . '

WHAT THE FUCK. Ohhhhh. Shit, I wasn't expecting this.

He's still racing through his speech. 'I had Candice and Peter over for dinner the other night – they're so lovely, he's so affectionate with her – and Candice kept saying "Alan, you need to get back out there!"'

He looks pensive for a moment. 'I think I need to get back out there, Lenny.'

Get back out there? Out where? The furthest he goes is to the Waitrose on Station Road for his weekly 'big shop'. What the fuck does out there mean and who are these people telling him that? I don't know Candice and Peter *at all*. They only moved in next door last year, just after Mum died, and I've only ever heard about them through Dad and the many terrible cakes I find haunting Dad's kitchen. There is some mouldy-looking banana and courgette bread waiting for us back home right now. I don't even know these people and here they are, pushing themselves into our lives. Telling my dad to 'get back out there', like he is a character in a stupid fucking book. I feel like storming round there right now and confronting Candice. Who is she to say that to *my* dad? Telling him to get back out there. Dad doesn't need anyone else. I look after him, don't I? I'm here for him. I listen to his complaints about the plants not growing how they should. I call him every day, see him every week. I give him everything he could need. Except the obvious – don't be revolting. But surely he doesn't need sex because that's disgusting. Jesus, if I still have to be having sex when I'm sixty, I will kill myself. No wonder Mum chose death if Dad kept insisting on having sex with her.

I don't say any of this, obviously. I just nod slowly.

He's looking at me, wounded puppy dog face waiting for me to say something.

'OK, I get it,' I say even though I don't get it and I will never get it.

He goes on. 'Candice said maybe I could try joining a dating website, or maybe going along to a singles' club. What do you think, Lenny? It's been thirty-five years since

I was single. I don't have any idea how it works any more.'

Neither do I.

'Will you help me, Lenny?' He looks so pained and shy.

I sigh. 'Of course I will, Dad. But maybe a singles' club is a bit premature?'

He looks relieved. 'Yes, yes, I thought probably not that. But how do you actually meet people these days? Your grandma set me up with your mum, because she was "respectable", and that was the only criteria.'

Mum wasn't respectable, that is nonsense.

Hmm. How do I break it to my dad that people no longer interact in real life – and that no one is respectable any more? That even meeting on a dating *website* seems somehow nostalgic these days? I'm definitely not putting Dad on a dating app . . .

He's looking at me expectantly.

'Well . . .' I start. 'It used to be that you'd just go to a bar and have conversations with people, but that's practically a museum move now.'

Dad sits up straighter.

'Can we go to a bar?' he asks excitedly, his voice quivering. 'Can we go to a *cocktail bar*?' he whispers urgently.

A picture of my fully round father trying to climb up on a stool flashes through my mind.

No way.

'Oh. Um . . . '

'Please, Lenny? Please, please can we go to a cocktail bar? I've never been to one in my life, but sometimes they talk about it on *Neighbours* and it sounds like so much fun. Please? Could we go for my birthday?'

No. Way.

It's Dad's sixtieth birthday in a couple of weeks and I've

planned nothing. I keep asking Jen if she's coming home from LA for it and she keeps telling me to get a life.

Dad's looking at me again; he's practically shaking with excitement.

Right. I make a decision.

'Yes. Of course we can, Dad!' I stand up, finger in the air and kicking at the scattering pigeons that squawk in protest. 'Of course we can go to a cocktail bar, and I'll help you find a girlfriend and I will be fine with all of this. Did I mention I am fine because I really am fine with all of this. Fine.'

He stands up too, mirroring my triumphant pose. 'Oh, thank you, Lenny! I'm thrilled! Now, let's go home and watch one of my soaps. Don't worry, I've got them on record.'

He sits back down and reaches for his bag. 'Hold on, I just have to feed the pigeons first.'

Back at Dad's house, we FaceTime Jen from the sofa. This is Dad's favourite bit of my visits. He loves Jen and his granddaughter Milly so much, but it's not really that part that gets him excited. It's FaceTiming. He is delighted by the novelty. He cannot get over the joy of seeing a person's tiny face on that tiny screen. He will talk about the experience and how clever it is for a whole hour after this call. The phone rings, and Milly's little face answers. She screams in terror at the sight of Grandpa's face, way too close, his nose hair almost brushing my screen. Must remember to clean it later.

Milly is six (nearly seven, she keeps telling me) (in six months), and, if Sophie's daughter, Ciara, is the best child in the world, Milly is the worst. She's only in the second grade but she's already in constant trouble at school. She's incredibly argumentative and throws temper tantrums everywhere she goes. Her favourite place for a screaming fit, she says, is a Whole Foods because the aisles are wide enough to really stretch out her fists, and the acoustics are good for all the shrieking. You need to be able to hear her from the vegetable aisle all the way over at the alcohol or the tantrum is a failure.

She's awful, but she's also the funniest, smartest kid I've ever met. In fact, she's in my top five humans on the planet (Dolly Parton is number four) (Dad will overtake her the day he writes a song as good as 'Jolene').

Dad backs up from the phone a little bit and smiles widely at his granddaughter. She ignores him.

'Ellie!' she exclaims happily, pawing at the screen. Milly thinks I'm super cool. When she was younger, and couldn't pronounce words properly, she thought we had the same name, and regularly informed me that we were twins. When I pointed out that I am a grown-up, she would laugh gently, pat me like I'm an idiot, and explain in a kindly voice that of course I'm not. Which is probably about right.

'Hello!' Dad and I shout awkwardly at the same time. 'How are you, little one?' he adds. She ignores him again.

'Ellie, I need to talk to you,' she says precociously, pointedly staring her grandpa out until he heaves himself up off the sofa making loud, old-people-getting-up noises.

'I'll go make a cup of tea,' he says mildly.

When he's gone, I turn back to her. 'Are you all right? What's going on?' I'm only vaguely concerned – Milly often has big important crises that she likes to discuss with me in detail. The last one was about learning to swim and the likelihood of a crocodile appearing in her school's pool.

She flicks her long blonde hair over her shoulder, exactly

like a teenager. 'I need to ask you about *periods*,' she stage whispers the last word.

'Oh?' I say, trying not to react.

OK, this is worse than I thought. First Dad wants to start dating, and now my six-year-old niece wants to discuss womanhood. Today is turning out to be totally excellent and I am still really fine with my life.

Milly glances furtively over her shoulder. No sign of her mum.

'Connie says I'm going to have periods when I'm older and it's going to be totally disgusting and being a girl is the worst.'

'Who's Connie?'

She looks impatient. 'My best friend. She's in the third grade. She says girls have periods and boys have tractors.'

'That's sexist,' I say automatically, but I don't know if it is. If in doubt, get angry and shout, that's my motto.

She ignores my comment because we've talked about sexism before. She says she finds the subject 'tedious' because all the boys in her class are 'morons' and there's 'no way they would get picked to be an astronaut over her'.

'So?' She is irritated. 'What are periods? Tell me and you better not lie to me, Ellie, because I'll know.'

I think for a second. How best to answer this? I should just be honest, shouldn't I? De-mystify it? Because periods happen to all of us and we shouldn't be grossed out or frightened by them. Except I am nearly thirty and I am still a bit grossed out and frightened by them. Sexism, see? (Wait, is it?)

'OK, Milly, it's not something that will happen to you for a long time,' I start cautiously, praying Jen will turn up and save me before I have to get to womb shedding. 'But when you're becoming a woman –' (shoot me in the face, this very second please please, please) '– part of that means once a month, you will have a, uh, menstrual cycle.'

'Ermmmmm,' she interrupts, indignant. 'Excuse me, if it only happens to girls, why is it a "mens"- trilicle?'

'Menstrual cycle,' I correct her. 'But still, that's a good question. And well done on the early years feminist indignation.'

She nods, pleased with herself, and waits for me to continue.

'Um. So your menstrual cycle means that you . . . uh, bleed a bit from your woowoo every month.'

I shouldn't have said that last bit. I should've left it vague. She looks horrified.

'But I hate blood!' she says, her lip trembling. 'I don't want that to happen. And why would it come out of that bit? That's where I wee! I don't want blood to wee out.'

'I know,' I say soothingly. 'It's pretty shi— annoying. But it's not so bad once you get used to—'

She interrupts me again. 'Wait, every month? Every single month? Even during the summer holidays? Even if you're at Disney World? What if I meet Mickey Mouse and my wee starts bleeding on him? *Every month*?'

'Well yes,' I say, trying to picture Mickey's outfit – I think he wears red shorts anyway. 'But some women take the pill –' (nope, don't say this, why would you be saying this) '– to stop their periods for a holiday, or for a wedding when a friend is making you wear a clingy cream bridesmaid dress even though you can't find a single person who thinks it looks nice.'

She looks relieved. 'Oh, that's fine then. Easy. I'll just take that pill and stop periods ever arriving.'

Of course, this is when Jen walks into the living-room and spots us. Milly turns round and shrieks, 'Mommy, I need you to put me on the pill.'

Oh fuck.

Jen looks appalled.

'FOR GOD'S SAKE,' she shouts. 'Don't call me "Mommy" – you're British. I don't know what to do with you. We've only been here a year and your accent is already going to hell. Next you'll be telling me you don't like queuing any more.'

They glare at each other for a moment and then Milly dumps the phone and wanders off. I stare at their ornate living-room ceiling for thirty seconds before Jen's face looms in. She looks me over, coolly.

'She asked you about periods then? I am going to murder that little bitch Connie.'

From the kitchen, Dad's voice wobbles; 'Have you finished your chat?' He pops his head in and the rest of him follows. He's holding a Custard Cream and looking a bit traumatised.

'You heard?' I say sympathetically and he nods sadly, sitting back down. I hand him the phone and he leans right into the camera so only his eye is visible to Jen.

'Hi, Jenny, you look very well,' he says.

'I know,' Jen nods smugly. 'I've been ill for a week so I've lost four pounds. I look amazing.'

'Oh, er, all right then. I'm glad you're better now,' says Dad, unsure of himself.

'I look thin, don't I?' She's asking me, and I nod enthusiastically.

'Yes, Jen, you look very frail indeed. Some might say close to death.'

She smiles, she's pleased.

Jen loves being thin. She loves it more than she loves anything – more than she loves her family. Moving to L.A. has been like coming home to her people. Finally she can talk about kale all day long. Even the waiters over there want to talk about kale apparently. I haven't been to visit yet, because kale isn't my thing, but she says she loves the place, and never wants to come back. I hope that's not true. I really miss her.

'Jen, how's your husband?' I say, changing the subject. Dad looks at me. He's worried I'm going to say something to annoy Jen. He knows I'm not a fan of my sister's husband, Andrew. He's just a bit dull and cold. Mum disliked him too, but we are all aware that Jen is a difficult breed, and as long as he continues to make her happy, we can make nice. It's not like we ever really see him anyway. Even at the rare family events where we've all been together, he's usually on his phone with work, or staring out of a window pretending to be contemplative, so he doesn't have to talk to us. Actually, the last time I saw him was at Mum's funeral. That was a bad day. But after hours of awkward empty apologies and head tilts, it was the first time I really appreciated Andrew making no effort to speak to me.

Jen shrugs. 'He's fine,' she says. 'Work is keeping him really busy, so it doesn't look like we're going to be able to get back to England for a while. I definitely won't be able to make your birthday, Dad.'

He waves his hand and shakes his head to say don't worry, but I can see he's disappointed. She pauses and looks at each of us. I'm waiting for her to say she's sorry she won't be there and that she misses us.

Instead she says, 'I see you're both still alone and fat.'

Dad and I glance down at our bellies and burst out laughing. Jen is brutal, but I don't think Dad really understands what she means most of the time, and I enjoy it. I don't mind being fat by her standards.

I mean. Obviously, of course, for a long time, I did mind. For most of my life I dutifully hated myself and my body, like women are supposed to. I am – what is the suitably elegant word? – a bit *lumpy*. Not hugely, I'm still human shaped, but I have never been thin. And for years I did the standard crying at the mirror, singing Mariah Carey songs at myself and wishing for magic lipo. Or at least magic money to pay for real lipo. Growing up with a thin and beautiful older sister was a little burdensome, and I regularly used it as an excuse to feel very sorry for myself. It was Mum – her death – that actually changed things. One day, not long after she died, I was going through my attic things (that's something no one warns you about when a parent dies, that you have to take possession of the accumulated childhood stuff you left at your parents' house because you don't want it but you don't want it thrown away either. 'Attic things'). Anyway, I found my old teenage diary and it was awful. Pages and pages of self-hatred. Seeing all that there – knowing I was using the same vile words about myself in the mirror fifteen years later – it made me realise I didn't want to do that any more. I didn't want to spend another fifteen years calling myself names I would never use when speaking to a friend. I didn't want to be old and look back at a life spent hating myself. That seemed so very sad. So, instead of starting yet another diet, I stopped weighing myself and starting following a bunch of body positive Instagram accounts. I slowly realised fat women are HOT. And so are thin women. And that we all want what we don't have. Thin girls want more curves, not-thin girls want less of them – we are programmed to look down and feel dissatisfied. But we can re-programme ourselves, I know we can. That's what I've tried to do; rewire my brain and reset my thinking, so every time I accidentally flip my camera phone onto selfie mode and want to scream at the sight of my stupid face, I stop that abuse there.

Obviously, the whole thing is still a work in progress, because I am a human being who likes crying in the mirror with Mariah, on occasion, but mostly I am achieving success in my own small way. Plus, you know what I realised? Men totally still want to have sex with me. Even if they do pointedly say, 'You have such a pretty face' and, 'I don't even find thin women attractive,' a little more often than I would prefer. It's like, *Dude, you don't have to body shame other women to make me feel good about myself!* (OK, maybe it helps a tiny bit.)

Jen tuts at our giggling. 'And you still don't care enough to do anything about it, clearly,' she adds.

I shake my head, I'm not sorry, and change the subject yet again. 'Is Milly OK? She seemed less confrontational than usual.'

Jen nods. 'Yes, she's going through a semi-nice phase at the moment. It's odd. Her head teacher said she hasn't even bullied anyone yet this semester.'

'Weird.'

Dad clears his throat. Oh right, he's going to make the speech again. He's seizing his moment. I sit back to observe the process.

'Ahem,' he begins. 'I'm very proud of you, Jenny, and I was hoping to talk to you about something, if it's OK?'

She rolls her eyes. 'Do I have to? I don't really have time for this. Wait, is it anything to do with the bird shit all over your trousers?'

I wince, but Dad doesn't seem to notice. He continues, 'Jenny, you know I've been lonely since your mum . . . er, since your mum passed away.'

'No, I didn't know that,' she says indignantly. 'Nobody tells me anything. Ellie, why aren't you being nicer to Dad?'

I sit up. 'He's your dad too, Jen, and you're the one living in California.'

Dad shushes us. He's mid-flow:

'And I've been thinking a lot lately. I wanted to talk to you about the possibility of me maybe starting to date again. I just thought, maybe I could try it. Try meeting someone. Obviously I'm not looking to replace your mum, and you wouldn't have to call her 'Mum'. I mean, unless you wanted to . . . '

Jesus, it's almost word for word. Even the intonation is the same. He must've been practising this for weeks.

'I had Candice and Peter over for dinner the other night – they're so lovely, he's so affectionate with her – and Candice kept saying "you need to get back out there". I need to get back out there, I think, Jenny.'

Jen looks bored AF.

'Do what you want,' she says, examining her nails. Then she looks up. 'Hold on, I don't have to do anything, do I? To be honest, it's better you find someone now, to save Ellie looking after you when you have a stroke and are stuck in a wheelchair for the rest of your life.'

Dad sighs, relieved.

'No no, you don't have to do anything,' he says, adding excitably, 'Lenny's going to take me to a cocktail bar!'

'She's what?' Jen snorts. 'Good luck with that, Ellie. I'm glad you've finally found a friend to do exciting things with at long last.'

'Yes, yes, very funny,' I say, looking at my watch, it's coming up to three o'clock. I only have an hour or so to get back to London. 'I better go, I've got a date.'

Dad looks panicked. 'At this time of day?'

I nod. 'Yes, it's just a coffee.'

'Have you got the right day?' Jen sniffs. She's promised not to say anything more about the Tax Lawyer Incident, but a blanket ban is too much to expect from my big sister.

'Yes, Jen, thanks, Jen, bye, Jen,' I say, getting up.

'Milly, come and say goodbye to Ellie and Grandpa,' Jen shouts, reaching for Milly, who leans across her mother into shot.

'Ellie, Mommy says you're going to be alone forever because your standards are too high,' she informs me.

Jen nods, approvingly.

I sigh. 'Having standards – *mandards* – is nothing to be ashamed of, Milly,' I explain. 'And I like being alone. Think of all the old lady cats I can have. You like cats, don't you?'

'I prefer foxes,' she says, thinking about it. 'One of them attacked a boy at my school.'

'That is great. Was he—'

'OK bye.'

She hangs up.

Dad turns to me, smiling. 'She's turning into such a nice little girl, isn't she?'

By the time Dad drops me off at the station with a hug and a five pound note shoved into my bag, I know I'm going to be late for this date. 'Don't spend all of that on rent,' Dad says in hushed tones as I clamber onto my train. 'Get yourself something nice with it too.' No problem, I'm going to use it for a nice M&S G&T in a can.

I sit down next to a heavy breather and get out my phone to text 'Adam' to apologise for running fifteen minutes behind schedule. I wonder if he'll mind. Is he the type of person who minds when someone changes plans an hour before? And am I the type of person who minds when someone minds about a change of plans? I realise I don't even know what I'm looking for from all this Tinder-ing. What's my type? Do I have a type? I glance at my phone. Adam hasn't replied, so maybe he does mind. And maybe I do mind that he minds. Maybe I already hate this uptight prick.

Jesus, the man next to me sounds like he has a collapsed lung, who breathes that loudly?

So here's all I know so far about Adam. He's thirty-two, quite handsome, and he likes playing squash. He was one of the first 'matches' I made on Tinder, thanks to Sophie and Thomas' exhaustive swiping, and he sent me a reasonably spelled message that very evening – one that actually said 'hello' instead of 'hey'. So that is basically where my oh-so high standards/mandards are at right now; a person who uses a slightly longer greeting word than others. We exchanged a few messages and he seemed to vaguely have a sense of humour. He suggested the coffee date almost immediately and explained that he has a policy of meeting dates as quickly as possible, because there 'isn't any point wasting time talking'. Apparently you don't know if you're interested in a person until you 'meet in real life, see each other face to face'. I think he's probably more interested in checking out my arse than my face but there it is. I got the impression that this is a seasoned Tinderer who is methodically working his way through the entire country's single females, and I quite enjoy efficiency, so here we are.

Actually, I feel fairly relaxed about the whole thing – I have to start somewhere – and it'll probably be fine. The only part I'm concerned about is the 'coffee' bit. Coffee. Not alcohol. A *sober* blind date. I'm meeting a stranger for the first time – a stranger I'm in theory probably supposed to flirt with – and we're not imbibing alcohol. Hmm. I wish I'd already bought that train G&T, but it seems a little uncouth to be drinking alone so publicly. Especially when the man next to me may need resuscitating any moment now.

I awkwardly pull out some make-up and start applying it, thinking about good conversation starters. If I'm going to be a person who dates, I'm going to need to seem worldly and intelligent. I want to seem cultured and intelligent, obviously, but also just shallow enough for a shag. What are your thoughts on global warming, did you catch Caitlin Moran's latest column in *The Times*, what is your favourite new restaurant in Soho, do you spiralise your courgettes, sir?

Maybe I should write this down.

I could have conversation prompts with me on dates? I'll become known as the girl who Tinders with cue cards.

I feel the eye of Puff the magic dragon next to me, watching me apply lipstick. His disapproval wafts towards me on a wave of furious heavy breathing. I don't really understand why people get angry about women doing their make-up on public transport. So much rage. The amount of times I've made eye contact, across my mirror, with a simmering, seething middle-aged man, glaring at me as he reads his *Financial Times*. But how is it really any different to reading that paper? I'm not doing anything that encroaches on his space or affects him in any way. If I were using powder or spraying a toxic cloud of deodorant, maybe I would understand the anger a little better. No one in close quarters with strangers wants foundation or scents flying around them. But lipstick? That's between me and my compact. The man next to me huffs again. Maybe he just doesn't like women betraying the illusion.

My phone vibrates with a reply at last from Adam:

Fine.

Ah, the awkward one-word response. What does that mean? Is he angry? Maybe he's in a hurry? But I'm running late, he shouldn't be. I firmly believe that people who respond with one-word texts should all be gathered up and burned to death in a public place. And then their ashes should be displayed for all to see, *Game of Thrones* style, as a warning to those of us who might think to power trip with a one-word text reply.

I'm still wondering if Adam is cross or disinterested when I arrive at the café.

It quickly becomes clear that it is neither of those things.

Adam is not cross or disinterested, he's just very, very drunk.

'Heeeeeeeeeeeeeeey!' he greets me enthusiastically, pulling me in for a long, weird stranger hug. I look down. He only has one shoe on.

I take a deep breath. This could be interesting. You know, in that car crash-y way everyone secretly enjoys.

'Ellie, right?' he shout-spits at me happily, releasing me from the hug and trying really hard to focus on my face. 'I BOUGHT YOU A COFFEE!'

I can feel everyone in the room looking at us and I whisper, as if that will balance out our public offensiveness. 'Oh that's kind, thank you.'

'I'VE BEEN AT THE FOOTIE WITH THE LADSSSSssssss,' he explains. 'We won, so we started drinking at eleven this morning. I'M A TINY BIT DRUNK SSHORRY.'

I laugh and immediately hear how forced it sounds. 'That's no problem,' I say, adding, 'I'm jealous, I love drunk people.' He picks up his coffee mug and stares at it, entranced. I take a moment to look him over. He's posher and better looking than I thought he would be. But he's also turned up to a first date – at four fifteen in the afternoon – totally trashed. Oh well, it's all good fodder for my friends later, right? And, I reassure myself, at least if he's drunk, he's probably going to think I'm cool. Beer goggles are my ally.

Oh, here we go, he's lost interest in the cup and he's shouting again. 'AFTER THIS WE SHOULD GO GET A COCK [high-pitched giggle] TAIL. ARE YOU UP FOR SOME COCK [high-pitched giggle] TAILS?'

I glance around, suspiciously. This feels like a joke, like a prank. Maybe he's one of those dreadful guys on YouTube who think a funny prank is running up to women in the street and yanking their tops up. So hilariously funny, yeah?!

I can't see anyone who looks like they'd be filming me. No one seems to care too much about the tall drunk man shouting cock in the middle of a coffee shop. Not unless that elderly couple eating flapjacks are in on the prank.

I turn back to Adam. Looks like this is actually really happening then. Whoopee.

I nod and we fall into silence. Shit, where are my conversation cards?

He's beaming at me, apparently happy with how things are going so far. I smile weakly back and sip my coffee. I hate these chairs, I think, shifting uncomfortably on the squeaky plastic. I can already feel a bum sweat coming on. Let's hope he doesn't try to Danny Arringford me later or he'll get a handful of sweat for his trouble.

Suddenly he's shouting again. 'I BOUGHT SOME SHOES!' Ah, that is presumably why he only has one shoe on. 'They are GREEN,' he explains, his eyes focusing in and out of my face.

'That sounds fun,' I say supportively. 'Can I see them?'

Adam reaches down enthusiastically to collect the shoe box and slams it down on the table, knocking over my coffee as he does. I jump up, and three seconds later, so does he (they call it the drunk people delay).

'OH SHIT,' he shouts, as staff come running over with tiny paper napkins and dap ineffectively at the brown pool.

Oh Christ, this is mortifying. 'I'm so sorry,' I say over and over to everyone around us. 'I'm *so* sorry.'

'I'll get more tissue paper,' says Adam, and he wanders off. He comes back a few minutes later with a handful of sugar sachets.

'I forgot what I was getting,' he explains, looking down at the spill, and then up at me, frowning, as if I'm responsible. It's semi-funny, but it's also a train wreck, and I wonder if I'm allowed to leave yet. How bad does it have to be before I'm permitted to ditch a date after only twenty minutes?

I take the sugar packets from him – maybe they'll work as tiny sandbags for the spilled coffee – and we sit back down. I ask him what he's been doing this week, and he looks confused. 'I BOUGHT SOME SHOES,' he tells me again, like I'm an idiot.

'Oh right, cool,' I say, nodding. 'Er, for a special occasion or did you just need new shoes?'

He rests an elbow on the table, leaning in some leftover coffee. I feel some satisfaction as the liquid seeps into his shirt. 'My style consultant says it's important we invest in shoes at least every two weeks,' he says slowly, carefully enunciating each word and only succeeding in sounding drunker. He pauses and squints at me, adding, 'Do you have a personal stylist or do you just not care about yourself?'

Ohhhh-kay. I think underneath the drunk is just a pompous cock.

'Actually, I might pop to the loo,' I say, getting up.

'They're over there,' he says pointing at the gents.

'Thanks.'

Hiding in the loo (the ladies), I WhatsApp Thomas and Sophie.

'This is dreadful. He is the worst. I hate him and he's wearing dungarees.'

He's not wearing dungarees, but I need them to think the situation is worse than it is to get more sympathy. I stare at my phone, waiting for a blue tick. No blue tick. The bastards got me into this and now they're off having lives and fun without me. I look at myself in the mirror and wipe some mascara flakes away. Hmm, maybe I shouldn't do my make-up on the train after all.

What should I do? I need emotional support, for someone to tell me I can leave if it's bad – I need permission. But if I hide in here much longer, he's going to think I'm doing a number two in a cafe bathroom.

'Right,' I tell my miserable-looking reflection. 'Give this a bit longer. Maybe he's just nervous and the alcohol is making him say lame things. Another half an hour and you can fuck off home and get into bed.'

I run my fingers through my hair feeling pepped, and head back out there.

Back at the table, Adam has his head in his hands.

'Sorry about before,' he says at a normal volume, and then he smiles. He has a nice smile. 'I'm behaving like a total idiot. Really bad form for a first date, isn't it, turning up trolleyed?' I wince at the cut glass way he says 'trolleyed', but I can see he's trying. He seems a little more sober. He adds, 'So, Eleanor Knight, tell me about yourself.'

I breathe a sigh of relief and start telling him about my visit with Dad and FaceTiming my sister. He tells me about working in the City and I laugh when he complains about having to wear a tie every day.

We smile at each other. This isn't terrible.

'So, what's wrong with you?' he says suddenly, looking me up and down. 'You seem nice, you have a job, you've got a pretty face –' (eye roll) '– so why are you still single at thirty?'

I laugh, a short, shocked laugh. I've been asked this before but it never feels any the less rude with repetition.

There's a silence and I say petulantly, 'I'm not thirty, I'm twenty-nine.'

He laughs and I add, 'What about you? You're older than me and single. So what's wrong with you, Adam?'

He looks put out. 'No one's ever asked me that before.'

We fall into another awkward silence and I try to move the conversation back to work, telling him about a project we finished this week, and how Derek cried because he said he was 'so proud' of all of us.

Adam frowns.

'My ex was like that. She'd cry about everything. She was crazy.'

Ah, the ex-bashing, welcome back my old friend, I was expecting you. I thoroughly disapprove of this. I think men say this kind of thing so that you – as a future potential girlfriend – feel you cannot cry or be 'crazy'. But I am very into crying and being crazy, so this form of gaslighting doesn't work for me. It just makes me wonder what he did to his ex to make her so 'crazy'.

'You don't like emotions much then?' I say, playfully, and he frowns again.

Then his face clears and he leans in, 'I've just remembered I've got some coke in my bag, let's do a line in the loo!'

I almost laugh in his face. Drugs in a Costa loo at five in the afternoon, with a stranger who I hate? Sign me up! But for real though, do not sign me up, I'm so done here.

'No thanks,' I say smoothly, standing up. 'I'm sorry, I'm going to head off actually.' I pick up my bag, hesitate and add unconvincingly, 'It was great to meet you!'

He looks genuinely surprised.

'Oh? I thought you were going to come back to mine after this?'

I want to laugh again. We've only known each other forty-five minutes, but I can already tell he's the kind of man who thinks foreplay is watching *The Human Centipede* and that he would then fall asleep while still inside me. Hard pass.

'I'm not sure what gave you that idea,' I say, putting my coat on over my sweaty bum. 'Sorry.'

I walk to the door, cursing myself for apologising and wishing I could take it back. I glance back as I go and he waves awkwardly, looking very put out.

Half an hour later I get a text from him:

Hey, did you leave?

5

4.15 p.m. Friday, 1 March
Location: Sitting on Maddie's messy desk, which is two down from my own. Her desk is piled high with stuff. In addition to my bottom, she has stacks of folders, stationery of all kinds (who needs paperclips in this day and age?) and the whole Beaver Family from the Sylvanian Family range – obvs. Lord help her if they bring in the hot-desking policy they keep threatening.

Rich, the guy who sits between Maddie and I, has been out at some shoot all day but he's back now, just in time for his four thirty crisp ritual. In a minute, he will get out a packet of Quavers, open them in a way that is somehow louder than any person who has ever opened a bag of crisps before, and then he will suck each crisp until it disintegrates in his mouth. He does this twice daily – we've missed the eleven o'clock showing – and it takes him between fourteen minutes twelve seconds, and sixteen minutes forty-two seconds to get through a bag. We know this, because either side of him, Maddie and I time it and instant message each other about piercing our own ear drums. He's the worst. The Worst.

Hold on, here he comes.

'Hey, Ellie! Hey, Maddie!' he says cheerfully sitting down. 'How are your days going? Isn't the weather lovely for this time of year? Oh, hey, did you see that polar bear documentary last night? Isn't it sad what's happening with them? I actually cried a bit!'

God I hate him.

I don't look up. 'Rich, no one cares about your polar bear fetish.'

'Haha, oh Ellie, you are hilarious.'

His laugh is the worst. And here it comes, the thundering sound of the Quaver packet. I shudder as he thrusts the bag at me.

'Would you like a crisp, Ellie?'

'Before or after you've sucked it to death, Rich?'

'Oh, hahaha, you're so funny! You want one Maddie?'

She shrieks and bats the packet away from her.

He continues, undeterred. 'Are you two excited about to-night? It's going to be weird seeing everyone get drunk, isn't it? I've never seen Derek tipsy, I bet he's hilarious!'

He's so earnest about everything. And he thinks everyone is hilarious – even *Derek*. He's the worst.

I'm going to send him another article from *The Onion*. I like watching him get outraged and tell everyone about it like it's real.

It's been a long, busy week, but tonight is the official launch party for the Nationwide Artist Hunt. Everyone's calling it NAH for short and everyone's also getting told off for calling it NAH for short. The whole office has used the party as an excuse not to do any work this afternoon, and I've seen at least four people swigging wine out of bags under their desks. But, honestly, I don't know if it's because of the party or if I'm only just noticing their everyday survival tool. Maddie and I haven't started drinking yet, but Madds has been applying layer after layer of make-up since eleven forty-five this morning. I'm all for it – she's really starting to look like my favourite drag queen; Alaska Thunderfvck.

Next to me, Madds is adding yet more blusher to her cheeks and shouting at Rich.

'Oh God, shut *up*, Rich. *God*,' she says, delightedly. She's having the best day ever. Last night she broke up with Ben, and she can't believe how not sad she is.

'I kept thinking I would be so miserable if I ever actually did it,' she keeps telling me. 'But I feel AMAZING.'

'It has only been twelve hours,' I keep reminding her, cautiously. I'm worried the novelty and excitement is suddenly going to drop away and the devastation will hit her. I am fully expecting to find her crying on the floor of the loos later. She gets like that after a wine anyway, and it's surely not going to take much to knock through her denial walls. You can't throw away that many years of a relationship and not fall apart, can you?

'It was so easy,' she says again now. 'I came home after work last night and Ben was playing with Alfred. I looked at him and I thought to myself, "He'd make such a wonderful Dad," and then I opened my mouth and I said, "Ben, I think we should break up." I don't know where it came from but as soon as it was out of my mouth I knew it was the right decision. I felt so fucking *relieved*. And I can't keep throwing away his grandmother's jewellery in case he proposes with it. We sat there in the living-room for an hour and a half holding hands and talking about how we'd become best friends, instead of lovers.'

She pauses. 'And then Ben told me he was happy because he couldn't stop thinking about sucking cock.'

Oh. This part of the story is new.

I look at Maddie, blinking. 'Um, Madds, is Ben . . . gay?' I ask hesitantly.

'Yeah, I think he might be!' she says enthusiastically. 'It's something I've thought for a while now because he talks a lot about guy on guy stuff in the bedroom. I once told him about this three-way fantasy I have with two blokes, and he said he had the exact same fantasy. I thought he meant with me and another man, but he explained he meant him and two blokes. But I just thought everyone fantasised about it. And I thought we'd stopped having sex because everyone does after the first two years.'

I nod.

'And I don't mind at all!' she adds. 'I've always wanted a gay best friend, like in *Sex and the City*! I've offered to help him with Grindr if he helps me go shopping for my summer wardrobe in a couple of weeks.'

I wince a bit at the clichés. Especially since the last time I saw Ben, he was wearing all brown, head to toe, including a brown flat cap he found on the train.

'And now I'm *single*,' she says, awed. 'For the first time in my adult life, I'm actually, really single.' She turns to face me, taking both my hands, like we're in a movie. 'I need you to tell me everything, Ellie, *everything*. I need you to do some single-splaining. Remember that I know nothing at all. Like, God, Ellie, do single people still talk about sex in detail like they did on *Sex and the City*?'

I shake my head. 'Nah, calm down, Samantha. I mean, sure, you can tell me you had sex if you like, and you can tell me if it was fine or good sex, but it's not the noughties any more, we don't want to hear details or positions. No one cares about your clitoris.'

She claps her hands, delightedly. 'I have a clitoris and straight men are going to see it!' she shouts.

That's Rich done, and he gets up, muttering about tea and speed walking towards the kitchen. He hasn't even finished his crisps. Rich is single – duh! Who would date him – but I think he's totally asexual. In fact, I would guess that he has no penis at all. I think he has, like, a smooth Ken-doll crotch down there. I get an impulse to check, and then feel sick. Instead, I tut at Maddie.

'I literally just told you I don't want to hear about your clitoris. OK, look, we'll compromise. You can tell me if it's *bad* sex and how you had to, like, Febreeze his penis before you put it in your mouth. Because that's funny, and funny bad sex never goes out of fashion. But having good sex is totally passé.'

Maddie nods. 'Oh right, OK. Ooh, this is so exciting! I'm so Charlotte right now!' She paces up and down in front of her desk. 'Maybe I'll meet someone tonight. A rich art collector! Everything is a possibility now, Ellie. Every new person I meet could be The One. Except, of course I'm going to be single for a while and really make the most of it. Make sure I get my number up to double figures. I can't wait to try a dating app! Oh my God, hold on, I'm going to make Ursula tell me the wifi password and download Plenty of Fish right now.'

I grimace at the choice of dating app, and glance over at Ursula, who is dressed even more like a gothic art teacher than usual today. It's like a Halloween Death costume you would order off eBay – it's just missing the scythe. Next to Derek, she looks even more terrifying. He's wearing a tie that features Mr Blobby from *Noel's House Party*. It's like he's projectile vomited down himself after a night of drinking pink and yellow cocktails. It's actually pretty hypnotic.

Maddie jogs over to the pair of them and I can see her and Ursula arguing. Ursula's in charge of office admin, which includes changing the building's wifi password daily. She then treats that password like it is a nuclear code and the rest of us are North Koreans. Maddie will only get that password if she can offer Ursula something of worth.

The arguing suddenly stops and they smile at each other. Maddie returns.

'What did it cost you, Ariel?' I ask, curiously. 'Just your voice?'

Maddie smirks. 'I told her my boyfriend is gay. There's nothing she prizes more than gossip, and I don't care if everyone finds out. It saves me having to tell them.'

I snort and pick up Mrs Beaver from Maddie's desk to check under her skirt. Smooth like a Barbie doll – and like Rich.

Several hours later, looking around the large hotel banquet room The Hales have hired for the event, I resentfully have to admit this looks pretty good. I was expecting, I don't know, streamers and party poppers draped across every surface, but the hotel must've put their foot down with Derek. They've arranged a few nice flowers and some candles, and that's it. The effect is understated and almost bordering on elegant. Maddie and I have been here since 5 p.m., when Derek excitedly announced to the team that we could all finish up and head on over to the venue. Obviously everyone immediately left and went to the pub 'for one'. But they must be drinking very slowly because it's nearly half seven now and so far there's only thirteen of us here. Maddie and

I keep exchanging angry glances because we wanted to go to the pub, too, but a sweaty, sweaty Derek cornered us as we were leaving, and begged us to go with him to the party. He's promised around a hundred guests and you can see he's starting to panic at the sparse room. He keeps asking Maddie and I to dance 'to liven things up' and 'get the mood going', which we have obviously point blank refused to do. Dancing alone in an empty room at a work event is not the way to earn respect from your peers. Derek came over to ask again a few minutes ago, so I said would he mind us including HR in this conversation about our boss 'forcing us to dance for him'. He scuttled away and is now sulking in the corner.

Just when I start to give up hope for this event, a large group of eight or so bland-looking men arrive, stopping at the door to regard the room with disapproval. There's one woman with them, mid-forties I'd guess, dark blue trouser suit, and taller than all of them. She's frowning too, but in a sort-of amused way as she surveys the scene. She seems relaxed, like she's used to being the one lonely smurfette in the group at events like these, and I get a sudden rush of feeling that I want to be her when I grow up. She's got that that kind of gravitas – that *pull* some people are just born with. I can't imagine ever being impressive. Maybe if I won the lottery I could pay people to *pretend* I'm impressive? I want to be the kind of person who can walk into a room full of strangers and not feel like I'm pretending to belong. Imagine that.

Derek rushes over to the new arrivals, shaking hands and welcoming each of the men. And then the woman too, as an afterthought. He points towards the bar, saying something enthusiastically, and they all nod, unsmiling, and move in that direction, marching as one. It reminds me of the scene in *The Matrix* where the Agent Smiths arrive en masse to take down Neo. I practise some martial arts moves in my head in case they move to kill me.

I turn back to the conversation. Maddie's talking to Aaron from the post room about – in what I can only assume is an attempt at flirting – signing for 'packages', giggle giggle. Good for her, maybe she'll finally get off with him. I hope so because I really, really don't want to. Derek moves to join us, awkwardly introducing himself to Aaron, even though they see each other every day, and had a long conversation just yesterday about a lost ASOS delivery. Aaron stares back at him, heavy-eyed and resentful.

Derek clears his throat and awkwardly turns to me, instead. 'They're from Windsor,' he tells me in a hushed, conspiratorial voice, leaning in and nodding over at the Agent Smiths. We watch as they circle the bar suspiciously, staring at their box wine in plastic cups with genuine horror.

'Ooh, Windsor,' I say semi-sarcastically, but I am secretly impressed. Windsor is one of the biggest chains of art galleries in the U.K. They own a string of them across the country, and NAH is actually their competition that we've latched on to with the bare minimum of sponsorship allowed.

'I hope tonight goes OK,' Derek says again, anxiously, staring over at the important people. 'This is more money than The Hales has ever invested in a project. This competition really needs to raise our profile. We want to be taken seriously by the art community.'

I nod supportively, thinking about the project I've just

finished working on – yet another *Peppa Pig* rip off. 'Have you sent your entry in yet?' I ask him, politely.

'Oh, are we allowed to enter?' Maddie interrupts, turning away from Aaron.

Derek's eyes bulge.

Yes, we're allowed to enter. Very much encouraged to do so. Derek has talked about this in every meeting we've had since entries officially opened two weeks ago. But, to be fair, Maddie's just got really involved in Kim Kardashian's Hollywood game on her phone, so I understand how hard it's been for her to pay attention. Either way, as one of the smaller sponsors, the bosses at Hales have been drilling it into us that we should get involved urgently, in order to 'inspire others' (bolster the number of entries). The whole competition is being totally independently adjudicated so there's no conflict of interest, and Derek keeps going on about how we are 'bringing art to everyone' like it's so far been trapped in a box. Schrodinger's Art.

'Yes, Maddie, you can enter, we'd really like everyone to,' he says exasperated.

She looks at me excitedly, 'Ellie should enter! She's amazing.'

Everyone turns to look at me and I feel my face turning bright red.

Maddie's never seen my paintings, but in between waiting for her Kardashian energy to recharge during meetings, she's watched me sketch the faces of people around the table. Faces – people – are my favourite thing to draw. There's so much to a face. So many weird, ugly, amazing little intricacies. Have you ever really looked at a nose, close up? It's fascinating. So weird and complicated and colourful. All these strange tiny colours running across an awkward bony lump inexplicably positioned in the middle of your face. For a while, I was all about ears, now I'm obsessed with noses. I love drawing Ursula, with her Resting Bitch Octopus Face. Maddie keeps a caricature I did of her, tentacles flailing, on her desk, and regularly, innocently asks Ursula if she likes it.

Maddie's still talking. 'Ellie made me my birthday card last year!' It's true, I did – and she looked pleased for half a second because she thought I'd bought it from Moonpig. When I said I'd drawn it myself, she just looked a bit alarmed and asked me if I needed to borrow some money from Alfred's trust fund (duh, of course the dog has a trust fund, how else is he going to attend university?).

'Yeah, I'll think about entering,' I say, pretending to consider it. I've already been thinking about it a lot. Hard not to with all this propaganda around me.

Maddie opens her mouth to argue the point some more, but right then I spot Sophie coming in the door, looking flustered but beautiful in a flowing green dress.

I'm so happy to see her.

I hurry over to greet her and we hug, giggling excitedly. It feels naughty, somehow, having my best friend at a work event, around colleagues she's never met. These are two worlds that don't usually collide.

More people are arriving now and I take her arm and guide her over to the bar. I explain to her that we have to drink the plastic cups full of bright yellow wine as fast as possible before it runs out. Sophie gabbles about the babysitter and arguing with New Ryan over putting Ciara to bed, and I side-eye the Agents Smith. They're still sticking tightly together by the bar, talking quietly among themselves. My girl crush in blue stands slightly separately, not bothering to include herself in the small talk and confidently regarding the room.

She's so cool. I could never just stand there doing nothing. I'd have my phone out pretending to be checking vitally important messages but secretly playing Candy Crush.

We take a gulp of our disgusting wine and grimace simultaneously. Sophie nudges me excitedly. 'So, how is Tinder? Any more promising dates coming up? Tell me about them, show me pictures!'

'Oh, it's awful,' I say, waving my wine in the air. 'I was talking to a guy last night who felt compelled to tell me that he only showers once a week. He said it's not even an environmental thing, he just reckons he doesn't smell and he doesn't like water. Who doesn't like water? We are literally mostly water.'

Sophie laughs. 'So he's like a cat? Maybe that's cute?' She pats me. 'There is someone amazing out there for you, Ellie, I know it. Just stick with it. You only need that one decent guy to come along and you could be married in a year!' I shift uncomfortably from foot to foot. I was hoping she'd tell me I should come off Tinder and forget about all these weirdos.

I see Maddie heading over. This could be interesting – they've never met. I excitedly introduce them, watching them watching each other. They smile awkwardly at each other and there's half a second of silence as my two circles collide.

'I can't believe you guys have never spoken before,' I say into the strange atmosphere. 'Two of my best friends!' I laugh and add, 'Don't fight over me!'

I wish I hadn't said that last bit. The tension prickles and my stomach clenches. Maybe they'll hate each other. Maybe they will actually fight! It's always bizarre when two friendship worlds are brought together. They know everything about the other – Maddie saw pictures of Sophie's mastitis nipples when she was breastfeeding and Sophie saw pictures of Alfred's tiny dog penis after he got the snip – but they don't *know* each other. Sophie clears her throat and asks after Maddie's day. They are mentally circling each other like wild beasts, each of them sizing the other up. It's hard to know what will happen next. *Please don't hate each other*, I silently plead.

There's a pause, a lull in weather talk, and then Maddie, looking mischievous, says, 'Was Ellie this much of a loser at school too?'

Sophie shrieks and puts her arm round Maddie. 'Absolutely. She had the giant tits, but still couldn't get a boyfriend.'

They start exchanging Ellie stories and I laugh and hit them both. There is nothing to bond two British people more than slagging off a third. Ugh, wait, Rich is coming over. UGH, he's introducing himself to Sophie. UGH.

'Hi there! It's *so* great to meet you, haha,' he's saying. 'I'm Rich. I expect Ellie's told you all about me – don't believe a word of it HAHA!'

That is the worst kind of introduction and only embarrassing old men should be allowed to say it.

'Sophie Ellis,' she says, giving him a limp hand to shake – because she has indeed heard all about him.

'Oh, haha, like Sophie Ellis Bex . . . ' (OH GOD PLEASE DON'T SAY IT) ' . . . tor?' Rich says, laughing. Sophie's face goes dark. She withdraws her hand. Rich pales. He knows he has made a mistake. But he can't quite see how. He's like a frightened animal, twitching, unsure which way to run but knowing his life may depend on the decision.

I think about trying to save him. I decide not to.

'Not –' (her voice is icy) '– particularly like it.'

Rich bites his lip. He is desperate to make a joke about there being Murder on the Dancefloor, I can see he is, everyone does, but he shouldn't.

He laughs again nervously and then licks his chewed lip. 'But . . . ' (oh God, he's going to try again with the joke) '. . . it *is* like Sophie . . . Ellis Bextor. Like her name.'

There's silence. I shouldn't be enjoying this as much as I am.

'The singer?' he tries again, beginning to sweat. 'The DJ?'

'Nice to meet you,' she says, staring at him and not moving.

He nods and backs away, head down, turning in the direction of the loo. She's ruined his night. Serves him and his polar bears right.

'Oh my God, he is the worst!' Sophie says, turning back to us.

Maddie's nodding. 'The worst!' I've already warned her that Sophie's name is not to be trifled with. But come on, she shouldn't have taken her husband's name when they got married. We all warned her this very thing would keep happening. Oh well. If only Sophie Ellis Bextor had enjoyed more than one big hit, maybe the jokes would at least be varied.

I realise someone else has taken Rich's place beside us.

It's *her*.

'Hello,' she says smoothly to me. I stare at her, she stares back.

'Hi! I'm Sophie,' Sophie says, happily, offering a much more enthusiastic hand and leaving off her last name to avoid a repeat of what just happened.

'Maddie,' says Maddie, barely feigning interest and staring off at Aaron across the room again.

'Elizabeth Shelley,' says blue suit, smiling, showing big white teeth. It has a sort of predator affect, I like it.

'Eleanor Knight,' I eventually volunteer, my voice higher than usual.

We smile at each other and there's silence. Sophie looks at each of us, feeling the awkwardness and recognising my intimidated face.

'So what brings you to The Hales' party, Elizabeth?' she says, saving me.

Elizabeth picks a long dark hair off her arm. It's probably mine, I shed a lot. That means I've sort of touched her.

'I work for Windsor,' she replies. 'I run one of their galleries in north London. And, of course, I'm helping with entries on this art competition.' She smiles again. 'It's proving entertaining so far.'

Sophie raises her eyebrows and glances at me. 'Have you had many entries yet?'

'A surprising number,' she confirms. 'We're displaying them all across the South Bank – have you been down? There seems to be a lot of talk over one in particular. It's rather beautiful. An anonymous entry, so people are calling the artist the "New Banksy".' She laughs and I realise she's nice. Beautiful, successful *and nice*. Fucksake.

'I'm going down there tomorrow,' I say, my voice returning

to a normal pitch. 'I'm an illustrator here at The Hales, but I also paint . . . sometimes.'

'She's wonderful,' Sophie adds loyally, as Elizabeth smiles nicely.

'You should enter. We don't have very many paintings so far. It's a lot of modern stuff, installation pieces and the like.'

'That's what I've told her, I don't know why she hasn't already entered,' Sophie says, and I can hear the irritation entering her voice. I change the subject.

'What's it like, working in a gallery?' I ask, adding quickly, 'I think it would be pretty much my dream job.'

Her smile gets wider.

'Mine too. I've been doing it for eighteen years now and every day is still exciting and new. I feel very lucky.'

I sigh. This is what I want. I want to feel lucky. I want to spend all day looking at art and talking to people about it. Elizabeth glances over at the Windsor agents. They're still not mingling, standing rigid side by side.

'Actually, don't mention this to anyone,' she says, her voice lowered. 'I'm in the process of opening my very own gallery. It's a big step – a big risk – but I'm thrilled about it. I can't wait. I want to give new artists a chance to show their work and discover new talent. I think that's why I'm enjoying this competition so much, there's so much out there and the art world can be so cliquey and closed off.'

I gasp, a little too dramatically, and she looks at me carefully, probably assessing whether I'm mocking her.

I'm not and hastily add, 'That's incredible. You must be thrilled. Will you be . . . will you . . . ' I trail off, glancing helplessly at Soph, and once more she steps in.

'Will you be hiring staff for the gallery?'

Elizabeth nods. 'Not immediately. I'm still speaking to investors and looking for the right location. But I will be, most definitely.' She looks at me directly. 'Shall I give you my card?'

I can't say anything, so just nod while Sophie grins and takes it from Elizabeth. Unzipping my bag, she pops it in.

'Thank you!' she says for me, as Elizabeth excuses herself and glides like an Egyptian queen over to Derek.

Watching her walk away, I feel a bit shell shocked. I know it's probably not going to come to anything. It's just party small talk. She was being polite. I probably won't even be able to recover that card from the recesses of my bag, where receipts, pens and breakfast biscuit crumbs go to die. But it's exciting enough – this feeling. Recognising what I want. It's like my ambition has come flooding back, and it feels familiar. I used to have this drive, ages ago, and I forgot about it. I didn't notice when it went away but now it's back and I want it to stay. I've been coasting for years, going through the motions. I want to achieve things and do something with my work that excites the hell out of me. This is an amazing feeling.

I take a big gulp of my now-warm wine and gag a bit.

From: Alan Knight <Alanknightinshiningarmour@BTInternet.co.uk>
To: Eleanor.knight@gmail.com, Jennifer.seevy@hotmail.com

5th March

Alan Knight
106 Castle Rise
Judfield

East Sussex
TN22 5UN

Dear Eleanor and Jennifer,

I've sorry you've had to wait a couple of weeks for the latest "instalment" of my "novel". I hope you weren't on the edge of your seat because you probably would have fallen off! L.O.L. I've had such a busy few days! Maybe you already know that Psychic Sharon has set up a "Psychic YouTube Channel" (I do not know what this means). She says she sent an "email blast" to everyone, so I am sure you were on that list. I have "attached" a picture I took of the email, in case you were not. As you can see, she is now a "YouTuber" (I do not know what this means either), and on Tuesday, she "Facetimed" me to say that she'd had a premonition about really terrible things happening to me if I didn't get straight over to Church Road to help her film her latest "Vlog". As it turned out, it was mostly me holding a bedside lamp really close to her face while she talked. She says the "lighting" is very, very important for "subscribers". I didn't mind, but my arms were really aching after two days of "Vlogging"! Psychic Sharon says I have now, thankfully, averted the terrible things, and she is giving me an "executive producer" title.

But I was happy to get back to my writing, I can tell you! I read the latest chapter to Candice and Peter, and Candice says it's really "hotting up". I hope you agree.

Lenny – Thank you for your feedback. I think tracksuits can be attractive? What about the red one your Aunt Susie gave me for Christmas in 2004? You said I looked like David Hasselhoff from "Baywatch"?

Jenny – I hope you're OK. Your "email address" seems to be "out of action"? I'm getting a reply saying I have been "blocked"? Hope this gets through to you but don't worry if not because Candice printed it out on her "colour printer" for me and I've put it in the "post" for you. Bernard at the Post Office said it would probably take a few days but who knows with the postal system being the way it is. L.O.L. I am only joking, I know they work very hard.

Love you both very much and I'm very proud of both of you.

Best wishes,
Dad

---

75 HUES OF TONY
A novel, by Alan Bernard Knight

Tony Braxton is very, very nervous, which is incredibly unusual for Tony. As everyone is always saying, Tony Braxton is the calmest person in the whole world. He has even been asked to defuse several bombs by the government even though he doesn't really know how to defuse bombs, just because he is so calm at difficult times. But not today. Today he is the bomb that needs defusing. He is very, very nervous.

Tony is nervous because he is on his way to Svetlana's house!! He cannot believe he is actually on his way to see her and he cannot believe how nervous he feels. He has never before met a woman who has had such a big effect on him or created such amazing sexual tensions in rooms with him before. It wasn't even like this with Anita and anyone would tell you that Anita was a deeply, deeply satisfied woman. If you were to ask her right now she might even say she was too satisfied, but only if you really put her on the spot and probably she would just say deeply satisfied, not too satisfied.

But anyway, as Tony drives the ten minute drive to Svetlana's house right now in his brand new yellow Ford Mondeo, he wonders again if he should turn back. After all he has been warned off this woman many, many times by the women at the Book Club. He knows it is wrong but that just makes it more exciting. He feels compelled to keep driving and he is forced to admit to himself and to Radio Four that he has on in the car, that he is very excited.

When he arrives outside the address Svetlana has texted to him, Tony opens the car door to get out and then gets out and closes the car door behind him, rubbing his nodding dog for luck as he does. He then locks his car and looks up at the enormous house. He is very impressed by the enormous house before him. It is enormous.

He walks up the path and knocks on the really enormous door using the big door knob, which is an erotic metaphor for what may be about to happen. A butler answers, which is really impressive as well, and he leads Tony through the house to the back garden, where Svetlana is waiting by the indoor pool in a really attractive swimsuit and a hat. She is holding a cocktail of some sort. Tony has definitely tried all the cocktails and he would guess that this one is a Commopolitane cocktail.

'You look very handsome, Tony,' says Svetlana, who stands up to greet him and looks him up and down, admiring the brown corduroy trousers and red Adidas jumper he has chosen specially for this occasion. They look amazing on him but they are also flexible and work-friendly in case he needs to climb on things or under things when he is fixing Svetlana's phone which is why he's here. Although they both know that was a pretence.

'Hello, Svetlana!' Tony says sensually.

'Please, Tony,' she says in her Russian accent, 'Call me Lana. Would you like a Commopolitane cocktail?'

Tony was right.

'Yes please, Lana,' says Tony politely, and the butler dashes to fetch the drink.

'Please sit down,' says Lana, and Tony does so, admiring the big pool in front of them. He has, of course, had many pools over the years, but this one is really special and big.

'Your pool is really special and big, Lana,' says Tony erotically, and the air is thick with unspoken words about things being special and big, like the door knob earlier.

They stare at each other for a moment and then Lana leans towards him.

What is about to happen? wonders Tony.

Just then the butler returns with Tony's drink and Lana leans away again. Tony takes the drink from the butler and says thank you very much because he is always polite. People comment on his manners nearly as much as his beautiful calves.

'Can I ask you a question, please?' says Lana and Tony nods generously. 'I know you are quite new to being single but are you interested in anyone yet?' And then she adds surprisingly, 'Do you like Wanda?'

Tony is surprised. He has known Wanda a long time and although everyone always says she fancies him and she is always talking about his calves and chiselled features, Tony is sure there is no more to it than that.

'We are just friends and book clubbers, there is no more to it than that,' says Tony.

'That is good news!' says Lana, downing the rest of her cocktail in one go. 'Because, Tony, I will tell you now, I am very interested in you and I wish to have you as my own.'

Tony cannot believe his ears and neither can the butler who is still standing there with them. Lana is so forward! Tony has never met a more forward woman in his life, and he has met almost every woman in the world. He is alarmed, but he cannot deny he is excited as well. Lana is incredibly good-looking and sophisticated. But he must not get carried away. Perhaps this is moving too fast?

'Maybe I should fix your phone before we go any further?' suggests Tony nervously.

Lana leads him through the house and into the study where a landline sits. The phone looks like it has been smashed by a shoe but Tony politely examines it anyway.

'I'm afraid I cannot fix this, it is beyond repair!' says Tony sadly. He is usually able to fix just about anything but this has pieces of phone smashed all over the desk.

'That's a shame,' whispers Lana, who is standing very close to Tony.

Tony steps away, very afraid. 'I will buy you a new phone, though!' he suggests very generously.

Lana takes another erotic step towards Tony, cornering him, and Tony thinks he should perhaps leave.

'Perhaps I should leave now?' he says.

'Before you go let me show you around my house!' says Lana, looking very sad at the prospect of Tony leaving her already.

Tony agrees and they look around. He is amazed to discover that she has her very own lift in her house, and they get in to go up to the second floor. Once the doors close, Lana POUNCES. She kisses Tony and before Tony thinks about what he is doing, he is kissing her back. They really, really kiss each other for what feels like years but is probably only a few seconds because the second floor isn't actually that far away. But it is an AMAZING kiss. Tony uses his tongue really successfully and it's clear Lana is really aroused and happy about the tongue he is giving her.

When the doors bing open, Lana and Tony stop kissing and look at each other. Lana is panting and Tony is licking his lips to replenish the lubrication there. There is a lot going on.

'That was the best kiss I've ever had,' says Lana as they wander round the second floor. 'I think it's clear we are very sexually compatible, Tony.'

But Tony isn't so sure. Yes, it was an amazing kiss and Lana is incredibly good-looking, but they still don't even know each other! He can't believe it happened. Tony has never kissed a woman he hasn't had at least three conversations with before.

When they reach the bedroom, Lana smiles seductively. 'Would you like to join me?' she says and Tony quivers. He is not ready to take that step and excuses himself saying he has forgotten to feed his pet tiger and must rush home. It is a good excuse and Lana waves him goodbye, looking very sad but also very impressed by his chick-magnet Ford Mondeo.

Driving away, Tony doesn't know what to think. He cannot deny that he is very attracted to Lana, and that six-second kiss in the lift was incredibly erotic with just exactly the right amount of tongue, but what does it mean? He has so many questions and he will list just a few of them here: They have sexual chemistry but do they have anything else? How is she so rich? Why do all the other women in the Book Club dislike her? What will happen next? And can she cook nut roast? There are so many questions and so few answers.

END SCENE

6

4.45 p.m. Friday, 8 March
Location: At The Windsor's flagship gallery in north London, waiting in reception. There's a bored AF girl behind the desk playing on her phone, and a giant landscape painting on the wall. It's such an impressive, expansive space and I would be completely in awe – if there wasn't sweat pooling underneath me on my chair.

I. Am. Shitting. Myself. I haven't been to a job interview for so long and I'm so nervous. I had no idea what to wear. Sophie was useless on FaceTime – too distracted by Ciara to give me advice – so I ended up resorting to my one nice shirt (I made Thomas iron it for me late last night), a dark green blazer, and a pencil skirt, that I'm finding useful for wiping my sweaty hands on.

So, I finally worked up the courage yesterday to get in touch with Elizabeth Shelley after our awkward party exchange. She replied surprisingly quickly, asking if I'd like to come in today to discuss 'possible opportunities'. I've got no real clue what that means, but obviously I said yes please, thank you very much, ma'am. And here I am, with my CV, and portfolio of artwork, hoping this is everything I need.

I shift in my seat, uncomfortably, clearing my throat. I've been waiting for fifteen minutes and I'm really paranoid the receptionist has forgotten to let Elizabeth know that I'm here. I don't want her to think I'm late. I keep standing up and loudly – pointedly – yawning in the receptionist's direction to remind her of my presence. But she is studiously ignoring me, too engrossed in her phone.

Just when I'm considering another attention-seeking cough, Elizabeth calls my name, warmly, from across reception. She's smiling that predator smile as she reaches out to shake my hand.

'Thank you so much for coming in,' she says. 'It's nice to see you again.'

'Oh, you too!' I reply, the feelings of inadequacy already creeping up my neck like a rash, as I follow this gloriously cool woman down a corridor and into her office.

There's a man already in here and he stands up to greet me. He's wearing a suit, holding a pile of papers self-importantly and giving off uptight, *I-don't-have-time-for-this* vibes. I thought this was just going to be me and Elizabeth. Shit, this all suddenly feels very official.

'This is Cameron Bourne,' says Elizabeth smoothly. 'He's a potential partner in the new venture.' He nods coolly at me and I wave back, stupidly. Elizabeth gestures for me to sit down in front of her desk and then smiles. 'Thank you for coming in,' she says again, nicely. 'I wanted to continue the conversation we started at The Hales' event. Obviously, this is all highly confidential, and I hope we can rely on your discretion?'

I nod dumbly.

She pauses for dramatic effect and adds, 'But there might be a job opening coming up, and I think that you—'

The man interrupts. 'So, *Eleanor*, what unique qualities do you think you would be bringing to the role?' He says my name like it is in quote marks. Like he doesn't believe it is my real name.

I stare at him, trying to comprehend and failing. I'm awful at these kinds of stock interview questions, I always have been. My brain melts when I hear them. How can anyone be judged on their ability to do a job, based on how well they can trot out the right bullshit adjectives? I don't even know what the job is, how do I answer this?

I clear my throat and Elizabeth glances over at her colleague. She seems peeved. 'Well,' I start, lamely. 'It depends a little on what the role would be, but I'm hard-working, committed—'

He rolls his eyes and interrupts again. 'OK, "Eleanor" –' (if that is your real name) '– where do you see yourself in five years?'

'In a girl band?' I say, my smile sagging when I catch his stony expression. 'Er, sorry, just a joke.' I steal another look at Elizabeth. She's hiding her mouth behind her hand.

I wipe my face with the back of my hand, the panic taking hold, and start again. 'In five years, I would hope to be helping run a gallery like this one and spending more of my free time painting. I brought some of my work along if you'd like –'

Cameron, his face bored, sticks his hand out for the portfolio and I gingerly hand it over. He flicks through it, unimpressed. Halfway through, he sighs and dumps it back on the table, leaning forward.

'Give me an example of a time when you overcame conflict with a colleague,' he says.

FuckOffJackie FuckOffJackie FuckOffJackie FuckOff Jackie FuckOffJackie

'Er.' My mind stays blank. Elizabeth has stopped listening and is studying my portfolio. She looks up at me questioningly, and then back at the art. I hold my breath, I can't tell if she likes it or not.

'Well,' I slowly breathe out, and then I stop. Sweat is tickling the back of my neck and my mind's still blank. What was the question? Was it the five years one? This is the problem in job interviews, I get so nervous I forget what's happening and usually end up talking round and round in circles until someone cuts me off, or I kill myself. I can't believe I'm nearly thirty and still haven't mastered interviews. I really should have by now – other people can do them, can't they? I should be able to play this game. I should be able to string a fucking sentence to-fucking-gether without falling a-fucking-part.

I can't let this happen, this means too much to me.

I lean forward, matching his body language, and try honesty. 'Look, Mr Bourne, I have no idea what you just asked me, but please believe me when I say that I would do anything to work with you both. I'm so passionate about art, it means so much to me. I've been drawing since I was a kid, and it's all I want to do with my life. Being around art is . . . ' My mind goes blank again and I trail off.

There's silence.

Cameron stands up. 'Thanks for coming in, "Eleanor",' he says, heading for the door and opening it.

I've fucked it up.

My shoulders sink and I look at Elizabeth. She looks embarrassed.

I've embarrassed her. She put her faith in me, and I made her look like an idiot in front of an investor. I've ruined everything.

I get up and shake her hand limply. 'Thanks,' I say curtly,

and there's pity in her expression. I wait until I'm in the lift before I start crying. Fuck everything.

Two hours later I'm in a bar, swigging wine and replaying the awful interview over and over in my head. As if this day couldn't get any worse, I have a date tonight. I'll have to paste on a smile and be my best self again for a few hours. God this process – life, dating – is exhausting. But at least I get to drink heavily, I think, cheers-ing myself. The barman watches me, alarmed, as I reach down my top and start awkwardly rearranging my boobs. I found this bra in my underwear drawer this morning, and like the moron I am, I thought, *Oh how lovely, I forgot I owned this bra. There can be no reason why I don't wear it any more. Let me put it on and spend the entire day trying not to scream in agony as my poor breasts are squeezed and scratched*. I forgot it was one of *those* bras.

I would take it off, but then I would have to go home immediately.

As I take another sip, my date, Gary, walks in, scanning the room. And I almost gag.

The man is huge, stacked, cut. He looks like he spends every waking hour in the gym, and then every sleeping hour under a sunbed. He could've just walked off the set of *Geordie Shore*, I think, in awe, as he spots me.

'Hello, love – Ellie, right?' he winks.

I giggle. And then giggle again.

That's weird.

Another giggle.

Holy shit, *I fancy him*, I realise. Gross, what's wrong with me? I don't usually find these kind of men attractive. I like nice, geeky boys, not orange *ladz*. But there's something about this guy. Something about his BIGness, it's making me turn into a simpering puddle of jelly. He confidently orders a JD and coke – 'with a straw, mate' – and turns his attention back to me.

'Can I get you another drink?' he offers, nodding at my wine with a cheeky grin.

His T-shirt is so tight.

I giggle again by way of an answer. He looks amused and gestures to the barman to fill my glass. We take our drinks and find a table in a corner.

I can see his nipples through that T-shirt. Oh fuck.

Three hours later, and my vocal skills are still failing me badly. I don't know what's wrong with me today, speaking has never been more difficult. I've gone from being unable to do anything but giggle, to giving bizarre speeches like this one:

'Sorry I was ages in the loo. It was one of those wees that keeps going forever! You know? You think it's all out and you're like "Phew! At last!" But then you squeeze and a whole new stream starts. And it was a mad colour cos I had a Berocca before I got here in preparation for the hangover. It's funny because sometimes I don't wee for like two days!'

'You're kind of a hot mess, huh?' he says, after my speech about urine.

I am perplexed. 'Did you just call me hot?' I ask, slightly turned on.

'Yes, pet,' he hoots. 'But I also called you a mess.'

'That's fine,' I wave my hand dismissively. 'I don't care about that, just the hot part.'

He scoots closer, grinning, and whispers, 'Are we going to bone tonight?'

I giggle again, not nearly as horrified as I should be. It seems to be all I'm capable of this evening.

I mean, I could go have sex with him. But can I be bothered? It's an awful lot of effort, and I'd always much prefer to wake up in my own bed. I'm not taking him back to TS though. If we call it a night now, I could be home in thirty minutes, eating discounted Terry's chocolate orange slices from Christmas, and reading the 'best rated' comments on the *Daily Mail* website to make myself feel outraged and superior. I think about my bed now and I ache with longing. This is what I love about being single – the total selfishness. I could go home now and watch *Made in Chelsea* all night. I could paint, I could eat biscuits and get crumbs all over my duvet. I could carry on the hilarious Tinder chat I've been having with a guy who makes dolls that look like real babies. I only report to myself, I only have myself to consult. I can do anything. And God, I like having the bed to myself. I like bundling myself up in seven layers of ugly old pyjamas, and tucking myself in like a burrito.

And, like, if I have sex with him, it will take my number up to seventeen, and I really hate odd numbers.

He smiles at me, wiggling his eyebrows suggestively.

I can't believe I'm even considering it. This is a man who said *supposably* several times earlier.

'Go on, pet,' he says, winking again. 'I promise I'll give you the best orgasm of your life. I'll massage your passage.'

Oh fuck no.

OK, I did have sex with him, but HEAR ME OUT.

I hadn't intended to, but then we left and there was a giant Derren Brown billboard outside the bar and Gary got really freaked out and kept telling me not to look 'the sorcerer' in the eyes because he'd curse us both. It was sooo adorable. And then we were kissing and I felt so tiny in his arms, and there we have it. I am blameless.

Which is how I've ended up sneaking out of his apartment in south London at eight in the morning. As I leave his house, I look around with surprise. I know exactly where I am, I know this area – Thomas lives down that road over there. I send him a WhatsApp.

> You home? Can you cook me breakfast?

His reply is instant.

> Yes! Where are you? How was your date? Are you walk-of-shaming?

I glance down at my dress and the heels shoved into my bag.

> I'm walk of priding it, actually. I'll be there in two.

Thomas has coffee waiting for me as I arrive, and he ushers me through to the kitchen. He has a proper house that he actually has a mortgage for, like some kind of aberrant millionaire.

'How's the head?' he asks in a soothing voice.

'Not terrible,' I say, sipping my coffee. 'Not yet, anyway. Can you make me scrambled eggs, please? I have such a craving.'

Thomas nods, laughing. 'You've been working up an appetite then? How was – what was his name? Gary?'

I wince. 'Yes, Gary.' Is it weird to tell Thomas about this?

I usually do, but Sophie's generally there too as a buffer. I don't want to hurt him or make him jealous.

'He had really tiny nipples,' I say thoughtfully. 'Big lad, but cute baby nipples.'

'You know what they say about men with tiny nipples!' Thomas laughs awkwardly.

'No?' I say blankly.

'Never mind,' Thomas rolls his eyes, cracking eggs into a pan. He's so nice to me.

'But yeah,' I babble. 'It was fun. And his loo had two flushes! So fancy. The sex did go on for ages though and I got bored and started counting sheep.'

'Isn't that for sleeping?' Thomas looks perplexed.

A thought occurs to him, and he looks up from his cooking. 'Oh wait, doesn't this mean you're back onto an odd sex number again? I know how you hate that.'

Damn, I'd forgotten. I laugh. 'I guess I'll just have to climb on someone else really soon,' I say. Thomas laughs too, and then looks at me a little pointedly.

Wait, did that sound like I was flirting? Does this feel like a date? Question: is it OK to feel like this is a date when I can still feel the imprint of another man's fingers inside me?

Thomas puts eggs in front of us both and tops up my coffee.

'Will you see him again?' he says, sitting down. 'Will Sophie at last see her double dating dreams come true?'

I make a face, shaking my head. 'Nah. It was fun, but Gary is not for me. I didn't even mean to have sex with him. I'm actually on my period! Day five, so it's, like, almost cute levels of blood, but still.' I look down at my food. 'I let his penis potentially get close to bits of my womb. Do you think I'm disgusting?'

Thomas laughs. 'No, don't be ridiculous! Boys don't care about that. I have period sex all the time. I just lay a towel down, it's not a big deal.'

Wait. Thomas has sex 'all the time'? WTF? Why doesn't he tell us about it? Is he telling Sophie and not me?

A wave of nausea overwhelms me. My hangover's really kicking in.

Josh is in the kitchen when I get back to TS, and I watch from the doorway, blank with fury, as he dumps his dirty breakfast plate in the sink. There's already a huge pile of crusty pans in there that he must be responsible for. When I left this place yesterday, the kitchen was clean and tidy, after two solid hours of scrubbing and grunting. But twenty-four hours with Josh Day, and it's back to the exact same gross rat hole it was before. Josh slumps back onto the sofa, grunting a greeting in my vague direction as he cranks up the volume on the TV. God I hate him. The eggs I had at Thomas' are rolling around in my stomach, and I can feel the pent up frustration of yesterday – my failed job interview and sad period sex – building up inside me.

'FUCKING CLEAN YOUR FUCKING PLATE,' I suddenly scream at Josh, who jumps in shock. I breathe out slowly. 'Please fucking clean your fucking stuff, Josh,' I say again, more calmly this time. 'I'm so sick of coming home to a wreck of a kitchen. Please, Josh, at least soak the nastier plates so they don't congeal for all time?'

He looks at me for a second and then laughs. 'You seriously need to chill out, Ellie. I will get to that stuff later. Or you can do it if you're really bothered about it. I'm busy right now.'

He turns back to *The Simpsons* and I dig my nails into the

palms of my hands. I know there is no point in screaming at him again. I swear he gets off on my anger, enjoys upsetting me. The only thing I can do is turn around and walk away.

'And hey,' his voice follows me out of the room. 'Let me know if you need a pity bang to help relax you.'

I stomp upstairs to shower Gary – and Josh – off my skin.

7

5 p.m. Saturday, 9 March
Location: Dad's heavily floral living-room (he hasn't changed anything since Mum died). I've put up a few birthday banners screaming HAPPY 60TH! and a few bright yellow balloons are bouncing around the floor, but the effect is still pretty depressing. I tried to find extra decorations, but the blue balloons I found in the cupboard under the stairs must've been from circa 1984, because they burst in my face when I tried to blow them up.

Dad is REALLY nervous. It's making me want to cry, but also shake him and tell him to pull himself together. When he opened the door, he was already dressed up in his best formal suit, with a glistening red tie I've never seen before. He's clearly been shopping in the local Next, especially for this evening – he looks nice, but is completely overdressed for the nearby All Bar One that I'm taking him to. He's sitting on the sofa now, poker straight and staring at the TV with the eyes of a man waiting for death. I wonder again now if I should try and get him to change, but I don't want to make him feel even more nervous. Oh God, I've just noticed – he's even put gel in his hair. Hmm. And, possibly, in his – yes definitely – in his eyebrows. The effect is disturbing. And it somehow makes him look even more like a middle-aged woman.

I stand up and he jumps, startled. 'You look lovely,' he

tells me again as I pull uncomfortably at my pale blue dress. I don't wear dresses often, more of a jeans person, but I wanted to make an effort for him. Except that now our combined efforts make us look like we're going to a wedding. I head for the kitchen to fetch the M&S Colin the Caterpillar cake I've bought.

'So do you,' I shout back enthusiastically as I stick six candles into Colin and try and get the stupid fucking match to light. I laugh at Earlier Today Ellie, who had genuinely considered buying sixty candles. The Earlier Today Ellie who would now be setting the house on fire in a literal blaze of furious frustration (except no doubt the match wouldn't light). I slowly pick Colin up, eyeing Candice's homemade red pepper cheesecake creation sitting forlornly on the side, and head for the living-room, shouting, 'Happy birthday!' again, with as much jolly as I can muster.

I've been dreading today. Taking Dad to a cocktail bar. Taking my father, the man whose sperm I am made from, to a cocktail bar. A dad and his crotch fruit, hitting up a bar to chat up women who could potentially – y'know, fingers crossed! – replace my dead mum. I am my father's pimp. I keep asking myself why I agreed to this. I should've just thrown the standard party everyone around here has when they turn sixty. The whole neighbourhood gathers to get drunk on sherry, play cards and watch a two-hour 'set' from Aunt Susie and Psychic Sharon in leather trousers, singing a *Grease* medley. I've had five separate, furious emails from Psychic Sharon about hosting it – she said she'd bought the extension pack for Cards Against Humanity specially for the occasion – and I kept saying no. Apparently I'm on my sixth curse this month. But why did I say no? It would've been much more sensible. And then the other part of me points out that it is *his* sixtieth goddammit, and this is what he wanted to do. He gives me so much and is such a lovely dad. He wants to try a 'Commopolitane' and who am I to tell him he can't? Just because I'm still not old enough to get over the embarrassment of hanging out in public with a parent. All week long I've been telling people about this and asking advice. Maddie didn't seem to think it was a big deal, she said she goes to her father's golf club with him all the time. Sophie bravely offered to come with me, but I didn't want Dad to feel like I needed back-up. I even told stupid Josh about it this morning when we were eating breakfast in the living-room. He couldn't stop laughing and asking if I was that desperate for a date. He's never met my dad, but he's heard the stories and even seen a picture of him – at which point he said my dad was a 'sexy older lady' and he would 'hit that'. After he stopped laughing, he suggested I should just get drunk really fast so I didn't mind when Dad tried to snog girls my age in front of me. And then he did actually help me choose the dress for tonight. In fact I'd just decided maybe Cunt Josh wasn't so bad, when I heard his bedroom door open and a furious-looking girl with bed hair stomped out and headed straight for the front door, slamming it behind her. Josh had been hanging around, chatting to me (laughing at me) for nearly two whole hours while a girl who'd stayed over waited for him in his room. And so then we had a big row about the way he treats women and he said he couldn't understand why it was rude – he said he would've brought her the cup of tea 'eventually' – and she could've just gone back to sleep. Unbelievable.

Dad's laid out his unopened cards and gifts on the table and I shove a few out the way to make room for the Colin cake. I recognise Aunt Susie and Psychic Sharon's handwriting – and there are Jen and Milly's cards waiting too. Dad blows out the candles and I cheer appropriately, then glance at the clock on the wall. We told Jen we'd call her at this time, and she gets really angry about tardiness (not her own, her own is fine). She answers on the first ring and I wave, holding her face up in the air so she can see the underwhelming table display and decorations.

'Stop that, it's making me feel seasick,' she snaps. 'Put me on the mantelpiece. I'll be able to watch from up there.'

I balance her up against a racially concerning porcelain statue and unnecessarily shout, 'Present time!' clapping my hands. Dad surveys the table and his limited popularity proudly.

'I'm glad my card arrived. Fucking international post,' Jen sniffs from her position above us. I laugh, she looks happy up there – I imagine she's enjoying literally looking down on us.

'Don't swear, Mommy,' says an indignant Milly, who's just arrived and is now peering at us through the phone. 'Happy birthday, Grandpa. I hope you live at least another year,' she says, very seriously.

'Oh, hello, darling!' he says, looking delighted. 'I'll open yours first, shall I?' he says, already snaffling at the envelope.

Milly's is handmade; a beautifully intricate drawing of Dad out at sea on a boat, waving. It's actually very good. We used to draw together quite a lot when they lived over here. She's really talented, much better than I was at her age. My heart sinks, I miss her.

'That's wonderful!' Dad exclaims, admiring the carefully drawn, appropriately elaborate eyebrows. 'You did that all by yourself?'

Milly nods. 'Yes, Grandpa. I'm saving up for the real boat for your next birthday because soon you'll be so old and we'll need to send you off to sea to die. Mommy says we can't afford to put you in a home.'

'We can afford it,' Jen interjects. 'We just don't want to waste the money.'

Dad tries not to laugh as he props the card up on the table and picks up Jen's, ripping open the envelope. He reads out the card's inscription on the front; 'Happy birthday to a man who is like a dad to me'.

I snort. 'That's pretty funny,' I direct at Jen, who narrows her eyes back at me.

'What's funny about it?'

'Nothing, Jen, sorry.'

Dad seems pleased. 'Ah thank you, love, you're a good girl, Jenny.'

He makes his way through the rest of the bland cards – all decorated with Vaseline-lensed photographs of waterlilies (and the one outrageously sweary card from Aunt Susie, who accidentally bought a job lot of Modern Toss cards a while ago – you should've seen the wildly inappropriate sympathy card she gave us at Mum's funeral). Dad makes enthusiastic noises about the various socks and books he's been given and Milly provides a musical accompaniment to the festivities with a song about penises she learned this week in the school playground. Candice and Peter from next door have bought him a really beautiful pocket watch. That is so nice of them. Dad seems completely thrilled, admiring it from every angle and then attaching it to his jacket pocket. At the same time, his eyebrows suddenly spring out, the gel worn off, and he begins to look like the white rabbit from *Alice in Wonderland*. I suppress a giggle.

From the mantelpiece Jen tells us she's bored, and shoots Dad a look.

'I can't believe you're going to a cocktail bar,' she sneers again. 'You know you're making a tit of yourself? Even Ellie's too old to drink cocktails.'

'I am not!' I say, 'I'm in my twenties!'

'Barely,' she snorts.

I glance over at Dad, he looks alarmed.

I want to reassure him it will be fine. Because it probably will be. We probably won't even get a seat and after ten minutes he'll admit he doesn't really like the noise, or understand why the drinks are in jam jars, and then we can leave. We'll head over to his local pub instead, where we'll make a half pint of shandy last all evening, and try to avoid talking to Letchy Arthur who props up the bar every night. Just like Dad usually does on a Saturday evening. I could even send a last-minute group text to his friends and hopefully get a few to come down to the pub to celebrate properly with him.

'Are you all right?' I say softly, patting his arm.

'Yes,' he says, suddenly determined as he takes my hand. 'Really, Ellie, I want to spend my birthday with my beautiful daughter and try something new. If you're not too embarrassed by me – and I wouldn't blame you if you were – I want to be sixty years young with just you tonight.'

I smile and reach over for a hug. 'OK, well, is there anything about the bar itself that you're worried about?' I ask, but he shakes his head and smiles distractedly, fiddling with his new pocket watch.

Milly pipes up from inside the phone. 'There are quite a few things I'm worried about,' she says, and starts counting them off on her fingers: 'Drowning, drowning in my own blood, global warming, being eaten by a crocodile, getting murdered by Finley at school, periods, the pill, what "virgin" means, never seeing Ellie again because her cats kill her—'

'Oh my God,' I interrupt, exasperated. 'I'm a dog person! I don't even have any cats!'

'Not yet,' Jen mutters.

'Right, I think we better get going,' I say, standing up and advancing on the phone.

'Wait, I need to ask you about something, Ellie,' says Milly, panic in her voice.

It cannot be about periods again, surely.

'Ellie, there's a school disco coming up and I've promised my class I'll bring cocktails – just like you and Grandpa are having.'

Dad and I exchange an uneasy look.

'I need you to help me make them. I've got fruit juice and lots of ice, but what else do I need? I asked Mrs Andrews at school and she said they'd have to be virgin, so where can I get virgins? What does virgin mean? I asked everyone in my class and they didn't know either. I told them to ask their parents and get back to me but then no one would talk to me the next day because they were all grounded.'

'You know what, Mill?' I say, smiling at Jen, who is ignoring the exchange as she examines her cuticles. 'Your mum can talk you through all of this.'

She looks up. 'What?'

'Bye everyone!' I shout, and stand up.

'That outfit really got away from you, didn't it?' Jen observes darkly as I press the button and end the call.

*

In the taxi, I cringe again at the prospect of spending my Saturday night with my dad in an All Bar One. But at least things are looking up on the work front. After my disastrous interview, Elizabeth called and apologised. Said she hadn't realised it would be so formal. She said she'd been looking through my work though and loved it. And then we had a proper chat. We talked about artists we love, our favourite pieces, what we would buy if we had unlimited money, how neither of us are particular fans of the 'modern' installation pieces you see so much of nowadays. It was pretentious as fuck but I *loved* it. I have never felt smarter in my life. I finally felt like I knew what I was talking about – for probably the first time ever – and I came away from the call feeling so inspired. It'll be a while yet before anything happens – Elizabeth's still looking around for investors – but I feel so much more hopeful about my life. I've even started painting properly again. It's much tougher work in the cramped blank-walled confines of TS, and I might be getting brain damage from the fumes in my room – slash hypothermia from having my window wide open at all times – but it's such a nice feeling to be back at my canvas. My latest portrait is of Milly. A big, bright, shining painting of her face, contorted with fury, from a photo I took when I last saw her in real life. The eyes worked almost immediately, the brightness and the intelligence – it was easy to capture – but her nose is proving challenging. It's such an angry little protrusion. Either way, I think it's some of the best work I've done in a long time. I even let Josh have a look – and I never let anyone see my work half done – and he seemed genuinely impressed. The fumes must have got to him too because he didn't even make a snarky comment.

*

As we pull up in town, I think again how astonishing it is that Dad's nearby town actually has a cocktail bar. There's so little here – the Next, the old Woolworths that turned into a Pound Shop but everyone still refers to as Woolworths, Psychic Sharon's candle shop that sells candles from the Pound Shop but substantially marked up in price because she's 'blessed' them, and that's basically it. Last year everyone went nuts over a rumour that a Nando's was opening up a branch in town. It was in all the local papers and the mayor made an announcement welcoming the news. For literally two or three months, it was all anyone was talking about. It didn't turn out to be true, but still, it was a pretty exciting time to be a resident of Judfield. So the fact that they have a legitimate cocktail bar here, just down the alley by Pound-Shop-Woolworths, is fairly amazing.

But that amazingness also means it's always dead busy, as the local teenagers flock there in an attempt to escape the grandparents they're staying with for half term. I'm aware of its popularity and I thought about ringing ahead to book a booth, or even try to get Dad and me on the guest list. But then I was worried they'd ask for our ages. I'm sure they couldn't actually have an upper age limit on patrons – that's probably age-discrimination, right? – but I can't imagine they're desperate to welcome in the local sixty-year-olds. Or even the local thirty-year-olds. I assume they just rely on old people preferring bingo and *Antiques Roadshow* (TBF, Dad loves both those things) to dark rooms and sticky floors filled with teen strangers groping each other.

I've made us get here super early – it's only six forty-five – partly in the hope that the place will still be fairly empty, and partly because I thought I could swoop Dad in without anyone noticing and hide us both in a dark corner. But as we approach, I can see that plan was idiotic. There's already a long queue, snaking down the alleyway, and two bouncers are prowling up and down, snarling at terrified teenagers who are quietly practising their fake year of birth and star sign. Dad grips my arm with terror as a couple of sixteen-year-olds give us a funny look. I square my chin at them, meeting their eyes defiantly as I take my dad and we join the back of the queue.

It's not moving.

OK, maybe this is the answer to my problem. If we can't even get in, problem/potential mortification solved. If we can't get in the door, we don't have to see anyone. I glance at Dad and feel bad. He looks so anxious, his eyebrows – now free from the gel constraints – are throbbing with anticipation and panic.

Shit, one of the bouncers has spotted us. He's glaring over at the pair of elderly oddballs at the back of the queue, and he looks furious. They're never going to let us in. This could be very humiliating. The bouncers confer, one of them – at least 17ft tall with dark eyes – is gesturing angrily in our direction.

Oh no, here he comes. Dad looks like he might cry as the angry giant beckons us to come over, out of the queue. Everyone's staring. God, we're actually being asked to leave. I'm being thrown out of a club I hadn't even managed to get into yet. And not for fighting or excessively boozy reasons – AKA cool stuff – but because I'm out with my *dad*. This is a whole other level of mortification.

'You two want to come in here?' the giant is shouting, threatening violence with those dark eyes.

I tremble as Dad whispers, 'Yes please, sir,' adding quickly,

'It's my birthday. My daughter and I wanted to try our first Commopolitane cocktail.'

'Cosmopolitan,' I mutter petulantly, avoiding eye contact. 'And I've already tried one.'

There's a long, angry pause, and then the violent-eyed giant breaks into a terrifying grin. 'Of course! Come right in, mate. Just didn't want you standing out here in the cold if you were coming in. Happy birthday – that is a lovely suit you're wearing. Is that tie from Next? My wife got me the blue one. Nice to have a couple of people in here with some CLASS.' He shouts the last word and a few of the classless people in the queue look a bit miffed. Even more so as the giant leads us past them, straight in and up to the bar.

'Get out of the way,' he growls at two terrified students sitting there. They make a run for it and the BFG gestures for us to sit. 'You want to try Cosmos, right? Two?' He waves a buxom barmaid over. 'Liza? Two Cosmos for these two please – on me – can you believe they've never tried them before?' He laughs, and looks at me pityingly for my sad, sheltered life.

'I have actually,' I mutter again to nobody in particular but Dad is already talking animatedly to Liza the barmaid and introducing us. She's grinning as she takes us in. 'I'm Alan,' says Dad. 'It's my birthday today! I am sixty years young! And this is my daughter, Eleanor! You can call her Ellie, or Elle, or Lenny. Lenny is what I call her, have done since she was a baby. We're absolutely thrilled to be here. Very excited, very excited. Thank you for having us.' He's shouting over the music.

'I'm not excited,' I say petulantly. This is not what I was expecting.

The giant bouncer elbows me as he casually leans on the bar between us, forcing me further out of the newly formed fun group. He booms at Dad, 'Your name's Alan? That's my name too, Alan, mate!' He offers an enormous hand for my dad to shake and they laugh, marvelling at the *extraordinary* coincidence, while I roll my eyes. Of course the giant is called Alan. Every bouncer is called Alan. If you're called Alan, you either have to work in security or be born immediately into your fifties with a grey moustache. My dad was the latter, but if he'd ever managed to grow over five foot five, I'm sure he would've worked in security as well.

Liza carefully places the much-discussed Cosmos in front of Dad and me, and excitedly sings 'Happy Birthday'. I sip mine a bit forlornly, feeling left out of the buzz around my dad. He said he wanted to come out with me but he seems much more interested in Liza and the giant called Alan.

I shake myself out of my sulk. For God's sake, Ellie, every time you're around your dad you turn back into a stroppy teenager. It's pathetic. This is his birthday, pull yourself together and act happy. Give him an evening of fun for once.

I look at him now as he takes his first sip of cocktail with everyone watching carefully. 'Oh my goodness!' he splutters, smiling. 'It's delicious, Liza! Thank you so much!'

She smiles, laughing, turning to me. 'Do you like it too?' she says.

OH MY GOD I'VE HAD ONE BEFORE I'VE HAD LOADS BEFORE I'VE EVEN SICKED UP A BUNCH OF COSMOS BEFORE.

I don't say that. I smile and nod, offering a thumbs up and taking a longer sip.

Liza gives me a thumbs up back, and returns her attention

to my dad, who is trying to guess ingredients. Liza is lovely, but can't be more than eleven years old. I look around the busy bar. Apart from giant Alan, Dad and me, everyone here is eleven. Liza is laughing again – she seems totally delighted to have met her very first old people – and I include myself in that. She brings us two more cocktails, these ones are dark and rich looking. Might as well follow Josh's advice and get really drunk.

'Free drinks for you two all night!' Liza declares happily.

OK, maybe hanging out with Dad won't be so bad actually.

Two hours later and a couple more people have joined our gang at the bar. Alan never went back outside, because he says the other bouncer – 'Oh, Alan, mate, him outside is also called Alan, mate! That's three of us! We should form a band, mate!' – will be fine without him. Apparently the place was already at 'one in one out' capacity by five thirty, so the third Alan just needs to stand there, glaring at people.

As well as me, Dad, Alan the Giant and Liza, a lovely couple called Zoe and Lois are sitting with us, sharing a tube of Original Pringles that Lois smuggled in. Alan the giant says that's OK, and he won't confiscate them as long as Lois shares them. So that's where we are now, sipping cocktails and passing round a tube of Pringles. It gets to Dad again, who's never before experienced Pringles, and is close to tears with the excitement of it all.

'They're in a TUBE,' he tells me again, picking up the Pringles and waving them next to my face for inspection. 'Could you ever have imagined such clever packaging, Lenny?'

'Have you never had Pringles before either?' says Liza to me, who is apparently actually nineteen, not eleven.

I sigh. 'Yes, I've had Pringles.'

She looks sympathetic. She doesn't believe me.

Alan the Giant leans over me again towards my dad. 'Keep going, Alan, mate, you'd got us as far as your thirties.'

Dad is telling his life story and we just got to the eighties, when Mum gave birth to me, and Jen came to the hospital to visit her new sister and said I was 'gross'.

'I am not ashamed to tell you, Liza, Alan, Lois, Zoe, I cried a lot,' he says, wiping a tear away now.

'Wait,' Lois interrupts. 'Are you two not a couple then?' she points accusingly at me and Dad.

'Oh, that is disgusting,' I shout, standing up with the horror of it all. And then sitting back down again because I'm trapped inside the circle by a BFG.

Dad chuckles and pats me kindly. 'No, this is Lenny, my youngest daughter,' he explains to Lois, looking at me misty eyed.

Dad is the only person who calls me Lenny. He's been doing it since as long as I can remember – he said he liked the simple loveliness of having a Jenny and a Lenny. I like it too.

Lois shrugs, 'Soz,' she says, not seeming all that soz.

Dad looks at me a little sadly. 'It was a difficult period for your mum though, Lenny,' he adds. 'She had postnatal depression for quite a long time after you were born. She loved you so much, but everything was very dark. It took a long time to diagnose and even once she was sorted, she used to cry a lot, asking me if she was doing enough to show you how much she loved you. She felt like she had to make it up to you.'

I never knew this. I certainly never felt a lack of love in my house. Too much, if anything. Dad and I look at each other and there's silence at the table. I can't say anything because there's a lump in my throat, so I take a long sip of the sweet cocktail in front of me. I have no idea what we're drinking at this point but apparently we've been working our way through every elaborate item on the menu.

'And where's your wife now?' Alan the Giant asks, gently.

Dad looks down and I clear my throat.

'She died, Alan,' I tell him, as smoothly as I can. 'She had cancer and we lost her about fifteen months ago, after Christmas. My dad's been on his own since.'

'Fucking cancer,' Lois says quietly, as Alan the Giant pats my hand.

'He's not on his own, love. He's got you, hasn't he?'

Another hour passes and Lois is shouting that she wants to get married. Zoe is slightly less drunk, and therefore, less into it.

'Look at this AMAZING MAN,' Lois is shouting, pointing into Dad's face. 'HE HAS SEEN REAL LOVE. Marriage means something and I fucking love you, Zo.'

Zoe nods, looking amused. She doesn't say much.

'I know we've never really believed in straight conventions,' says Lois, with conviction. 'But I've seen the light this evening. This man has helped me realise what marriage means. Marry me, Zoe?'

We all applaud but Zoe looks annoyed.

Dad looks thrilled. His first Cosmos, his first Pringles and his first lesbians, all in one night. What a sixtieth.

'We'll talk about this later,' Zoe hisses. But Lois isn't listening.

Lois turns to Dad, taking his hands. 'You must come, Alan. You can give me away! Will you give me away?'

Dad nods. They hug. They're both crying.

'What about your actual dad?' Alan the Giant asks.

'Fuck him!' says Lois, angrily, and then makes an awkward face. 'Oh, actually, my dad is pretty lovely. He's the reason I've always accepted who I am and he was so proud when I came out. I should probably let him give me away. Sorry, Alan.'

Dad wipes his eyes and tells Lois not to worry. She says maybe Dad can be a bridesmaid of sorts and Alan the Giant can officiate, because apparently that has been a life-long dream of his. Dad wants to know if there will be Cosmos and Pringles available at the wedding. 'You two *should* get married,' he's saying, eyes shining again.

God he's cried a lot tonight.

Zoe sighs, annoyed. 'Lois, stop it, for fuck's sake. I'm not getting engaged in an All Bar One. Stop being such an attention seeker.'

Alan the Giant looks a bit huffy. 'And what's wrong with an All Bar One, young lady? We've had plenty of proposals in here, haven't we, Liza?'

She's nodding emphatically as Dad turns, a little more sober-faced, to the group.

'I'm very proud of you all,' he starts. 'I was hoping to talk to you all about something.'

Oh fuck, it's that fucking speech again.

I interrupt, hastily. 'My dad's hoping to start dating again,' I explain.

He looks embarrassed. 'I am very lonely,' he tells the already emotional group, who lose it yet again at this statement. Even Alan the Giant is fisting his eye.

'We'll find you someone!' Liza says triumphantly, pulling out her phone and opening Facebook. Good idea, because obviously all her eleven-year-old friends will be gagging for a date with my tiny, sixty-year-old dad.

'Have you tried Tinder yet, Alan?' Lois asks.

Zoe looks excited.

'Yeah, let's get Alan on Tinder!' Liza joins in.

Dad is nodding enthusiastically but definitely doesn't know what Tinder is.

Oh God, this is the worst.

'Erm, is this a good idea . . . ?' I try but Lois interrupts me.

'Have you got a smartphone, Alan?' she says. Dad hands it over and she starts fiddling. I realise with a start that this whole situation is horribly familiar. It's like a parallel reality version of my night at Sophie's house a few weeks ago. A Kafkaesque version of my life, and I'm trapped inside it.

Alan the Giant is leaning over. 'Gosh, Alan, mate, you've got a lot of photos on Facebook, haven't you, mate?'

Dad nods excitedly. 'You must add me!'

They pick a photo of him and start searching for matches in the vicinity. I watch in total horror as the first woman's face pops up.

Me.

I'm the first suggestion.

Of course.

Of. Fucking. Course.

I take the phone as Lois gives the group an I-told-you-so face.

'Let's definitely not, shall we?'

It's close to 1 a.m. and Dad is telling the group about his recent retiree project; investigating the family tree.

'. . . of course, the war criminals were only on Lenny's mum's side of the family,' he explains blithely. 'My side were just in prison for thieving and raping the locals.'

I yawn loudly and Liza leans across.

'So, Ellie, tell me about you,' she starts. We haven't really spoken much yet tonight, and I smile, wondering if I could tell her about my painting and the gallery, and my newfound ambition and –

She interrupts my thought process. 'You're single, right? Why are you single? High standards?'

Cool. Straight in there.

Liza's already told us all about her own love life – in graphic detail – and asked for advice on what to do about her boyfriend of four months, who, she says, just doesn't seem ready to commit yet. We suggested she be patient, but she says she doesn't want to be an 'old mum'.

OK, I'm ready for this.

I take a deep breath and explain, 'Actually, honestly, Liza, I have really low standards, so I don't think it's that. I don't know what the answer is. I can only tell you that I like being single. I like my freedom, I like being selfish. My life isn't exactly how I pictured it, but being on my own has never been an issue. I love my own space and I worry what a relationship would do to that. Even the best boyfriends in the world are difficult and need shouting at occasionally. I haven't had to shout at anyone at all since I broke up with my ex, Tim. Or been shouted at. I can just be who I want to be. So yeah, I just like being single.'

The group has turned to face me during my speech, and the Alan the Giant is nodding encouragingly.

Hurray! Maybe I got through to these people. I'm so bored of the pity.

'Don't worry, love, you'll meet someone soon,' he offers reassuringly.

Trying not to roll my eyes, I try one final time. 'Thanks, but I'm happy on my own.'

Liza looks thoughtful. 'Have you considered therapy?'

'For what?' I am perplexed.

'To fix that,' she adds helpfully.

'Fix . . . happiness?' I say carefully, and she's nodding.

'You shouldn't be happy being single, that's just weird and wrong.'

This is pointless. 'Oh hey, Lois,' I grin, changing the subject. 'If I were gay, would you fancy m—'

She cuts me off. 'Oh my God, if you ask me if I would date you if you were gay, I am going to punch you in the vagina.'

Oh.

'I wasn't going to ask that!' I say, fake laughing.

I was.

'That's not even anatomically possible anyway,' I add, muttering. 'You're probably thinking of the vulva.'

She rolls her eyes but smiles and ruffles my hair.

Dad watches us, half smiling.

'You know, Ellie, I want you to know you can tell me absolutely anything,' he says, haltingly.

'Er, sure?' I reply, cautiously.

'I know you've been on your own since Timothy, and I'd want you to feel like you could speak to me if you decided that he – or, er, any other man – wasn't the right life path for you. You could talk to me about that if you wanted.'

Interesting.

'What do you mean?' I ask, curious.

He shifts in his seat. 'Well, I just mean, I see you here,

getting on so well with lovely Zoe and Lois, and they're very happy together, and I thought maybe . . . '

'Dad.' I narrow my eyes. 'Are you asking me if I'm gay?'

'Oh my goodness, no I wouldn't!' he looks alarmed, adding. 'There is no pressure for you to tell me that. Not now. I would never make you tell me anything like that until you were totally ready. Whenever. You must do it at your own pace. I just wanted you to know that whenever you feel comfortable, I'm here for you.'

'And you'd be all right with it, if I were gay?' I ask, genuinely curious.

'Oh my darling, of course I would.' He hugs me and I think how lucky I am to have such a warm, loving dad. My family might be dysfunctional as fuck, but there's a lot of kindness here. Even if I had to lose one of my parents, I know I'm still streets ahead of a lot of other people.

'Dad, that is so nice,' I tell him. 'But I'm not gay.'

He looks disappointed.

'But you've been single for so long. Are you sure?'

'It's not that long,' I say exasperated. 'And yes, I'm totally sure.'

I consider telling him about a girl I kissed in my second year of university and how little it did for me. And then I remember that this is my father, and it would be the worst conversation we could ever have – and that includes the one where he told me Mum was dying.

'You're very sweet, Dad, but being single doesn't mean I'm a lesbian. Although hey . . .' I turn, laughing towards Lois, '. . . I think sometimes it would be easier if I w—'

She rolls her eyes again and cuts me off. 'Don't say that either. God, be a cliché some more, why don't you, Ellie?

Oh. My bad.

Dad finishes his cocktail and slowly chews on the Jammy Dodger that came with the drink.

'OK,' he says slowly. 'Well, whoever you are and whatever you do, I am so proud of you, Lenny.'

'I know, Dad, I'm proud of you too. Shall we get an Uber?'

He looks suspicious. 'Is that number seven on the menu? You know I'm not a big fan of rum.'

I laugh. 'Happy birthday, Dad.'

8

6.20 p.m. Friday, 15 March
Location: My cramped, mould-ridden shower, which is dribbling alternately hot and cold water from a shower head coated in immoveable limescale. There's hair blocking the drain, and several almost-empty Radox bottles lining the floor. All belonging to Josh. But he says he 'needs them' so no I can't throw them away. I will viciously knock each and every one of them over before I get out.

For God's sake. I'm nearly thirty and have still not worked out what to do about my body hair. I'm in the shower having an actual out-loud argument with myself about it. Of course, objectively I know it is nonsense that I should consider it a problem. It's hair, it's fucking hair – WHY DOES IT MATTER? – but I'm not immune to society telling me everything below my neck is disgusting. I have a date tonight with a guy who actually seems genuinely promising, and I know I should do something about it, just in case, but I'm paralysed. I always leave it too late for a wax (mostly deliberately because it's awful and mortifying and painful, and when exactly are you supposed to go? Three days before? The day before? Seven days after? I have no idea). I could shave, and I usually persuade myself to do that, but that's awful too. If I shave now, it'll be fine for exactly an hour and a half, and then I will be covered in red spots, unable to wear jeans for at least a week, and trying not to scratch myself in public too much. I should just leave my bush alone. But I also don't want him to think I'm disgusting if we do end up having sex.

Sigh. It's not like it matters; everyone knows the rule – if you shave, nothing will happen, and if you don't, you'll somehow end up shooting a porno and it will have to be in the 'fetish' category because you've got hair down there. Right, I am a feminist who does not have to do anything I'm not comfortable with, so decision made. I will leave my poor vulva alone. Free the bush. I climb out of the shower, feeling proud, like a naked Germaine Greer.

Tonight's date is with thirty-four-year-old Nathan. He's a politics teacher and we've already had some really smart WhatsApp conversations about the latest happenings with this government, and the situation across the Atlantic at the White House. I think I came across as really intelligent and well-informed, thanks to the comments I copy and pasted directly from the *Guardian*. As I stare in the mirror, trying to find my one long chin hair and wondering if I should've shaved my face, I feel a tiny bit of excitement unfurling in my stomach. I'm not getting carried away or anything, but Nathan actually seems funny and interesting. And he wanted to know about me and my life. There's the smallest possibility that he could actually – shock horror – be a decent guy. Hey, it's a small chance, but it's definitely there. Which is why I feel so worried about making a good impression with the presentation of my vagina. Oh, come on, I shake myself, if he's really a decent person, he won't care either way.

As I leave the bathroom, I bump into Josh. He smirks at my towel and cocks a sexy eyebrow at me.

'Going somewhere, Knight?' he asks.

'Actually, yes,' I say huffily, pulling my towel tighter round me. 'I've got a date tonight. His name is Nathan and he's really good-looking. Much better looking than you, since you asked. And he's a much nicer human too. He doesn't abandon women he's shagged in his room while he eats breakfast.'

Josh smirks again.

I pause. 'Well, actually he might, I don't know yet. But he doesn't seem like the type to do that.'

'Blind date then?' says Josh, still looking amused. 'Where is he taking you?'

'We're going to an Italian restaurant near him, in east London.'

'Near his place?' His smile gets wider. 'Good move, Nathan. Classic.' And then because he's a dick, he adds playfully, 'Did you shave?'

'Fuck off, Josh,' I bark. 'I don't have to conform to your patriarchal standards of beauty. Go watch your glossy Barbie porn in your room.'

He shrugs, gives my legs another lingering look, and heads into his room.

What a dick.

I go back into the bathroom, climb back into the shower and shave it all off. I am such a shit feminist.

I'm early, for once, and ask the waiter for water. I've made a decision that I won't get too drunk. At least, not before my date actually arrives. Not again, I mean. It's a pretty nice place. It's a great date setting, lots of posh paintings on the wall and big fat candles on the tables. You know a restaurant is romantic when you can hardly see anyone else. I've learned that romance means as few light bulbs as possible. Which can be tricky when you're blind dating, but never mind. I'll just be on my phone when he arrives, so he has to make the awkward approach. I flashback to a date earlier this week where we arranged to meet outside a tube station and I approached three different men who all seemed to be waiting on dates before I located the right guy. It turns out, every single person waiting outside a station is waiting for a Tinder date.

Nathan arrives five minutes later, and I stand up to greet him. Honestly, I'm delighted. He's very good-looking – tallish, dark green eyes, wide smile – and he seems pleased to see me, giving me a kiss on the cheek and laughing at himself when he goes for two kisses and I sit down. I apologise and laugh too, feeling my nerves draining away. I fancy him, I realise with surprise. What a nice feeling. It's been a long time since I felt physically attracted to anyone – apart from the Josh hate-fancy and the weird crush on tiny-nipples-Gaz – and it's a relief to know I'm still physically capable of it. Could he be that rare find, a nice, normal man who is also attractive? Nathan starts chattering about his day, taking off his Paddington Bear-style blue duffel coat, and I realise from here on out, I will probably want to have sex with Paddington Bear.

'Thanks for coming all this way across London,' he says nicely, sitting down and picking up his menu. 'I know us Londoners don't really like to leave our own boroughs, but I love this place. It has such great food.'

'Don't be silly,' I say. 'I'm looking forward to trying it. And thank you for booking.'

To be honest, I never usually like to eat on a first date. I love food a little too much, and my shovelling technique is not conducive to falling in love with a stranger. I'd rather keep up the pretence that I'm a dainty little fucking flower for as long as possible. But it was so refreshing for a guy to actually suggest somewhere and make arrangements, I didn't want to discourage him. God, I'm sick of suggesting the same bar in Angel over and over again for dates because no one is capable of making a decision. I need a break from that place, because seriously, after that many nights in there, always leaving with a different man, at this point the barman in there definitely thinks I'm a prostitute. And not even one of those high-class, expensive ones.

We both study the menu for a minute, and I wonder whether the silence is comfortable or not. How do people know?

He looks over at me and smiles.

'You're so pretty,' he says, sweetly.

'Oh, shush,' I wave my hand at him, feeling horribly awkward. I've never been able to take a compliment like other normal humans. Tim used to tell everyone that the first time he'd said I had nice hair, I threw my food at him and shouted MERRY CHRISTMAS even though it was May, just to offer a distraction. I don't remember, so can neither confirm nor deny, but it does sound like me.

'Thank you,' I stutter a little, aware I'm going red and grateful for the dim lighting. 'You're not so bad yourself.'

He grins again and closes his menu, keeping eye contact. 'I know what I'm having, how about you?'

Two hours later and I'm on the loo, doing a little drunk dance as I wee. Nathan is great fun. We've been playing a series of drinking games, and we're both cheating constantly, so a lot of wine has been consumed on both sides. We've just finished one he plays with his students at the beginning of term (minus the alcohol, obvs), that's designed to help people get to know each other. The idea is that you offer up two facts about yourself and the other person has to guess which one is true. Except our version of the game quickly descended into who could tell the most outlandish two lies without laughing. We've also eaten a lot of food. Nathan insisted we get all three courses and has just now ordered a second dessert to share. It's so lovely not to be expected to just eat a side salad, and it's really helped soak up those alcohol percentages. But I'm still drunk enough to weave a bit as I stagger from the loo to the sink. I wash my hands and stare in the mirror, humming to myself as I think about how well tonight is going. As well as the sillier stuff, we've covered most standard date topics; family, work, friends. He seems genuinely interested in my life, and God, I'm certainly interested in his. He's been a secondary school teacher for the last four years, and before that he was living in Barcelona for a while, teaching English. That was in between backpacking around Europe. And before that, he spent some time in Africa, helping build villages, and presumably generally making everyone who's ever known him feel totally inadequate. Including me. He's got his life in order, he's got his own flat, a job he likes – he's a high achiever but he's not an arsehole about it. It's intimidating, sure, but it's also very attractive.

I check my face and reapply my dark purple lipstick.

God I love lipstick. I love putting it on, I love the way it looks, I love how powerful it makes me feel. Boys always talk about my hair and eyes (and tits, duh) when they're complimenting me/trying to have sex with me, but I've always thought my lips should get more attention. I pout in the mirror now, wondering if Nathan will want to bite my bottom lip.

Two girls barge in, arguing about how much they would have to be paid to get off with Donald Trump. I grab my bag, hoping they didn't catch me making sex faces at the mirror.

Back at the table, Nathan asks me how long I've been on Tinder.

'Not long – a few weeks – but it's already been life changingly bad,' I say, smiling. 'How about you?'

'About six months,' he replies, making a face. 'It's . . . it's been a mixed bag. Some great dates –' (he makes that lingering eye contact again) '– and some dreadful.'

I grin. 'My theory is that the dreadful ones are really the best,' I say. 'At least they give you a funny story to tell your friends later on. Nobody really wants to hear about a nice date where everyone got on fine and no one got set on fire. And isn't that really why we're all on Tinder? To entertain our mates?'

He laughs but doesn't look so sure. 'Hmm. I think my friends are bored of hearing about it. And I don't think an amusing pub tale was worth the horror of my last date with Sister Sandra.' He grimaces and I laugh. 'She was on a Christianity recruitment drive and told me I was going to hell when I ordered us some wine. I thought she was joking and then she gave me a leaflet about saving my soul.'

'Of course she did. Do you still have the leaflet? I'd really like to read it.'

He nods. 'Of course, I take it everywhere I go, I'm going

to read you some passages later – are you more of a New or Old Testament kind of gal?'

'Old, of course,' I say lightly. 'I like big beards and shouting. Didn't I put that on my Tinder profile? Hey, let me know if you ever lose that leaflet, I keep spares in my bag for sinners like you.'

We giggle and he reaches over to top up my wine, brushing my hand. My skin tingles a bit.

'I had a date recently where the guy took me to his "favourite Pret",' I tell him. 'About four minutes in, it became clear I was just there to make Natalie – the girl making lattes – jealous. He studiously ignored me, while repeatedly trying to get Natalie's attention. I actually felt sorry for him, she just totally ignored him. It was all kinds of awkward.'

We laugh again and start telling competitively bad Tinder stories.

He tells me about a girl who kept asking him how often he pissed sitting down, and then revealed that she kept a PG Tips mug by her bed to wee in when she couldn't be bothered to get up and go to the loo. I tell him about the guy who asked me, twenty minutes into the date, if I'd like to have my toes sucked. And how he then, in a romantic voice, told me that he hadn't had his usual wank that day because he was saving himself for me.

And so it went on.

It's freezing as we leave the restaurant, the last patrons standing, and he puts his arm round me.

'This was fun,' I say, the fear settling over me again. What happens now? I haven't had a date I actually liked before.

'It really was,' he smiles, adding casually, 'Do you want

to come back to mine? It's only a few minutes this way.' He nods along the high street and I stare down the road, undecided. I do like Nathan, he's fun and sexy, but I'm picturing Josh smirking. Telling me this was the plan all along. Picturing myself creeping home in the morning, shoes in hand like last time, and hearing Josh crow that Nathan got exactly what he wanted. But who cares if inviting me here was a ploy, right? We're all animals who like sex, there shouldn't be any shame in that. Should there?

And I did shave.

But he'll think I'm a slag if I go back with him.

But that's totally outdated and ridiculous. Would I really be interested anyway, if this was a guy who would judge me for doing that?

I squirm.

But he'll tell his friends I put out on the first date.

But do I care?

But I quite like him, and Jen will tell me off.

But I'm horny.

But he'll judge me.

Nathan looks a bit bemused. My internal monologue has gone on that little bit too long, and I'm probably making faces.

'Go on, we're not far,' he says, taking my hand. 'I don't want this to end yet, we can just chat. I have wine in the fridge.'

Oh, how convenient. I hesitate again. 'Erm, actually, if it's OK,' I hear myself say, 'I'm going to head home, I've got so much to do in the morning and I'm heading over to visit my dad first thing. This was great, but . . . *y'know*.'

He looks perturbed.

'I wasn't trying to be pushy, I just thought we could have another drink,' he says, defensively.

'Oh, I know, I just . . . better get an Uber,' I say, pulling out my phone. His sexy eyes have turned into more of a death stare. I suddenly, definitely want to go home.

He sighs as I click the app. The car is two minutes away.

'OK,' he says, a little coolly. 'I'll wait with you.'

We stand in awkward silence and I feel very disappointed. Disappointed in him for his reaction, and disappointed in myself. I seem to have ruined the whole night and I don't really know how.

I should say something.

'I . . .' A car beeps as it draws up. My taxi.

Nathan opens the door for me and smiles a little tightly.

'Sorry,' I find myself saying, and then hating myself for it, as I climb in. 'I had a great time.'

He nods. 'I'll text you.'

He does text me. As I pull up back at my house twenty minutes later, my phone vibrates.

> Hi Ellie, I had a fun night, but I don't think we're really compatible, sorry. Take care. Good luck with your search. Bye.

I drop my phone into my bag like it's hot. Ouch. Ouuuuuuch. What is this? Was it just that I said no to sex? Am I sixteen again, being dumped by my boyfriend because I wouldn't put out? This was the first date where I've actually had a really, genuinely good time. Met someone I had chemistry with. And I got rejected. So what's the point of this? I am clearly never going to meet someone decent.

Thank God Josh isn't around as I drag myself to my room and collapse on my bed.

I'm so annoyed. There are such mixed messages given to women these days. I'm told over and over again that I'll never find love while I keep having all this fun sex. So I stop having all the fun sex and I'm still getting rejected.

I should've just had sex with him.

No! That's stupid! It's good that I didn't go back to his. I'd have felt much more humiliated afterwards, thinking he liked me and then getting this text message the next morning.

I don't know what to think. We had fun, didn't we? He just flipped so suddenly. It's so disappointing.

What a shit. Ugh.

I moan into my pillow, and check what the time is in California. Four thirty in the afternoon, which means Jen will be back from the school run. I call her.

'What?'

This is how she always answers the phone.

'Hi. How are you? What are you doing?'

'Busy.' She's not busy. 'How are you?'

'Um, I guess I'm OK. I just wanted to say hello.'

She sounds suspicious. 'Why?'

I sniff. 'I just got back from a date. A good and then very bad date. I'm pretty sick of all this, it's exhausting and a total headfuck. I wanted some support, a friendly voice, so I'm not sure why I rang you.'

'I can be supportive if I want to be.' She sounds indignant. 'It's not my fault you won't be helped. You're as bad as Dad. I offered to set him up with my friend's mum the other day. She's lovely and lives really near him. She's a widow too and they have so much in common. I arranged the whole thing but instead of giving her a chance, it was all complaints from him when he got home.'

I brighten up, thinking about how I'll hear all about this tomorrow at Dad's. At least he's going through the hell of dating too.

'What kind of complaints?' I say.

'Oh, you know, the usual excuses: "She's too old for me, Jen. She's eighty-two, Jen. She couldn't hear anything because her hearing aid wasn't on, Jen. The other residents at the care home asked if I was her son, Jen. We weren't even allowed outside because of her oxygen machine, Jen." What a load of nonsense. He says he wants to meet someone, so I go to the trouble of finding him someone perfect, and he's this ungrateful.'

'Hmm, yes, very ungrateful,' I agree, supportively. I'm trying not to laugh at the picture of an eighty-two-year-old woman trying to flirt with my dad.

'Look,' she says, suddenly sounding serious. 'Do you actually want to meet someone? Because you don't seem to be having any fun with this dating. And frankly, all this moaning is getting very tiring for me. I have a lot going on over here, you know?'

'Like what?' I say innocently.

Jen pauses. She doesn't have anything going on. She's got no friends in California – for obvious reasons – Andrew is busy with work all the time, and Milly is the most self-sufficient six year old I've ever met. She won't be helped by anyone or with anything. Seriously, do not try to help her, or you will lose your fingers.

'Are you OK over there, Jen?' I say, quietly, knowing there's no chance she'll admit to being lonely.

'Of course I fucking am,' she snaps. 'Don't patronise me.

I love it here. It's better than sad sack England, with that awful weather and that old man always hanging around going on about his garden.'

'Dad?'

'No, Prince Charles. So fuck off with your sympathy, I'm totally fine. You're the one everyone's worried about.'

I shouldn't have said anything. I know the rules with Jen. It's important she never thinks you're trying to offer advice or support of any kind. If she feels in any way patronised she will lash out, snarling that she doesn't need any 'JOLLYING FUCKING ON'. It's a tricky line though because I also get accused of 'NOT FUCKING CARING' regularly. But how do you ask questions about a person's life without seeming interested or supportive? Tricky, tricky.

'OK, well you know where I am' I say, cautiously.

'DON'T FUCKING JOLLY ME ALONG, I'M FINE,' she shrieks. 'It's you that needs to get your life in order. You'll be thirty soon and no man wants to date a thirty year old. Stop spending all your time with Dad, meet some actual men, bring down those *mandards* of yours, and get in line, for God's sake. Life is meant to follow a certain path: work, marriage, kids. That's how it's supposed to work, Ellie. Stop fighting it and just get on with it. Everyone's sick of you being so contrary.'

'I'm not contrary,' I mutter, contrarily.

'Look, I have to go,' she sighs. 'Stop dating if that's what you really want. If you really want to be on your own forever, then quit the apps. But bloody well be brave about it. Be your own person, tell Sophie and everyone else asking you about it to fuck off and stop letting everyone else tell you what to do. Do what you want to do. OK?'

'OK, Jen, I'll stop letting everyone else tell me what to do.

Thanks, sorry. Night.'

She hangs up.

From: Alan Knight <Alanknightinshiningarmour@BTInternet.co.uk>
To: Eleanor.knight@gmail.com, Jennifer.seevy@hotmail.com

22nd March

Alan Knight
106 Castle Rise
Judfield
East Sussex
TN22 5UN

Dear Eleanor and Jennifer,

I hope you are both very well. Did you catch that cracking episode of "Neighbours" yesterday? I just do not know how they continue to come up with such high quality stories, year after year. I went for a walk with Peter and Candice this morning and she suggested I should write episode reviews for "IMDb". What do you think?

Lenny – Thank you for your "reply". I don't understand. Is "EL James" a Mexican restaurant? And if it is, why would they want to sue me? If you are serious, Candice says she and Peter have been watching "The Good Wife" and she can find me a lawyer on the internet if need be.

Jenny – Someone has accidentally written "Return to sender" on the last few chapters I posted to you. It looks like your writing! L.O.L. But don't worry, I will post them out again. I don't want you to miss out because Candice says it's getting "really good" now.

Love you both very much and I'm so proud of you.

Best wishes,
Dad

---

75 HUES OF TONY
A novel, by Alan Bernard Knight

Tony cannot believe the last few days. Since all that snogging with tongues in the lift at Svetlana's house, Svetlana has been bombarding Tony with texts and gifts. She has sent him clothes and cufflinks and a laptop and a new car, but Tony is still unsure what to do. He likes Svetlana but he is overwhelmed by all this and after another conversation with Wanda last night who came over to make Tony a really nice dinner, although not chicken and nut roast, because it wasn't chicken and nut roast night, he is feeling even more uncertain. Wanda says that Svetlana has a dark past and has been single a long time which is a bad sign. She is to be avoided!!

But Tony is not sure he can avoid Svetlana. He is drawn to her dark and powerful aura.

Today she rang him up when he was on his way out the door to visit B&Q to get a new plant pot and it was on her landline so clearly she has been able to get it replaced without his help but Tony isn't annoyed about that, it is fine. She wanted to know where he was going and when he mentioned B&Q, Lana said she had some errands to run there too, and could they meet in the tools section? She said in a very flirtatious way that she needed a really big tool and Tony understood the innuendo immediately because he is very intelligent. Anyway, he agreed to meet her and he cannot deny how excited he is now as he climbs into his new

Lamborghini Veneno that Lana sent him. He thinks now maybe he should buy Lana something as she has bought him so many presents? He will pick up a box of Celebrations on his way to B&Q.

He smells Lana's intoxicating musk before he sees her, turning the corner on the plant-food aisle. There she is and she looks even more unbelievably good-looking than the last time he saw her. She's wearing a really, really nice purple top and purple skirt and her hair is up in a way that is really nice. Lana stops when she sees him perusing the seeds, and they stare at each other for about five minutes. Tony wonders if maybe they should stay this distance apart because he senses it would be dangerous to get any closer.

And then Lana comes over and in her basket Tony spies that she has eighteen rolls of duct tape. 'If you need to fix a puncture, I can change a tyre,' says Tony helpfully and Lana looks at him again.

'These aren't for a puncture,' she says, smiling mysteriously.

The sexual tension that is now a given between them is really filling up the aisle, and passers-by look over at them, no doubt thinking what a beautiful couple they make.

'Thank you for the gifts,' says Tony and then gives her the chocolates. He couldn't find any Celebrations in Tesco, so he had to settle for Quality Street.

'These are my favourites. You are so very thoughtful!' says Lana, putting them in her purple bag. Tony is very good at gift buying.

Lana reaches over and strokes Tony's arm and then they both drop their shopping baskets and start snogging again right there and then! It is very risqué, right in the middle of B&Q, but other customers who might usually be upset by it all actually seem really impressed because it's so clearly amazing kissing.

When they finally stop, they are both out of breath despite Tony's regular cardio on the step machine.

'That was amazing,' said Tony.

'It was the best kissing I've ever done,' said Lana. 'Tony, I would like you to consider signing a contract to be my boyfriend.'

A contract? thinks a very confused Tony. Tony is not one of those men who says all women are crazy but this particular woman does seem to be crazy even though she is a very good kisser.

'Why would you want me to sign a contract?' he says, and this time it is out loud.

'Because I want to be in charge of you,' says Lana. 'It's what everyone does where I come from.'

Tony is not sure he believes this. He has been to all of the countries in the world and he has never seen anyone sign a contract to become a boyfriend. And it will come as no surprise that loads of women have wanted him to be their boyfriend!!

'What would the contract say?' says Tony, still confused but not wishing to be rude.

'I will have it drawn up for you immediately,' says Lana. 'You can read it in full then. But know that signing it will mean you can have everything you've ever wanted. I am an amazingly generous girlfriend, Tony. You can have all my money, all my things and most importantly . . .' Lana starts whispering '. . . you can have my BODY, Tony.' Lana picks up her shopping basket full of duct tape as Tony tries to keep himself together. He is very overwhelmed by her words especially the part where she whispered the word BODY. Lana walks off and then turns around and says seductively, 'You will want to sign it, Tony, I promise you. Oh, and will you also be at home tomorrow to take delivery of a private jet?'

Tony confirms that he will and establishes the delivery slot between three and four in the afternoon, then they go their separate ways because Tony has not completed his B&Q purchases just yet. He is more confused than ever. Yes, he is very attracted to Svetlana, but he is not sure about being her boyfriend, and he is also not too sure about signing a contract? That seems a little bit too much. He might even say that it seems a tiny bit unnecessary. Especially after only meeting a few days ago. But he has not been single for a long time and maybe this is the way of the world now. Maybe Anita is somewhere out there signing a contract with a rich man too.

Tony heads home. He knows he has a LOT of thinking to do.

END SCENE

9

10.35 a.m. Monday, 25 March
Location: The glass-walled office boardroom for our regular Monday morning 'catch up'. There are never enough seats for everyone, so I mostly end up milling around at the back. And at least one of the old married dudes will offer to have me and/or Maddie on their laps *haha just being hilarious don't tell my wife haha or call HR just a joke*. And then they will look afraid for the next ten minutes, darting glances at us and wondering if I'm recording this because I'm the type to do that. And maybe I am.

Maddie is meant to be discussing what projects she's working on, updating Derek on how she's getting on with them. But she's mostly just telling everyone she's rubbish and how it was a group effort, while the men either side of her, who didn't help at all, look pleased with themselves and nod. I've told Maddie to stop doing this but she won't. Every Monday is the same. She says she doesn't want to come across as 'aggressive' by taking credit for her own accomplishments. I'm her self-appointed work wingwoman, so it's my duty to let her know when she's self-sabotaging, and also step in when she's getting interrupted over and over again by the office bros. I find it so frustrating, but she doesn't seem to notice. Actually, I don't think Madds would even know how to end a sentence during a meeting – she's so used to being shut down mid-word.

As we all file out, I prepare to tell her off again but she doesn't want to listen to my self-righteous speech this time, waving away my pleas with something 'much bigger and more important' than her 'stupid career'.

'I'm in love!' she hisses at me happily as I gape back at her. Rich falls into step with us. He's missed his 11 a.m. Quavers showing, but, *thank God*, he's got a packet ready now and is already diving in.

Maddie is glowing with excitement as she giggles at my shocked face. I know she had her very first Plenty of Fish date on Friday and she didn't reply to my pushy text on Saturday, demanding to know how it went, so I assumed it was a let-down. Because duh, dating. And duh, dating on Plenty of Fish.

'Sorry I didn't reply to your message, I was pretty caught up with Zack,' she sighs. 'That's also why I was late to the meeting this morning. Ellie, he's so completely wonderful, I can't even tell you. It was love at first sight. We met after work at my local Wetherspoons, and it was just . . . magical. We got drunk on tequila and just, fell in love, y'know? He came back to mine and we spent the whole weekend together. It was so romantic.' She looks overcome and says again, 'He's completely wonderful.'

'That does sound, erm, romantic,' I say agreeably, a bit overwhelmed with all the 'romance' of tequila and Wetherspoons.

Rich agrees enthusiastically, sucking on a Quaver. 'It does sound dead romantic, Maddie, I'm so happy for you! Do you think I should try Plenty of Fish? I was at a wedding at the weekend and every girl I spoke to told me they had a boyfriend before I'd even got past hello.'

We both ignore him and Maddie goes on. 'I know it's come out of nowhere, and I've only just broken up with Ben, but Zack and I have talked about it and we've agreed to take it really, really slow. He knows I'm very newly single and we wouldn't want to rush anything. But, Ellie, I totally know he's The One and I told him that, and he said it too! We even talked about marriage and babies!' She glances at my shocked face and adds quickly, 'But we're going really slow, I promise.'

I nod, enthusiastically. Marriage and babies. Really slow. 'So . . . ' I try. 'You won't be, like, talking about being boyfriend-girlfriend for a while yet?'

She looks caught out. 'Well yes, we did decide we would take that step, and commit to each other as boyfriend and girlfriend. But we're still going really slowly, honestly we are, Ellie.'

I laugh. We have different definitions of slow, clearly. 'That's lovely, Madds, I'm so excited for you.'

'So am I! Haha!' says Rich, unnecessarily. As if anyone cares about his opinion.

Maddie hums happily. 'Can you believe it was my very first date after Ben, and I've already met someone! And not just someone, but *the* someone! What a great story for the wedding too, don't you think? My first internet date and I met the perfect guy. It's a dream come true. You can just totally picture my dad making a wedding speech, can't you? I'm so lucky!'

I laugh again and squeeze her happily.

She stops suddenly, looking mortified. 'Oh Ellie, I'm throwing all of this in your face, aren't I? When you've been single for, like, years and been on a million dates!'

'One year, and it's not a million,' I correct her. I really

don't want this to turn into a conversation about me and my singleness. Not again.

I continue, 'And as if I care about that! I'm really happy for you, Madds, this is awesome, Zack sounds like perfection. I want to see pictures and I want to meet him as soon as possible!'

Maddie starts gabbing excitedly about his gorgeous silky hair as she pulls out her phone and shows me his Facebook. I smirk, noting that they've already added each other and tagged themselves as 'in a relationship'. But who am I to judge? It has been three days after all.

My snark aside, I wonder if I mean it, if I am genuinely happy for Maddie. Not totally, I realise, as she shows Rich baby pictures of Zack, and tells us how they have the same favourite colour (blue), and how Alfred went straight for his crotch when they met – which means he likes him.

It's not jealousy I feel. I guess I am just a bit . . . disappointed. Caught off guard, maybe. I was excited about having someone single to play with. And not even for dating together purposes. I think it was more that there would be someone else for everyone to pick on. That I wouldn't be the only curiosity around. That, by extension, my singleness wouldn't be so strange. That my situation would be less of an issue for everyone else if my friend was in the same boat. But this is good for Maddie – in a totally nuts, overly quick, rebound-y way – because I don't think she would've liked being single anyway. She's a relationship person. We all know those friends who can't be single; Maddie craves that security. And I've really never seen her this full of joy – she's bouncing off the walls. So I'm happy for her. At least, I'm happy enough.

We sit back down at our desks and Aaron from the post room wanders by, waving in our direction.

For a second Maddie looks horrified and wails, 'Oh my God, I forgot to have sex with Aaron! I forgot to have sex with *everyone*. That was my one window of opportunity and I blew it.' She looks disappointed and then quickly rallies. 'But Zack is The One, so it doesn't matter. I've met the best man in the world, I don't need to have sex with Aaron. I'm going to text Zack right now about how cute our babies will be. Look, I've downloaded that app that lets you put your pictures in and shows you what your offspring will look like.'

Rich makes a loud sucking noise on a Quaver and suddenly turns to me. 'Hey, Ellie, I've just thought. I know someone single!'

Oh, here we go. Everyone has one single friend and they always say they're perfect for you but it always turns out the 'perfect for you' part is just that they're also single.

'He'd be perfect for you!' says Rich.

There it is. I sigh. Getting set up by Rich. I've hit a new life low.

Maddie puts down her phone, squealing and doing excited jazz hands. She wheels over between us in her chair. 'Amazing! What's his name, Rich? What does he do?'

Traitor. Straight off the single train and immediately back on the out-of-control, hurtling-towards-death-at-breakneck-speeds, find-Ellie-a-boyfriend train.

Rich grins. 'He's called Ronald –' (I'm out) '– and he works in banking –' (I'm back in) '– finding loans for customers at the Watford branch of Natwest . . . '

But Maddie doesn't really care about the details of this man. Nobody does really, they just want you to settle. When you're twenty, everyone's like, 'Ewwwww, he said he prefers cats over dogs? Dump that creep.' And when you're nearly thirty, everyone's like, 'Oh dear, he's on the register, so not allowed to visit your house because it's near a playground? Just stay at his place or you could move house? – YOU CAN MAKE THIS WORK.'

Maddie's clapping her hands now and chanting, 'Show us a picture, show us a picture!'

'OK!' Rich agrees enthusiastically. This is the most attention we've given him in months. He turns back to his computer and logs in to Facebook, checking Derek is safely ensconced in his office. Of course Rich doesn't already have any social media open, what a goody two shoes. Look at that – it doesn't even have his password saved, he has to *enter it manually*. Monster.

I look away as he types into the search bar. Rich tried to add me on Facebook ages ago and I've always left it pending. His profile is open though and he's that weirdo who updates his status once a week like he's writing a family newsletter. And *tags himself into his own status.*

'Here he is!'

Rich proudly sits back and we review Ronald Havering's profile page.

OK, well, firstly, this man is clearly over fifty, and his cover photo features three children he's clinging on to with that distinct, divorced-dad-seeing-those-cherubs-on-his-only-weekend-in-a-month air.

Maddie's eyes widen a little, 'He looks . . . ' she's searching for the word, 'LOVELY!' She has declared herself, content with this choice of soulmate for me. 'I mean, he's, he's not really my type, but you . . . ' She trails off.

Reaching over Rich, Maddie clicks through some more photos. The third picture in is clearly with his wife, and to her credit, Maddie pauses and looks unsure, sensing a tiny hurdle.

Rich nods sadly. 'That's his ex-wife, they broke up in January, but,' he turns to me eagerly, 'he's definitely ready to start dating again, he told me so. And he's *such* a great guy. Loves his kids so much and is a major cat person. He's really close to his mum too, actually he lives with her, but that's just until the divorce goes through next year.'

God I hate Rich.

'Er, how old is Ronald?' I enquire politely.

'Oh.' Rich looks concerned. 'He is a bit older than you, is that a problem? I'm sorry, Ellie, I didn't think you minded an age difference. The pictures of you and your ex on Facebook—'

'Tim?' I interrupt, bewildered. Tim is my age, and if anything, he looks much younger than me. Every time we got a meal deal in M&S, he would get asked for ID; to the point where I always had to buy the wine for us. I got ID'd in there once too, and when I started delightedly looking in my bag for my driving license, the cashier laughed and said, 'I was only joking.'

Rich continues, 'Was Tim his name? I thought it was Alan?'

'Alan? ALAN?' I shout. 'MY DAD? You thought my dad was my boyfriend? OHMYGOD WHY DOES EVERYONE THINK MY DAD IS MY BOYFRIEND?'

Rich looks crestfallen. 'Oh Ellie, I'm sorry, it's just that you're all over Facebook together and I just . . . '

Fucksake. I don't really add things to Facebook – it is primarily a creeping tool for me – but my dad loves it and is constantly taking 'selfies' of us to post and then 'checking us in to' the Crown and Anchor seven doors down from his house. So yeah, of course people think we're dating. Of course. Everyone I went to school with, who I never spoke to but am now obviously friends with on there, all now probably think I'm dating my dad. That is fantastic.

Fan-bloody-tastic.

Hmm. At least they think I have a boyfriend.

Rich looks really disappointed. 'OK, I'm really sorry. Forget about Ron.' He logs out of his Facebook and shuts the page. Goody two shoes.

Maddie huffs, clearly disappointed we're giving up on this dreamboat so easily.

'Hey, I tell you what, Ellie,' Rich adds excitedly, turning back around. 'How about if we're both single when we're forty, we get married?' He laughs too loudly. 'Haha. Marriage pact? Haha.'

I narrow my eyes. 'Didn't you just turn thirty-nine, last week?'

Maddie giggles and Rich coughs awkwardly and then suddenly springs up out of his seat. 'Haha. Just a joke. Haha. You're so funny, Ellie. Just popping to the loo, haha.'

He stiffly turns to go and then turns back. 'So, no marriage pact then?'

I stare him out until he leaves. Sigh.

It's approaching lunchtime and I'm openly applying make-up at my desk. I've booked in a one o'clock Tinder date because I'm trying to be efficient about all this and I figured that an easily escapable hour here and there seems like the answer.

Especially since weekend dating appears to require me to shower and get out of bed, which is increasingly out of the question. I've been making a real effort to go on dates in the last couple of weeks, partly to get the taste of Nathan out of my mouth, and partly to appease Sophie and Jen, who told me I could stop when I got to thirty-five dates. I'm up to fourteen already and I think they've actually been impressed with my dedication. And also extremely disappointed in me because they've all come to nothing.

The trouble is, there seems to be only five types of men on dating apps, and I don't like any of them. There's:

1. The 'Nice Guy'.

This is the simmering-with-fury misogynist, who will tell you over and over how 'nice' he is, even as he calls women 'bitches' for not being interested in him. He wants you to know how many times this week he has opened a door for a lady who didn't even thank him, or paid for some ungrateful bitch's lunch, only for her to ignore him. He doesn't understand why being 'nice' doesn't entitle him to your vagina. He is the one who texts you after your coffee date when you've explained you're not interested, to ask you to give him back the £2.55 he paid for your latte.

2. The Shagger.

The guy who seems perfect and into you. You have a great time, share everything, talk about the next date; he wants to take you for drinks in the Shard – *Have you ever been? The view is almost as gorgeous as you are* – and you laugh together about the cheesy line. You go home thinking, actually, maybe a relationship wouldn't be so bad. And then he will totally fucking ghost you, and all your friends will try to convince you he's lost his phone/is in the hospital/is just scared by the intensity of his feelings. He's none of these things, he's just a prick who likes the validation of your attention, and/or your vagina.

3. The Bomber-Wearing Model with a Manbun.
It's not a model, it's a fifty-five-year-old guy living in his mum's basement masturbating over your enthusiasm to meet up. Sadly, he's always too busy with his, like, Save The Children volunteering and sexy mountaineering hobby to ever actually go on a date. He wants to keep texting you FOREVER AND EVER AND EVER though and if you could send a sexy selfie he'd be really grateful.

4. The Oversharer.
Dude just wants free therapy. He wants to tell you about his failed relationships, his failed career, his failed life. How he's been thinking about re-training as a life coach and what do you think about that? He's going to tell you about that time he stole a ten pound note from his mum's purse when he was seventeen and how he's been carrying that guilt around with him his whole life, eating his feelings late at night. And he's going to cry in your mouth when you sympathy-snog him. But at least it will shut him up for five minutes.

5. The Guy Who Wants a Wife.
At any cost. He just wants to settle down. Now. Whoever walked through that door, you were Her. He will text you when you go to the loo that he misses you. He wants to be your boyfriend that very night. When you have sex, he's going to look so deeply into your eyes and tell you he can't believe he's met you and he is so, so, so lucky. And when he texts you after that one date – about going to Canada for Easter to meet his cousins – you are going to have to spend the next week and a half trying to break up with him – with lengthy, emotionally charged texts back and forth about his FEELINGS. SO MANY FEELINGS.

Also, I've realised there are only four interests men on Tinder are allowed to have:

Music.

Photography.

Travelling.

Sports.

I'm not particularly into any of those things – I don't like hobbies at all – so that's tricky. And if one more guy passive-aggressively tells me their height, because apparently, 'It's all women on here seem to care about,' I will start removing the legs from everyone on the internet.

But here I am, on my way to yet another date. Today's lunch date is Robbie. He's twenty-nine, works in marketing – his office is round the corner from me – and is not good at all on texts. But I've learned that is also meaningless. A talent for messages has been no indicator of real personality so far. Some guys who've been hilarious on text have been absolute shambles of human beings in real life, less fun than the clichéd watching paint dry. More than once, I've had to resist the urge to ask if they're getting friends to compose texts for them – there can be no other explanation. I stop outside the restaurant to change my shoes, which is unfortunately when Robbie arrives and makes his approach.

'Ellie?' he asks, looking down at the one heel I'm wearing and the one Primark slipper (shut up, they're sooo comfy).

I laugh. 'Sorry about this,' I say, indicating my shoe. 'I was trying to make a decent impression with heels. Guess that didn't exactly work.'

He laughs and offers me his arm to balance on as I put the

other shoe on. His arm stays there as we head inside and I'm grateful. I forgot I totally can't walk in these heels.

He's handsome-ish and I'm touched by his laid back attitude to the shoe situation, but I quickly realise – after I've asked him about his life, his work, his family, his week, his journey to work this morning, his thoughts on the changeable weather, whether he thinks the loos here are nice, if his fork is clean – that he is one of those people who doesn't ask any questions. In fact, that 'Ellie?' at the beginning of the date is pretty much the only question mark I hear for the whole date.

I start to flounder. 'So how long have you been on Tinder?' I try.

'Four months.'

'How are you finding it?'

'Fine.'

'Any good date stories?'

'I don't think so.'

'Oh, so . . . all fine?'

'Yeah.'

'How, how . . . old . . . is . . . your . . . mum?'

I've run out.

'What?'

Oh! A question!

'Haha, sorry, I meant, do you have any pets?'

'No.'

'Not even, er, when you were growing up?'

'A goldfish.'

'Did you win him at the fair? I was always terrified that might happen. My mum told me she'd flush it down the loo if I ever brought one home.'

'No. It was from a pet shop.'

'What was its name?'

'Goldie.'

'That's a great name!'

I try again to volunteer some information about myself, in the hopes that it will spark a conversation. 'I never had fish for pets. Seems like a lot of hard work for not much return! They just sort of float there, looking shiny, don't they?'

[silence]

I keep going anyway. 'I had a dog, though, when I was little. Ralph. He was a Yorkshire terrier and the nicest little guy. He used to hide in my bed and surprise me when I got home from school. He died a few years ago, but my dad still has his little sister, Lily – although she's very old now and can't really see or hear.'

[silence]

'Bumps into things a lot.'

[silence]

'So that's nice.'

I breathe out slowly. Thank fuck this hour is nearly over. I have never wanted to get back to work so much before. Derek will be so impressed with my enthusiasm this afternoon, you just watch.

[silence]

OK, I can't take this any more. 'Right, this has been really *sooo* great, but I better head back to the office, work to do,' I say, getting up slowly, like it's just occurred to me and not, in fact, something I've been resisting doing for forty minutes. 'I've got a bunch of pig sketches to do,' I add, attempting to pique curiosity.

Nothing.

He nods. 'I better get back too, I guess.'

'Busy afternoon?' I try one final time.

'Probably. It usually is.' He half smiles and gives me a kiss on the cheek. We walk out together and he points in the direction of my office. 'I'm going that way.'

I panic. 'Oh, I'm down here,' I nod in the opposite direction and he looks a little disappointed. 'Bye then!' I wave in his face.

'I had a great time!' he says as I start walking away. He continues talking to my retreating back, 'I'd really like to see you again, it's not easy to find someone I can chat to so easily.' I don't look around.

I hide, crouching behind a car for a while until I'm sure he's gone, and then head back to my building. But when I get to the door, and see everyone busy, dashing about inside, I realise I can't quite face going in. I'm already late back, but it's not like Derek will say anything, so I head for the back stairwell to have a quiet sit for a few minutes more.

When I get there, Nick from across the other side of the office is already occupying my usual spot.

Nick and I have an unusual connection, in that we're on the same loo cycle. The Hales' office has a unisex bathroom, because we're just so unconventional, guys, and we reject society's societal social constructs, yeah? I'm being sarky but I do actually get irritated by the sexist signs on gender specific toilets. The 'quirky' representations of the sexes? Last week I saw one where the ladies' was a shopping bag, and the men's was a football. Nice. Anyway, having a unisex loo here essentially means there is regularly an unflushed poo in there. I'm not blaming the men of the office, but it is definitely the men of the office. I think sometimes constructs are about protecting you from men who don't know or care how buttons work. So Nick and I generally end up accidentally weeing together in side-by-side cubicles then complaining about the lack of hand towels, at least twice a day. We're bonded for life.

'Are you all right, Nick?' I ask, trying to be friendly, and then realising with horror that he's crying.

Erk. We're not *that* bonded. Maybe I should go.

'Yeah, I'm OK I suppose,' he says, wiping at his eyes.

'Can I do anything? Get you anything? Do you want some water?'

He smiles gratefully at me. 'Better not, wouldn't want to knock myself off our loo cycle, would I?'

I laugh a little, unsure what to do. 'I'm sorry, do you want me to leave you alone?'

'Not unless you really want to,' he says. 'Sorry about all the emotions. I've been having a rough few days.'

'Don't be silly. I'm sorry you're not having a good time.' I plop down next to him and we sit for a minute in companionable silence on the cold steps.

'I think my marriage is over,' he says suddenly, and the silent tears start again.

'Oh God, Nick, I'm so sorry. So sorry. How long have you been together?'

'Twenty-six years. Ellie, I love her so much.'

'If you love her, isn't it something you could work through?'

'Do you think that's possible?' He looks at me hopefully, through watery eyes.

'I don't know what's happened,' I say cautiously. 'But I

know that everyone makes stupid mistakes, and it doesn't mean you don't love that person a lot. I believe people can forgive each other.' I pause. 'Did you . . . have you . . .'

'She cheated on me,' he says quietly.

'Fuck.' I don't know what else to say.

'Do you think I should forgive her?'

'I can't really answer that. Do you want to forgive her?'

'I think I do. I really think I do. I want to. I love Emma so much. I know she's flawed, but that's what I've always loved about her. And like you say, Ellie, everyone makes mistakes, don't they? I have to get over it sometime. I can't keep holding on to this anger. Emma doesn't deserve that.'

He stands up, renewed.

'After all, like Emma says, I have another brother I can talk to, I don't, like, *need* Simon in my life. And like she says, I should stop moaning about the STD she gave me, because the antibiotics will clear that right up. There's really no reason I shouldn't forgive her, and like she says – has she *really* done anything *that* bad?'

I feel my eyebrows shoot up.

'You're right, Ellie,' he says again. 'Everyone deserves another chance. And I didn't like spending Christmas with my family anyway.' He pulls out his phone, presumably to call the unrepentant, riddled wife who has been sleeping with his brother.

'Thanks, Ellie, you've been great.' He wipes his face with his sleeve. 'You're so lucky to always be so happy and never have any issues. You should stay single forever! Life is a lot easier, trust me!'

He laughs, shouting, 'See you in the loo!' as he heads back into the office.

I sit there on the hard step for a few more minutes, feeling hollow.

Poor Nick. Imagine having to ditch your family over Christmas for a partner.

God, families are a mess. I have a flash of our last proper family Christmas together before Mum got ill. It was claustrophobic, overwhelming, and I spent the whole week begging Dad to please for the love of God turn the heating down, but it was also really nice. Mum, Jen and me were on the day-wine for five days straight, and we got so drunk on Christmas Day that we ended up spit-roasting the living-room furniture to a Liberty X album.

I wish my mum was here. I wish it so, so hard.

I miss her all the time. But that's not enough, those words aren't enough, because it's more than that. I read somewhere once about phantom limbs, how people who've lost a leg or an arm still feel an itch or pain in that missing limb. My mum being gone is like I've lost my arm. Every time I look down, expecting to see it, I feel the loss all over again. I'm getting by without her – I'm smiling, I'm doing what I need to do to survive – but my life will never be as good as it was with her in it. It still hits me sometimes, how fucked up it is, the way everyone just carries on, as if the most important person in the world hasn't left it.

The weight of it crushes down on me and I cry now, alone in the stairwell. And then I cry some more because I'm ashamed of crying.

Mum would know what to say to make me feel better in this moment. She'd tell me that everything – my work, the house, these terrible dates – will all figure itself out.

And then I laugh, because actually, she wouldn't have said anything remotely as comforting. She would've hugged me, and then she would've said the daftest thing she could think of, just to make us both laugh. She never put any pressure on me about finding The One, or getting married. She just wanted me to be happy, that was all that mattered to her.

I don't know how to talk about how much I miss laughing with her. How much I miss arguing with her. How much I miss the smell of her and the warmth. Dad talks about her sometimes, but he gets so emotional, I don't want to burden him with the depth of my feelings. He needs me to be strong. I can't fall apart with him.

I want so badly to talk to Jen about it, but she won't. Or can't, maybe, I guess. I wonder if she misses Mum like I do. I want to ask her how to do this – life – without Mum's help, because I feel like I don't know. And I don't know how to hold the family together without her. Mum was our glue. She was the one who dressed up as Father Christmas – the worst one you've ever seen – to hand out presents every year. Even that last horrible, horrible Christmas, when she was so sick she could barely get out of bed, she still insisted on wearing the hat and beard. And then she complained that we'd ruined the magic when we kept asking her if she was OK – if she needed her sick bucket.

It's so unfair. That's the worst of it, how angry I feel all the time. I feel angry with Mum for leaving us, I feel angry at Sophie and Thomas and everyone else for having their mums, I feel angry with Dad for being OK without her, I feel angry at Jen for moving away with Milly right after the funeral and not coming back. And I feel so angry with myself for feeling this way. I don't know how to get over losing her and I don't know if I'm even supposed to get over it.

I angrily wipe the wet tears from my face and follow Nick back in.

10

7.40 p.m. Friday, 29 March
Location: Sophie's large living-room. Things are somewhat, er, less perfect than usual. There are discarded toys lying on the floor, a smelly wet towel thrown over a chair, and a half-eaten ham sandwich that does *not* look organic, sitting disapprovingly on the sofa.

We've been here a couple of hours and, despite my best efforts, the mood is not improving. Sophie's quiet and snappy, frayed by a lack of sleep and a small child who is always present, even when, like now, she's out with her dad. We ordered pizza – usually forbidden because of E numbers or something (gluten? I think gluten is the one we don't like any more, right? E numbers was such an early noughties concern), but even melted cheese couldn't help relieve the weird tension. My usually immaculate best friend today is wearing a stained blue cashmere jumper, matched in no way with a pair of fetching grey, saggy jogging bottoms. Her usually glossy hair is still technically glossy, but today the shine is more grease than lustre. It's pulled back into a tight ponytail, with an attractive fat line of dry shampoo zigzagging along her unwashed parting. There's also the sweet tang of perfume in the air, like a person – let's say Sophie, specifically – has frantically sprayed an unwanted Christmas present around her living-room, just as guests are arriving, in order to mask a smell. Let's say a ham sandwich smell.

Sophie is, today, much more like I would be if I were to have a child.

Usually, I'd be delighted by the slip in protocol. I would've crowed about being allowed to eat gluten (and, what the heck, E numbers too). I would've eaten the stale ham sandwich as a pizza chaser, just to prove a point. But not today. Sophie is not in that kind of mood. Not in the mood for fun.

Thomas and I have carefully made small talk around the tension, which was ready and waiting for us when we arrived, and it's fine, I understand Sophie is tired, but I do feel a bit hard done by. I've had a shitty week too and was hoping I could rant tonight. Rant about dating, rant about my work, rant about Josh and TS. Obviously I don't want to make everything about me, but I was really secretly hoping we could make everything about me. I was hoping my best friends would tell me I'm awesome a bunch of times and send me home smiling, like they usually do. But I know this is not the day for that. My life and my stupid little problems would seem trivial and unimportant next to the real life difficulties of having a small child.

I squirm on the sofa, wondering if it's too early to leave. We were supposed to be watching a film – Sophie and I concocted a plan on Tuesday and rehearsed a whole script for today, one that would result in Thomas thinking he came up with the idea of watching one of the *Twilight* movies. But my partner in crime hasn't even properly sat down with us yet. She barely touched the food and now she's moving – prowling – between the kitchen and the living-room, where we're sitting, picking things up, tutting at them, and putting them back down again. She's snapped at Thomas twice now to take his feet off the sofa, which is something she doesn't usually care about. She has a child so, as we've discussed many times, the sofas will obviously need to be thrown away in a couple of years.

There's another lull in conversation, and hesitating, Thomas asks again, cautiously, 'Are you all right, Soph?'

She ignores him, her only response a loud, weary sigh in the direction of the ham sandwich.

'Come sit down with us?' I add, trying to be cheerful, even though I feel miserable. She glances over at us now, like she's forgotten we were here.

'I'm fine,' she snaps. 'I can't sit down, there's too much to do.'

'Then let us help you?' I offer, but she shakes her head.

The TV is playing episode after episode of *Come Dine with Me* and suddenly a drunk woman, with all of the cleavage you can imagine, shrieks with laughter. Her breasts shaking dangerously on screen. I snort and Sophie follows suit, the tension in the room slightly easing. I breathe out, as she finally sinks down onto a chair behind her, and adds reluctantly, 'Ciara's been poorly, so I haven't really slept in two days. I'm a bit tired, but I'm fine.'

'Oh no,' I say feebly, unsure what to say.

'That's awful, poor little mite. What's wrong with her?' Thomas adds. He's better at this than I am.

'An ear infection,' Sophie says, picking up a cushion and then putting it back down again. 'She's got antibiotics, the doctor said not to be concerned, it's very normal. It's just . . .' She pauses and a cloud crosses her face as she continues, 'Never mind, you two wouldn't get it.'

I feel a wave of irritation. Why wouldn't we get it? We try to get it. I can certainly picture how exhausted I'd be if I'd been awake for two days straight, listening to a person

I'd barely known a couple of years screaming in my face at 4 a.m.

Actually, that reminds me of a couple of nights out after our GCSEs.

But Sophie knew this would happen when she had a baby. It's the one thing they're actually honest about when it comes to parenting – you will never sleep again. She knew that's what she was choosing. That's what she wanted. I don't want to sound melodramatic, but she *chose* this life over our old life – how can she act like we're the ones who've rejected her?

Sophie is speaking again. 'She just . . . Ciara never stops crying and crying and crying. And I can't do anything to help her, it's impossible. But it's just a phase, it's just because she's ill and she hates taking the medicine. Don't worry about it; I know you two find this stuff boring.'

'No, we don't,' I say, aiming for reassuring, and just sounding angry. I try a softer tone, 'We love Ciara and we love you.'

Sophie's head snaps in my direction. 'Well you never want to talk about her, you pretend she doesn't exist.'

I blink, shocked into silence. Thomas shifts uncomfortably on the sofa next to me. That is completely unfair. We do not pretend Ciara doesn't exist. We hang out with her, we buy her things and we play with her. And when she's not here, I try to talk about her with Soph, we both do. Sophie is the one who usually brushes us off – saying she wants to hear about the 'real world' – what's happening outside her four walls.

We all fall silent and Sophie picks up the TV remote, fiddling with the brightness controls. The drunk cleavage lady gets brighter and brighter, sitting in her taxi saying she's had the best night of her life and holding up an upside down ten.

I can't remember the last time it felt awkward like this between us. It's never awkward. I mean, apart from maybe that time in Year Eleven when Thomas got a girlfriend called Kelly who told him to spend less time with the trio, so we took her round the back of the science block and told her we would put chlamydia in her drinking water if she didn't back off. And then when he asked us about that a few days later, of course we said she was a lying bitch. I remember that as being pretty awkward too. Especially after he dumped her in front of everyone.

But not really since then.

It's true, we've seen Sophie do this occasionally – get in her moods. She'll get really tired and passive aggressive. I always feel bad for New Ryan when she's turned on him like this. But that's what couples do; they pass-agg each other, right? Like a couple of months ago, when we watched this conversation happen after dinner, when New Ryan abandoned crockery in the sink:

Sophie: 'Are you going to leave that plate there?'

New Ryan: 'Oh. No, sorry, where should I put it?'

Sophie: 'No, no, please feel free to leave the plate exactly where is easiest for you. The most important thing here in this house – where you help me *sooo* much – is that everything is convenient for you.'

New Ryan: 'Sophie, I'm sorry, please tell me where to put it?'

Sophie: 'I don't care, I really don't care.'

New Ryan: 'You do care.'

Sophie: [pass-agg snort] 'I might care, but you don't care, and obviously that's more important, so who cares whether I care or not? Because you do *not*.'

New Ryan: 'I do care.'

Sophie: 'You don't care.'

New Ryan: 'I do care!'

Sophie: 'It's interesting that you're pretending you care about what I care about.'

New Ryan: 'Of course I care about what you care about.'

Sophie: 'It's totally fine, Ryan. I don't care that you don't care what I care about. Nobody cares about me. I have to do everything. I'm the only one who cares about anything round here.'

And so on.

It was pretty entertaining. But I have to admit, it's far less entertaining being on the receiving end of it. I wish New Ryan were here to take the brunt of it (sorry, New Ryan), but he's at his mum's for the night with Ciara. He went over there, in theory, to give Sophie a break, but I think being a mum means never switching off. The worry and the pressure and the guilt never go away.

Thomas clears his throat. 'I'm sorry you feel that way, Sophie. We'll try to talk more about your family.' Sophie looks at me pointedly but I stay silent, feeling resentful.

'Ellie's not sorry,' she says, putting the remote down and glaring at me. Daring me to react.

I look back at her, trying to swallow my anger down. I know she doesn't mean this. 'I am sorry,' I say carefully. I don't want to do this, I don't want to have this conversation. I'm on edge, she's on edge – this is all sleep related. I'm the same when I miss a meal. This is just the exhausted version of being hangry. She's just tirate? That's probably a thing.

Thomas clears his throat again and turns to me. 'Ellie, how are the dates going?' he says, attempting to change the subject.

Sophie tuts loudly, adding a sarcastic 'HA!' She knows how the dates are going.

'Um, fine,' I say lamely, looking at the floor.

'She's not giving anyone a chance,' Sophie snaps.

'I am!' I protest, weakly.

Thomas looks uncomfortable. 'That's a shame. Never mind, hey? I'm sure the next guy . . . '

I interrupt him, suddenly sick of the whole thing and desperate to be honest. I'm not even sure there will be a next guy. 'I hate it; I just want to stop doing it. I want to come off Tinder,' I say.

There's a long echo-y pause that reverberates round the room.

'Why?' Sophie says, tersely, frozen in the action of reaching once again for the remote. The other *Come Dine with Me* participants are discussing how Drunk Cleavage Lady ruined their night.

'Have you met someone?' she adds, knowing I haven't.

'No!' I say, angry. 'I don't have to meet anyone; I'm fine on my own. Finding a boyfriend is not the most important thing in the world, Soph.'

I can't deal with this any more. I've had a bad week and I'm so sick of all of this, so sick of being patronised and spoken to like I'm an idiot.

Sophie stares at me. 'So quit then, Ellie,' she says slowly. 'Like you do with everything. This is just the latest white flag of surrender in a long line of half-hearted attempts at changing your life. You're so afraid to try anything, so scared to try. I had to force you into speaking to that woman from Windsor at The Hales' party. I had to force you on Tinder. I had to force you to actually go on dates. You wouldn't even enter that art competition at work, even though everyone told you to. That could've been an amazing opportunity. And now the deadline's gone and you've missed your shot. All because you're too afraid to try something and maybe fail.'

I bite my lip, she doesn't understand.

She goes on. 'You won't change your easy, boring life for anything, will you? Not even if it means something better might actually come along and challenge you.'

I stand up. It's a reflex move when I'm angry, I need to be on my feet, but it's also a confrontational move. We are now both standing up, eyeball to eyeball.

'You think my life is so easy?' I demand, suddenly furious. 'So what if it is? Yours could've been too. You chose to do this. You chose to trap yourself with a baby. Trap yourself in this perfect life, with your perfect suburban beige house with your perfect suburban beige husband. And you're trying to force me to do the same, forcing your choices on me, forcing me on Tinder. Even if it's not something I want. But that has never occurred to you, has it? Not once? It hasn't occurred to you that maybe I don't want the same life as you, Sophie. Maybe I don't want all this fucking beigeness everywhere. You've never stopped to think that maybe I want my life to be different? To be actually *fun*.'

I can feel the heat pulsing from my face and I can feel Thomas' horrified discomfort from his position on the sofa behind me.

Sophie's face is blank. She takes a step towards me. 'You're afraid of it all,' she says quietly. 'It's pathetic. You complain about your life, you make joke after joke about it, but you won't do anything about it. And when there's a chance to actually change things, to do something exciting and try something new, you close your eyes, put your fingers in your ears, sing *la-la-la*, and run in the opposite direction. You're always running away from anything that could be real. You pretend you're so happy and carefree but you're a fucking mess, Ellie. You don't seem to understand that you're getting left behind. You're using your mum as an excuse to stay in one place forever. You're getting left behind and it's your own fault because you push everyone away. Just look at what you did to Tim.'

I feel like I've been slapped. My ears are roaring and I'm peripherally aware of Thomas standing up, picking up his bag, and silently leaving the room.

Sophie points a finger at the door closing behind him.

'And what about him?' she hisses. 'You won't give him a chance either, even though you know he could make you happy. That he does already make you happy. Why are you so afraid of actually falling in love? What is so broken in you that you don't want to even try it?'

I throw my hands in the air and laugh, nastily. 'I'm not afraid of it, Sophie. I just don't want to settle for the first guy to come along, and then spend the rest of my life pretending my life is perfect all the time.' I'm shouting now. 'And better to be afraid than never being able to admit things aren't the fairytale you expected. You think I'm a mess? Look at you.' I gesture at her jogging bottoms and she winces. 'Look how broken you are. But will you actually come out and say how hard all of this is? That you're struggling? That you can't cope? Of course you won't. You can never admit this isn't living up to what you wanted and that it isn't the perfect dream you thought it would be. Instead of asking for help, you'll just throw your life in our faces until you're sure we feel inadequate. Until we agree to follow you blindly into the boring beige oblivion of suburbia. God forbid anyone should notice you're not blissfully happy.'

We stare at each other furiously, the toxic words filling the air between us. I'm panting, out of breath, my brain roaring with adrenaline and venom.

I turn around, grab my coat, and leave, slamming the front door behind me as I go.

Thomas is waiting outside, smoking. I haven't seen him smoke since our sixth form leavers' ball when he was trying to persuade cool girl Louise Venditti to lose her virginity to him. I smile at him tightly, but don't stop, striding off in the direction of the train station.

I hear him following, falling into step a few paces behind me.

'Come on then if you're coming,' I say fake brightly. Like everything is fine. Like I'm not going to scream and cry at any moment.

He catches up and for a couple of minutes, we walk in silence.

'I . . . ' I start

'I don't want to take sides,' he interrupts.

Fuck him.

This is something I hate about Thomas, he's always such a good guy. Sitting on the fence, refusing to get stuck in the middle. Even when someone has clearly been a prick.

I just don't know yet whether it's me or Sophie who's the prick.

'*Et tu, Brute*?' I mutter instead.

'Who's Brute?' he asks, amused.

'You are,' I say impatiently.

'I'm Thomas White.'

I roll my eyes. 'Read a book, dude.'

'OK, I will' He still sounds amused. 'Just tell me what book that quote is from.'

'I don't want to.'

'I'll go read it this very minute if you can tell me what you just quoted. Come on, Ellie, tell me about this Brute character, what does he do exactly?'

'It's from . . . Charles Dickens.'

'You don't fucking know!' he laughs.

'Oh shut up!' I say, tears prickling in my eyes. 'Why are you being mean to me?'

He stops me and we look at each other. For a moment I think he's going to kiss me and then he looks away, and starts talking quietly.

'I'm not trying to be mean to you, Ellie. I wanted to make you laugh.' There's a pause and he takes a long drag on his cigarette. 'I will say this though. Whatever else crazy, tired nonsense was going on in there, Sophie has a point about you taking control of your life. When you talk about your work – about dealing with Ursula and Derek – you sound so in charge of everything. Even, maybe, *too* in charge when it comes to poor Derek.' He snorts. 'I know you're unhappy there but you still do a good job and you're clearly respected. You know what you want and the people around you listen to you and follow your instructions. It's because you know your work is good, you believe in yourself, and you don't take any shit.' He pauses. 'Outside of that though? It's like you're scared to make a decision for yourself. Scared of your personal life changing or evolving. You have all this bravado, but there's a gulf between what you say and what you actually do.'

I half nod, but tough love isn't what I need right now. I need sympathy and a hug. I need to hear that Sophie was being unfair but she didn't mean it. I need to hear that she was just tired (tirate). And that what I said wasn't as awful as I know it was.

He puts his hand on my arm. 'Elle,' he says softly. 'It's awful seeing you like this. I'm only saying this so you can see part of where Sophie was coming from. And honestly, I hate seeing it happen. You let people push you around without telling them how you feel. Your sister and Sophie especially. You didn't have to go on Tinder, you didn't *have* to do all this. Even with your dad, you speak to him so much but you couldn't tell him how you really felt about his dating again. I'm not saying you should've told him not to do it, but you could've been open with him about how it made you feel. I know you've found it hard seeing him move on from your mum. And you won't talk to him about losing her. Or talk to any of us about her.'

I shrug his hand off and take a step back. That's more than I can listen to right now.

'I don't need you to tell me that,' I bark. 'I don't need to hear any of it. I've just had this shit from Sophie, and you think you need to inform me I'm a terrible person too? OK, well I get it, thank you so very much for letting me know. You want me to tell people how I really feel? I feel like you should fuck off, Thomas, and stop trying to help me. I get enough of that from everyone else.'

I start walking again. Big, angry strides, but he's with me, matching each step.

'Fine, I won't help you,' he says quietly.

'Great. Please don't.'

'No problem. No more help from me. Next time you're walking into the road without looking I'll just let you get hit by a car and die, shall I?'

I turn around to snap at him again, and he pulls me off the road and out of the path of a Peugeot, beeping furiously as it speeds past. I breathe hard, watching it go, and then turn to look at Thomas. We stand there staring at each other for a few seconds and I know I should say thank you and that I'm sorry and that I know he's just trying to look out for me.

But I can't.

My mouth opens and shuts and I turn and walk away. He doesn't follow me.

I go to the very far end carriage of the train and hide from Thomas in a corner seat. If he tries to look for me, he doesn't find me, and I sit in silence, trying not to hate everyone, trying not to punch the seats. Trying not to cry.

I think about what Sophie said. And about what Thomas said.

I think about the dozen or so dates I've had recently. Several really terrible but mostly pretty much *fine*. A couple of them were even actually quite nice. Why didn't I give any of them another chance? Why did I immediately give all those perfectly decent men the brush off?

I think about my great date with Nathan that ended so badly. I think about that text I got from him that said,

I don't think we're really compatible.

And then I think about the second text he sent me fifteen minutes later, that read,

Fuck, I'm so sorry I sent that. I'm so sorry I behaved like that at the end.

And then the text after that, explaining how he lashed out because he thought I was rejecting him. That he'd had his heart badly broken not so long ago, and that Tinder had been a rough ride of emotions. And that he was so sorry he reacted like a spoilt brat just because he thought I wasn't interested. He said that he really wanted to see me again.

I think about how genuine and heartfelt the message seemed, and how much I understood his childish reaction to the whole situation. I've been there, and I totally get it.

And I wonder why I didn't even reply.

And then I think about Tim, and how I treated him at the end.

11

11.02 p.m. Friday, 29 March
Location: A tiny – but very overgrown – public garden near my old house, with a small pond. It's closed for the night when I turn up, but it's only got a little gate, so I climb over, feeling like Hugh Grant in *Notting Hill* (whoopsidaisies). This is where Mum and I used to meet up for lunch when she was nearby – she loved it – and I needed to feel close to her for a few minutes tonight.

My mum was diagnosed with breast cancer around mid-April – on my birthday actually – and she died just after Christmas. So she kind of ruined all my favourite annual celebrations. But I guess that's not her fault. She tried really hard to hold on, and she said sorry about the whole thing a lot.

It's always seemed weird to me when people talk about *battling* cancer. I heard that so much over those next few months – *Your mum is a fighter, Ellie. She's not going to let this beat her, Ellie* – but there was nothing Mum could really do. She had the operation and the chemo, and the cancer spread to her bones anyway. There was nothing else to be done. She didn't have any other weapons. It didn't matter how hard she wanted to 'fight' the 'battle', because cancer didn't give her any options.

But I suppose we just say things, don't we? We say anything that might make us feel like we have some kind of control over our own lives. It's a way to pretend like you have a tiny bit of say in whether you get to live or die, isn't it? When the truth is, with something like cancer, you're actually just a helpless random victim being torn apart from the inside. It takes everything away from you, your independence, your spirit and, often, your life. And it doesn't care what that means. So I understand why we talk about fighting. But sitting on the sidelines, I couldn't even pretend I was doing that much. I just had to hold my mum's hand, tell her I loved her a lot, and watch it happen.

Tim was the only one who seemed to understand how I felt. He was the only person who seemed to get all of that helplessness that comes with a loved one being ill. His dad died when he was just a teenager – cancer *a-fucking-gain* – so he'd seen the same pain passing across the face of those people you always thought were invincible.

We'd been together a few years by that point, after meeting at a Christmas party when I was twenty-four. At the time, I was temping at an ad agency for eleven pounds an hour (nice, right?), answering phones and trying to make it as an artist (eyeroll) in my spare time. He was a colleague's brother, who'd crashed our festive work do at the local Green Man pub. It was a familial connection I didn't discover until after I'd drunkenly explained to him in which order my colleagues were the biggest cunts. His brother was the seventh biggest cunt, out of a possible thirty-two.

He agreed.

Tim thought I was so funny. The funniest person he'd ever met, he kept saying that night – and most nights after – and I deeply appreciated that he didn't say funniest 'girl'. We talked about *Antiques Roadshow*, and what nerds we were at school. I told him about being jealous of how badly behaved my rock star sister was – and that time the headmaster still talks about, when she held a student strike in the science block during third period. Tim told me more stories about his brother's cuntery and we agreed that maybe he should be upgraded to number six on the list. We kissed that night, and he asked to see me again, which I thought was dead romantic considering he'd seen me get off with two other guys as well during the course of the evening (What? I was drunk and it was Christmas, get off my case, GRANDMA GLADYS).

For our first date, a few days later, we went to Winter Wonderland in Hyde Park and spent eight hundred pounds (approx.) on rides and sweets. After one particularly upside-down-y ride, I had to sit down, dry-heaving for a few minutes, while my stomach settled. He sat with me on the muddy, wet grass, rubbing my back and feeding me sips from his tiny, four-pound bottle of Evian until I felt better. I remember standing back up, looking up at him, and wondering if it was the nausea making me feel dizzy, or just how totally beautiful I thought he was. We went back to his house that night, and I didn't ever really leave. We moved in together officially after six months and I thought that was that. Of course, everyone loved him. Mum and Dad would nudge each other when we visited, and talked about saving for the wedding. Sophie loved how kind he was, and told me he looked like a young Ed Miliband. He's her secret crush, so it was a compliment. And even Jen couldn't find too much to criticise about him. Except when she said he looked like Ed Miliband and it wasn't a compliment and she didn't say a younger version.

And so we started saving for our own place, our own mortgage. It was a project Tim was much better at than me. He was working as a marketing consultant and I was still temping and struggling to be an artist. But he got it, and always encouraged me to keep going with the art. He told me his boring job made it all the more important that I should 'follow my dream' (he was really cheesy, but it was cute). He said one of us had to do something cool with our careers. He bought me paint and canvas when I couldn't even afford my half of the rent. He was great. Eventually, though, I got my job as illustrator at The Hales, and with a regular income, we finally somehow managed to get a deposit together. We spent months looking for the right place to buy – the place that would be our home, where we could get a dog and talk about hosting BBQs for our neighbours and then avoid eye contact with them whenever we actually saw them. It was so exciting and brilliant. We settled on this lovely flat in a Victorian terrace in south London – zone five – which ticked all our boxes. It was the dream. It was in a long chain, but we were willing to wait for it.

We argued a lot, but it was fun, silly stuff like who was going to do the washing up, or how much of my mess was too much mess. And over his habit of leaving Post-it notes everywhere with to-do lists on them. I would hide them from him and leave him a ransom Post-it note with clues, which sounds cute but it always ended up with him screaming that my 'clues' were impossible. And then he would leave me a Post-it note on my pillow saying sorry, and we would have angry sex, and then I'd remember I hid his Post-it notes in the bed and they were now soiled. OK, that only happened once. But yeah.

It was stupid and complicated and lovely, and it really worked. He accepted me for who I am and made me feel like who I am was OK.

And when my brilliant mum got diagnosed with cancer out of nowhere after some routine tests, he was so kind and patient with me. He didn't say anything when I cried all night, and he didn't say anything when I didn't cry at all. He made me eat things that weren't just Mars Bars, but also bought me Mars Bars whenever I needed them. He stayed up with me when I couldn't sleep and he slept beside me in the daytime when I passed out with exhaustion. He took care of the house purchase, and didn't mind when I was too distracted to celebrate with him when it eventually went through. He took time off work to come with us for chemo appointments, and he understood when I told him to leave, so I could help my mum go to the loo. He looked after me when I couldn't look after myself.

I started cheating on him about three months after the diagnosis. I think he knew. But he didn't say anything. He just got needier and more intense. Which made me pull away even more.

I can't justify it. I don't know what made me do it. I just wanted to get away and have fun and not be around him. He reminded me too much of what was happening in my life, and I didn't want that. I wanted men who didn't look at me with sadness or pity. I needed to be around people who just wanted to fuck me, not someone who kept suggesting I have another Berocca to counteract the Mars Bar diet. I wanted the one night stands and the uncomplicated tongues in my ear. I hated myself for it, Sophie hated me for it, but I didn't stop. I didn't know how to stop and I didn't listen to her when she told me I was destroying my relationship, because I didn't want to stop. And the more I did it, the more I knew I'd ruined things with Tim anyway, so why should I stop? And then my mum died the day after Boxing Day and everything in me went numb.

Things came to a brutal head at her funeral. It was a freezing cold day in early January, the church was ugly, and the priest kept saying that my mum was nice.

'She was a very nice woman,' he said again and again, making eye contact with me from the pulpit.

Nice. Nice.

He had no idea if she was a nice woman. He never met her. I couldn't understand why we were having her funeral there – Mum wasn't religious, she said it was 'laughable nonsense', ranting about how ridiculous the whole concept was, even as she put on a coat for her weekly visit to Psychic Sharon.

Nice. Nice.

Surely funerals must be so boring for priests? Saying the same things over and over, about people you don't know, and pretending you feel so sad. Your neck must get permanent damage doing so much sympathy head tilt. So wouldn't you at least make it more interesting by coming up with jazzier adjectives for these dead people you didn't know? Something better than 'nice'? What about 'genial', or 'nifty'? I think my mum was pretty nifty.

Nice. Nice. Nice.

I remember wondering, as we sat there in the cold, ugly church, listening to this stranger talk about my mum, if I could pull up thesaurus.com on my phone. But then Tim gave my hand a squeeze and I decided to focus all my fury on him instead. God, I prayed, let me escape this man that I hate so much for no reason.

And an hour later, back at my dad's house for the wake with sandwiches and French Fancies, I told Tim it was over.

'What?' He looked so shocked.

'I know this isn't the time,' I said, the cold in my voice matching the cold of the church. 'But I don't think this is working any more, I think we should break up.'

I remember him shaking his head, like maybe he'd misheard, or like he wanted to shake my words out of his brain, out of his ear. I remember him putting down the two drinks he'd just been to fetch – one was meant to be for me – and I remember thinking *it's so weird that people drink alcohol at funerals*. I always think of getting drunk as a celebration. Although as Psychic Sharon and Aunt Susie kept telling me that day, spilling prosecco all the while – 'Today is a celebration of your mum's life.'

Personally, I couldn't really see how a dank church and cucumber sandwiches – that Jen pretended she made even though they were still in their M&S tray – was in any way a celebration of my mum. Or even representative of anything she was or anything she loved. If that day was really about my mum, we would have hosted the whole thing at a Britney Spears' concert. She loved Britney so much. Right from day one. Right from 'Baby One More Time' in '98. She talked about getting a white pet snake for a whole year in 2001, and in 2007 she set up a 'Save Britney' fund. Aunt Susie and her even went to see Britney in Vegas just before Mum got sick. She didn't stop talking about it for months afterwards, and they wore their Britney Bitch T-shirts everywhere they went – even to her work as office manager at a local playgroup. They didn't like the T-shirt – they made her put a jumper on over it.

She even wore it to chemo later on.

My *nice* mum.

'You're not serious?' Tim had said, his voice getting louder. A couple of people from Mum's salsa class had looked over at that point, hoping for drama, sandwiches hovering inches from their faces.

'Maybe we should go out here,' I'd said, pulling him into Dad's tiny hallway, and away from Psychic Sharon, who may not have a sixth sense for much, but she definitely does for arguments. But too late, she was already charging over, waving a cucumber sandwich in one hand, and 'yoohoo-ing' the pair of us.

'What's going on?' she stage-whispered, conspiratorially, as she squeezed into the small corridor alongside us.

I said nothing and Tim looked at me, a wounded, confused expression on his face that made me hate him all the more.

'Well?' said Psychic Sharon, aggressively, refusing to take silence for an answer.

He cleared his throat. 'I think Ellie's dumping me.'

Psychic Sharon looked askance at me.

'You're not serious?'

'That's what I said,' Tim exclaimed, bolstered by the unexpected support.

'I . . . I need the loo,' I said, feeling intensely claustrophobic, backing into the hallway toilet behind me and hooking the catch lock quickly before they could crowd in there too.

'Ellie, don't be ridiculous, come out,' said Tim, appearing at the door crack.

Psychic Sharon remained out there and I listened to the muffled arrival of yet more nosy mourners, wanting the inside track on the gossip. Tim's agitated voice carried through the door as he replied to the curious group forming outside the loo.

'No, she hasn't told me why.' 'No, nothing happened.' 'Yes, now she's hiding in there.'

'I'm not hiding,' I called out loudly, from my hiding place.

'I need a wee. Could everyone go away, please?'

Then I heard Jen's voice, butting in. 'She's what? Oh my God, she's such an embarrassment. Ellie, why are you being such a loser? Haha, "loo-ser"? Get it, everyone? Because she won't come out of the loo?' She laughed at her own joke again and then turned back to the door. 'Are you doing a poo in there, Ellie? Because you remember the flush doesn't work properly in that one? You'll have to pump the flush. And the bog brush is under the sink if you need it, do *not* leave a mess like Dad does. Why won't you come out? Are you jealous because everyone liked my eulogy better than yours?'

'I didn't do a eulogy,' I tried to say, but Psychic Sharon started howling in pain. 'Jenny just elbowed me! Why did you elbow me? It really hurts, why would you do that? I was just trying to get past.'

'Oh for God's sake, stop being such a whiny little bitch,' said Jen, hotly. 'It was an accident. And you know it's my mum's funeral today? Have some consideration for how I might be feeling. I'm allowed to elbow people today of all days. *God*, some people.'

It's a small hallway and Jen has very sharp elbows, it could've been an accident but I imagine it was not. She'd been annoyed with Psychic Sharon for weeks, saying she should've warned us this was going to happen – that Mum was going to die – even when I pointed out Psychic Sharon is a charlatan. Jen still hasn't forgiven her.

Psychic Sharon continued howling and someone else sniggered and asked her why she didn't predict it happening.

That joke did not go down well.

On the other side of the door, Jen turned her attention back to me again.

'Have you really broken up with Tim?' she shouted. 'He says you have but I can never tell whether he's joking or not. He's got one of those ridiculous clown faces that look like he's always telling a joke. Just like Ed Milliband. Is it a joke, Ellie? It's not very funny if it is. Because surely you know, even with Tim's stupid face, he's about as good a boyfriend as you're ever going to get? Yes, obviously he's a bit of a wet blanket—'

She got cut off at that point as an indignant Tim insisted he's never been a wet blanket, that he's just a nice person and—

That was the point he too got an elbow in the stomach.

Jen started again through the door. 'You don't want to be alone, do you, Ellie? That would be depressing for everyone around you – oh, and for you. Hold on, I'm going to get Andrew, he'll want to hear about his. GET OUT OF THE WAY, EVERYONE, YOU KNOW MY MUM IS DEAD, RIGHT?'

I heard her stomp off and continue to shriek in the living-room for her husband, who – I found out that night – was hiding outside in the garden with my dad the whole time. Dad told me later they almost bonded.

Psychic Sharon then started shouting that she needed the loo and I heard another voice – Sophie maybe – telling her to use the one upstairs, and that she'd find some Nurofen for the elbow-inflicted injury in the bathroom cabinet up there too. She told Sharon that Jen didn't mean to hurt her, and I heard Jen shriek from the other room; 'I BLOODY DID MEAN IT.'

The crowd had thinned a little then and Tim came back to the door crack, his voice soft and kind. A voice you'd use with a tantrum-prone child who's tuckered herself out after fifteen minutes of screaming. 'Ellie, I know this is a shitty, shitty time for you – especially today – but please don't do this,' he said. 'You shouldn't be making any decisions while you're upset about your mum. We don't have to talk about this now. We'll talk some more later, shall we? I'm sorry if I've got this wrong. I'll do better, I promise. We can fix this, I love you. I want to make this work. We can make this work. Fuck, Ellie, we've just bought a house!'

But I couldn't do it any more, I needed to be selfish. I moved out a week later, into Dad's.

12

10.30 p.m. Friday, 29 March
Location: The local Londis by my flat, which caters for all of my food and alcohol needs. They've recently expanded into the shop next door, and don't know what to do with all their new shelf space. For example, there is now a whole row for tartare sauce, which is great as far as I'm concerned. Can't have enough tartare sauce for fishfinger sandwich-related emergencies.

I'm here to buy alcohol. Exclusively alcohol. After my fight with Sophie, and then those quieter, but just as upsetting, words with Thomas, all I want is to get raging drunk and pass out. Ideally, to the point where I wake up with absolutely no memory of today. Potentially no memory at all, so I can start a brand new life somewhere, as a pitied amnesia victim. Thinking about everything with Mum and Tim hasn't blocked out the argument – the shitty things Sophie said, and the shitty things I said, too. I didn't even mean it, I don't think Sophie's pretending to be perfect, I think she's just doing her best and doing really, really well. In fact, she's doing a fantastic job, Ciara is totally amazing. Sophie might have started the fight, but everything she said was right, I am a loser, and I am afraid. And because I'm a loser and because I'm afraid, I lashed out at her. I had no right to say those things to her. This is all my fault. It's all me. I am broken and useless, Sophie was right.

'You're a stupid fucking bitch,' I mutter to myself as I throw two bottles of white wine into my basket.

'You're a fat, stupid, ugly bitch and nobody likes you,' I say again, a bit louder this time. A man at the other end of the aisle looks over at me, grinning, and I look down, avoiding his questioning eyes. Staring at the ground, I mutter again, 'God, look at that, even your shadow is fat. You are the worst, the absolute worst.'

The man looks over again and shouts down the aisle, 'Cheer up, love, it might never happen. Givvus a smile!'

My self-hatred briefly flickers outward. Lasers of red hot fury zoom in on him. Even when I haven't just had the worst night ever, I cannot stand being told to smile by strangers. I snarl in his direction, and he snorts.

'Just being friendly, love,' he says and happily meanders off in the direction of the vegetable aisle. I debate storming after him with a lecture on how women feel about this constant demand for them to appear polite and happy. If telling women to smile is so 'friendly' and well-intentioned, why don't men tell other men to smile? Sometimes, when a man tells me to smile, I want to point at other men – big, burly other men – and ask if he should be forced to smile too. I want to ask who made him the smile police. But I know I'll get called a bitch, so mostly I stay silent and just, well, smile. It is hot garbage and I'm sick of it.

It feels nice not to hate myself for two minutes.

Is two bottles of wine enough? I look at my phone, it's pretty late, two should be plenty. I throw three tubs of Häagen Dazs into the basket, too, and then look round for sanitary towels. I'm not on my period, but I need my basket to seem sympathetic. I know the lovely elderly couple who run the shop worry about me and my apparent diet of black coffee and sugar. Mrs Shannon recently brought up the fact that I only seem to buy Digestive biscuits and how maybe I should be varying my diet a little bit because I might get scurvy. I thought that was really sweet but pointed out that I do get variation in my diet. For example, sometimes I will buy dark chocolate Digestives, and other times I will get milk chocolate Digestives. And just so she would stop worrying, I've also started buying the newer caramel Digestives from time to time. See, variation. She didn't look totally convinced by this argument, but English isn't her first language, so maybe she just didn't understand.

I regard my basket. Two bottles of wine, three tubs of ice cream, and some sanitary towels.

Hmm. Maybe that's a little bit too pathetic.

I add in a bag of iceberg lettuce. It looks good with the rest of my shopping, and Mrs Shannon will approve of that addition. The colour will complement my fridge too, until it goes brown and I have to throw it away. Like all the rest.

Satisfied with my distraction items, I head determinedly for the till and barrel straight into Josh.

Shit.

He smirks as he realises it's me, and then his smile droops a little when he sees my face. Damn. I cried a lot on the train here and I know the effect isn't exactly attractive. I don't need a mirror to know my eyes are red and puffy, along with the rest of my stupid, fat, ugly face, smudged with lipstick and smeared with mascara. My self-hatred surges back in, worse than before.

'Jesus. Are you OK, Knight?' Josh says, sounding genuinely concerned.

'Yes,' I say, looking away, staring intently at the crisps aisle.

Hmm. Actually, maybe I do want some pickled onion Monster Munch. Would I have to also buy some courgettes to balance that out?

'What's happened, is everything all right? Tell me,' he tries again.

I shake my head, not trusting myself to say anything. Why is it always when someone is being nice to you that you get most upset? I really don't want to start crying again in the middle of Londis.

'Ellie,' he says again, gently. 'Can I do anything?'

I can't help it, and a small welp-sob escapes. Josh takes my basket from me gently and puts it on the ground. Then he pulls me in for a hug. And it's not until I'm wrapped up in his arms that I realise how much I needed this. Some human warmth. This is all I wanted from Thomas earlier. It was all I wanted from Sophie when I arrived at her house tonight. I start to quietly cry and we just stand there for a couple of minutes, surrounded by the comforting rows and rows of crisps. I hear Mrs Shannon come over and ask if everything's OK and I hear Josh quietly dismissing her, politely and nicely by name.

Eventually I let go of him, and laughing, embarrassed, I wipe my face with my sleeve. There's a wet patch on the shoulder of his grey jumper. I hope it's from my tears and not snot.

'Let's get you home,' he says, picking my basket up again and casually glancing at the contents. We look at each other and I wonder if he's ever been this close to the words WINGS and NIGHT TOWELS before. He doesn't seem the type to hang around girls long enough to encounter periods.

'Sanitary towels, eh?' I say for no reason. He better not

think I'm crying because I'm on my period. I think about explaining to him about distraction purchases but realise that would make me seem even more unstable.

With one arm round me, holding me up, Josh quietly pays Mrs Shannon for my 'groceries' and marches me across the road, squeezing me close, like we're doing a three-legged race, home to The Shithole.

In the living-room, sprawled across the sofa, I swig from the bottle directly. I spot an ingrown hair on my leg and pick at it, but even the satisfaction of pulling it out can't cheer me up. I feel so sad and alone. But Josh is here. I hand the bottle to him, beside me on the sofa. He's watching me a bit too intently and keeps asking me if I'm OK and what's happened. I've told him to mind his own business several times, but now the warmth of the booze is taking hold in my stomach, and I'm starting to feel like I want to tell him. I need an ally; I want someone who is on my side. It's the first time in a year I've felt like maybe a boyfriend would be really handy – someone to complain about my best friends to. I take another gulp of the wine and, swallowing the bitter liquid hard, I start to tell him about my dates, about the pressure I feel to meet someone, and how depressing I've found the whole experience. I tell him everything, about the judgemental heavy breather on the train, about the date who never asked questions, about Rich trying to set me up with a fifty-year-old divorcee. I tell him how my life and recent choices have caused this weird tension between Sophie and me – and how it erupted so horribly tonight at her house. I even tell him about Thomas and the strangeness between us that followed it, during our walk to the station.

Josh is silent for a minute and then he says, surprisingly perceptive, 'Thomas is in love with you?'

I sigh, drinking more. 'Yes. But shouldn't that mean he takes my side in all this? Isn't that what love is? Always being on your side?'

Josh smiles. 'I'm on your side, babe. I think Sophie's behaving like a crazy bitch.'

'No, she's not!' I say, instantly defensive of my best friend – if she's even still my best friend – despite the fact that I've just been complaining about her myself. I'm a hypocrite, too. We'll just add that to the list of things to hate about myself.

'Women be crazy,' he says again. I know he is deliberately trying to provoke me and I know I shouldn't let it wind me up, but I can't help it.

'Women be NOT crazy,' I say crossly.

'OK, but you have to admit, they can be pretty bitchy and mean to each other, can't they?' he says, his eyes dancing.

'That is total horseshit,' I say, taking the bait again. 'Like, what about groups of drunk people? Put a group of drunk girls who don't know each other in a room together, and they will inevitably all end up in the toilet together, sharing lipsticks and stories about their sex-pest bosses, and holding each other's hair back as they puke. Compare that to groups of drunk men, who call me a whore in the street – I know which of those I think are "bitchier".'

He laughs, 'Good point!'

I scowl. Why do I always let Josh get to me? He gets under my skin so much, winds me up more than anyone else. I know he only said those things to irritate me, and it still feels like he's winning.

He laughs again at my anger. 'I was only joking,' he says, taking the wine from me again and swigging from it, sloppily. 'I don't really think women are mad. Certainly no more so than men. We're all mad, right? People be crazy.' He hands me the bottle. 'Let's not talk about this,' he says suddenly standing up. 'You've had a bad few weeks, you need cheering up. So let's eat some of your full-fat ice cream and then just focus all our attention on getting really, really drunk.'

I feel his words wash over me like a soothing balm. I like this caring side of Josh. I needed someone to be kind.

An hour later and Josh and I are doing karaoke through an old PS3 he's found under the stairs. For once, I'm glad Gemma isn't around because we're being way too loud for someone sleeping to be cool about. We're actually – and I can't believe I'm saying this – having the best time. Josh is being really nice to me, he's totally cheered me up. I am hardly thinking about the seventeen-year friendships I've left in tatters. Hardly at all.

Oh, look at Josh, dancing. He's so good-looking and nice. Why did I think he was a cunt? I mean, apart from the fact that he is a cunt, there is totally no reason to think he's a cunt. Poor, misjudged Cunt Josh. And he can really sing! He's slurring a bit, but he's only just about missing the tune! And some of the words are wrong too, but he's really talented! If only he were hitting the notes at all, he could totally win *The X Factor*. He starts singing 'Your Song' by Elton John and I open my mouth to tell him about Simon Cowell, but instead I say:

'God, I fancy you.'

He laughs, and then pauses the telly, dropping his mic. He takes a step towards me.

'No, you don't,' he says, his voice low and deliberately husky. I've heard him use this seduction tone before.

It's nice though.

'Yes, I do,' I say nodding my fuzzy, fuzzy head.

'No, you don't,' he says again, shaking his head. 'You hate me, I know you do. It would be obvious, even if you didn't also tell me that all the time.'

'No, no!' I say, giggling. 'I don't hate you. I just don't like the way you treat women. I don't want to be yet another girl you shag and then discard the next morning.'

'You know, a lot of them discard me, actually,' he says, contemplatively. 'And honestly, Ellie, you would never be like those girls.'

He pauses and I wonder if I'm annoyed on behalf of the women he's just dismissed so easily. He continues, his words rolling off his tongue. 'You know, we're both drunk, Ellie. You're feeling sad, I could make you feel better. Sex would make you feel better. It's my duty as your mate to make you feel better.' He smiles like a fox and I laugh. For a second, he looks vulnerable. 'You drive me crazy,' he says suddenly, hotly. 'I want you so much, I always have. Right from the day you turned up here, looking disapprovingly at me and the wallpaper. I fancy you so much. You know, sometimes I think I love you. I try and get your attention all the time and you ignore me. It drives me nuts. I know I act like a dick, and I know it winds you up, but that's why I do it. It's the only time you pay me any attention. I just want you to notice me.'

He touches my face and my stomach flips over.

We're really drunk, and I know what he's saying is total nonsense. Total bullshit nonsense – lines he no doubt uses with every girl who doesn't seem interested in him – but, fuck, it's such lovely nonsense. It's so nice to hear.

He draws the lines around the edges of my face with his fingers and everything tingles. I study his beautiful features, illuminated in the dim glow of the paused Elton John lyrics, and feel lightheaded. I know that I either need to have sex with him right now, or I'm going to pass out. It's hard to know which one.

He kisses me.

Yep, it's sex.

Half kissing, half falling over, we head to his room, removing our clothes as we go.

Shit. I think about this bra I'm wearing, that I've been wearing day in day out for at least two weeks (OK, three). In one deft move, I remove it over my head, along with my T-shirt, and he looks delighted.

I should remember that – pretending to be a sex kitten when you're really trying to avoid the man about to put his penis in you seeing an old bra that is probably full of stale crumbs and whole sets of keys. Winner.

He trips over his trousers a bit and I drunkenly throw myself onto his bed, trying not to inhale too deeply. I know how often he washes his sheets. Which is not often.

He stops, standing over me with his T-shirt in hand, looking at me intensely again. His pupils are so dilated.

'Are you sure you want to do this?' he says again and I pull him down on top of me.

It's 4 a.m. and I'm staring at the ceiling, my head pounding from the booze and the humiliation. I had sex with Josh. I'm in bed with Josh. I promised myself I would never do this. What's wrong with me?

Don't get me wrong, sex with Josh was lovely. Really,

really, really. I mean, it was very drunken and lasted longer than I would've ideally liked because we'd both had so much to drink. But it was hot and sweaty and loud, just the way I like it. There was some awkward nipple moments, where he kept tweaking them and I wasn't sure what to say, so I just said 'Ooh,' and then he seemed encouraged and did it harder and then I had to say 'Ow' so he would stop. But apart from that, it was pretty great. I even nearly came. After we'd got his orgasm out of the way, we worked on mine for a reasonably solid few minutes. There were a few seconds where I thought it might even happen. Generally, I know if I concentrate really, really hard, and the guy keeps doing that one exact thing, without otherwise moving or breathing or speaking, and if I keep picturing Zack and A. C. Slater from *Saved By the Bell* having sex, sometimes I can come.

It's not Josh's fault he doesn't know that rule, and he only gave it a few seconds before he changed things around. But hey, the almost-possibility of an orgasm is better than I get with most men. At least he tried, got to give him points for that.

But it's Cunt Josh.

What was I thinking? I'm so ashamed of myself.

And on an important side note, I really need to fart. I tried to go to the loo a few minutes ago – ideally never to return – but he reached over in his sleep and pinned me down. Now I'm worried about moving too much in case he wakes up properly and starts pawing at me again. We did it twice, but even now, I can feel his erection poking my leg. Poor men, testosterone seems like such an exhausting burden.

*

I desperately want to sleep, but I know there's no chance now. Not here in Josh's bed. I'm wide awake, all the shame of the last few days piling in on me. I've ruined things with my best friends and I've humiliated and debased myself by sleeping with revolving door Josh. What is wrong with me? This is a new life-low, an absolute rock bottom with extra spiky pebbles poking into my back. Everything has gone wrong: Sophie, work, everything. I'm supposed to be an adult, I'll be thirty in a matter of weeks. This is when you're meant to be getting your shit together, not watching it all fall apart.

In the distance a fog horn blares and my stomach rolls over, jealously. Damned ice cream for dinner. FFS, Eleanor, you know dairy and sex don't mix.

I sigh into the dark. Am I really going to stay lying here uncomfortably for the next few hours? Afraid to sleep, in case I fog horn, and afraid to leave, in case he wakes up and we have to do sober sex? If I do stay here, it'll be just as awkward in the morning anyway. He's going to give me the speech I hear him giving to those blondes every week. Where he says how he thinks I'm great, but he's not ready for anything more serious. How he's emotionally damaged from his parents' divorce when he was seventeen. How he really likes me but he's a lone wolf.

To be fair, I don't think he's ever actually said the lone wolf thing, but that is the implication. It's going to be so humiliating.

Christ, I don't even like Josh, I can't believe I did this! Well, hold on, let's think about this – *do* I like him? I don't think I do. Yes, he was really fun last night, but that was the alcohol and the ice cream. Everyone's fun when you've drunk a bottle of wine and are singing karaoke with ice cream. We were just drunk, I was sad, and because of that, now I'm going to have to move out. And since I've wrecked things with Sophie and Thomas, I can't even go and stay with them. I'll have to move back in with Dad and watch *Neighbours* every day. And gah, I'm so far behind with the storylines now, I'll never catch up. Is Paul Robinson even still alive? I can't believe I let this happen, I'm so stupid.

OK, enough. I'm going to my own bed to fart in peace. I start to roll away, and Josh growls in his sleep. God that's hot.

No, stop that. Shit, I really thought having sex with him would've knocked all that out of my system. I guess I'm even dumber than I thought.

Slowly, glacially, I slide out of his bed feeling like a hung-over, naked ninja. I creep out, carefully collecting my pants and old bra (oh, my keys *were* in there!), trying not to stand on any of his stuff, and silently shut the door behind me. I tiptoe across to my room and close the door, letting out a huge sigh of relief – from my bum. I crawl into bed, my skin itching with shame, and swaddle myself in my own duvet like a newborn.

Staring at the ceiling, I think about what my mum would say about the decisions I've made over the last twenty-four hours. Over the last year, actually. I feel so ashamed. As I drift off, crying into my pillow, I wonder again how I've managed to mess everything up so badly.

13

9.51 a.m. Monday, 1 April
Location: Back in my subdued office, at my desk, where two of the account execs are laughing nearby about how one of them April Fooled his wife this morning by asking for a divorce. They both think this is the funniest thing ever and are crying and whacking each other on the back. There's a huge pile of work waiting for me in my in-tray, but instead I'm just fiddling with poor, neutered Mrs Beaver, stolen from Maddie's desk.

I somehow managed – like a total grown-up – to entirely avoid Josh all weekend. I would almost feel proud of this accomplishment, if I didn't hate myself so much for the whole thing. When I finally woke up late on Saturday – with a killer hangover and a mouth that tasted like rotten Cheesy Puffs, Twinkies and other things I've heard U.S. telly talk about but have never tried so what am I even talking about? – Josh was knocking on my bedroom door. So obviously I hid under the duvet and pretended to be out until he went away. I didn't come out until I heard him leave for the gym a couple of hours later.

Which reminds me, as well as moving house to avoid Josh, I'm also going to have to change gyms too. This would be so annoying if I ever went to the gym.

Once he'd gone, I quickly got showered, dressed and went to hide out at my dad's with my sketchbook for the next two days. I came straight from his to work this morning, and then wished I hadn't bothered because no one else seems to be here. Maddie's on a last minute Airbnb holiday with her new boyfriend – the one she's going super slowly with – along with his whole extended family. Derek's on a management course, and he's taken Rich the Quavers Master with him. The office gossip has it that Rich is being groomed to take over the deputy manager position, which is considered 'big news' apparently. Even Ursula's off sick. Usually on a day like this I'd spend the whole day messaging Thomas and Sophie. Not today. Today I feel like I'm totally alone, with no friends. I'm so depressed, I'm even considering buying some Quavers and sucking them to death.

I'm so sick of this place. Nothing about the work challenges me any more, I sit here in a trance, day after day. I've stayed too long.

It was a weird weekend. When I turned up with my overnight bag on Saturday, Dad asked if I was OK – I haven't stayed over since Tim and I split – but he didn't push it when I said I was fine. I mostly stayed in bed, sketching. It was the only way to clear my mind and stop everything that's happened lately crowding in on me. Dad tiptoed around, occasionally bringing me food – including a Candice special that he didn't warn me was hers until after I'd bitten into it. Lemon and broccoli.

On Sunday he offered to cancel a date to spend the day with me, watching back-to-back soaps. He's joined *Guardian* Soulmates, and had arranged dinner with a nice-looking lady called Eileen. He said Candice and Peter had helped pick her out, and he proudly showed me the profile pictures Candice had kindly printed out for him.

Obviously I insisted he went, and I got to spend most of yesterday evening on my own, wallowing in my stupid misery. Having barely slept since Thursday night, I was passed out by the time Dad got home last night, and I had to leave super early this morning to get to work on time. So I don't know how it went with Eileen. I'll call him in a bit.

I hope it was fun, I hope he is happy.

I sit at my desk, trying to figure out what to do with my life. I haven't spoken to Sophie or Thomas since our huge row on Friday and the longer this situation goes on, the more it's starting to feel a tiny bit irretrievable. They haven't made any effort to reach out to me, they don't seem to be missing me. Maybe they're realising they're better off without me in their life. It feels a bit like, if they were real friends, who really cared about me, they would've reached out by now, surely? They would've supported me more in the first place. I keep having visions of them hanging out together, just the two of them, without me. Laughing together about what an idiot I am and how glad they are to be rid of me at long last. I keep trying to remind myself that's not really who they are, but it's hard to shut my brain off.

Oh, I hate myself.

I should've just said sorry straight away. I should've sent a text to both of them immediately, apologising and pleading until they forgave me. Really, I should never have let myself get sucked into the row in the first place. It was so pointless. But now I've – we've all – gone so many days without any contact, it feels harder and harder to casually say I'm sorry. Our usually intensely busy WhatsApp group chat has been conspicuously silent since Friday, and I keep absentmindedly picking up my phone to check the seventy messages

I've usually managed to miss in the space of ten minutes.

I check my phone again. Nothing.

I don't know how to fix this. I'm worried I can't. What happens if I can't?

Maybe I could move to America.

It's an idea that's occurred to me before – there's something so appealing about a total change like that. It would be such an adventure, starting anew, making new friends, starting a whole other career. I could do anything I wanted, be anyone I wanted.

Mum's family was American, so we all have dual citizenship. Mum and Dad made sure of that when we were young, in case we ever needed to either – in my mum's words – 'escape a Tory government' or 'Be closer to Britney'. It's always been my plan to take advantage of that someday, try living in another country. Why not now? I've ruined everything here; maybe a fresh start is exactly what I need.

And it wouldn't just be about a fresh start, it would be about being close to Jen and Milly. I miss my sister and my niece so much. I could reconnect with them, watch Milly grow up. I could stay with Jen to begin with, look for a job and a place to stay. We have other, distant relatives out there, too – maybe I could travel a bit, CouchSurf. I glance out of the window at the grey rain covering London in sheets. Imagine all the sunshine in California. All that lovely greenery. All the shiny, happy people that R.E.M. were so excited about. And it's not like I'd be leaving a big, exciting career behind me. I pat the pile of papers on the desk in front of me. My job here at The Hales is going nowhere, I've heard nothing from Elizabeth in weeks and she didn't reply to my last email. I feel such *disappointment*. How is this how my life has turned out? I don't know how else to escape this cycle, other than smashing it up completely. Turning my vicious circle into an L.A.-shaped square.

But what about Dad? Could I leave him here? Maybe if he met someone. Maybe if Eileen turns out to be The One, maybe he'd be happy to get a bit of space from his needy, clingy children. I ring his mobile.

'Hello?' he answers suspiciously.

'It's Lenny, Dad.' You know, the person whose name just came up on your phone – I don't say.

'Lenny? Oh my goodness, hello, darling! How are you? Are you here? Are you in your room?' I can feel him looking over his shoulder at the stairs, up into his empty house.

'No, Dad, I'm at work. Why would I ring yo— never mind. How was it?' I say expectantly.

'How was what, darling?'

'The date! Eileen?' I say impatiently.

'Oh! Oh, well, darling, goodness, it's hard to say . . .'

That doesn't sound too promising.

'Well, what was she like?' I try. 'Was she nice? Did you find her attractive?'

'Um,' he hesitates. 'Yes, she was awfully nice. Very pretty red hair.'

'And?'

'Um,' he slows again. 'I don't think she was terribly keen on me, I'm afraid, Lenny.'

'Oh.'

'Yes, it's a bit of a shame. She said she didn't realise I'd be so old, and then she asked me if I'd put gel in my eyebrows and said it looked very silly. I'd only put a little in there, Lenny. Candice said it suited me.'

'Ah, I'm so sorry, Dad.' I'm instantly furious. Poor Dad.

Why would this woman be so rude? I've met some horrible people in my dating life, but I didn't realise things don't get any better in your sixties.

'Not to worry!' he says with fake cheer in his voice. 'You live and learn, don't you, Lenny? And I'll remember not to wear my red tie from Next for the next date I go on. Eileen said it made my face look really round and red.'

'Dad, that's not true, your red tie is lovely. And you're not old and your eyebrows are great,' I say, my voice high and indignant.

'That's very kind of you, my darling,' he says, not sounding very convinced. 'But you mustn't worry, I'm not upset. We had a nice time anyway, it just wasn't meant to be. Although it was a bit expensive in the end. She kept ordering champagne, which as you know, I'm not a big fan of myself.'

I can contain myself no longer. 'What a cow! And she let you pay, obviously?'

'Try not to use language like that, Lenny,' he says, scolding. 'And yes, I did pay, but I offered to. And she said it was only right because I'd let her think I was so much younger. I didn't mean to mislead her though, Lenny. My age is right there on my dating profile. And she's the same age as me.'

'Dad, you mustn't let this get to you, she's clearly just an awful cow.'

'Lenny,' he says gently, warning.

'Sorry,' I sigh. 'Please don't let it put you off dating, Dad. I know you'll meet someone wonderful. I'll come over again this weekend and we'll have another look at the website to see if we can find someone lovely for you. Someone who will think you're super brilliant, and who won't insult you and steal your money. Maybe you can even get Candice and

Peter over to help choose someone again too – it would be great to finally meet them.'

Dad laughs. 'Peter's not much help with these things, but yes, that sounds lovely.' He pauses, and then asks carefully, 'You're not coming back here again tonight then?'

'No,' I say, feeling determined. I need to go back to TS really, if not to be brave and face Josh, then at least to collect fresh pants.

'OK, love,' he says. 'And you're . . . you're all right? You seemed a bit sad this weekend.'

'I'm fine!' I say, and then remember what Thomas said. About how I never talk about my feelings. About how I can't even tell my lovely dad how I really feel.

'Actually, Dad,' I say. 'I had a bit of a fight with Sophie and Thomas on Friday. So, yes, you're right. I was, am, feeling a bit sad.'

'Oh, Lenny, I'm sorry.' He sounds it.

'Thanks,' I start to well up. This is why I don't talk about things, I get emotional. I hate crying and I hate putting anything on him. He's been through so much, he doesn't need me weeping down the phone to him.

He goes on, 'You don't have to tell me what it was about, but they're your best friends, Lenny. Nothing can change that. I'm sure it'll be all right. You just need to talk to them, set things right. I bet they're just as sad as you, waiting by the phone for you to call them.'

'Maybe,' I say, unconvinced.

'Definitely. Why don't you give them a call? Or pop over to see them now?'

'Dad, I'm at work . . . '

'You are?' His voice is incredulous. 'Listen, Lenny, Sophie and Thomas love you very much, darling, just like everyone does. You are wonderful and kind and very clever. I'm so proud of you, Lenny.'

'Thanks, Dad.' My voice breaks a bit again, I feel like none of those things.

'This will work itself out, I promise. Is there anything else bothering you, darling? I'm here if you ever want to talk about anything at all. I'm always here for you.'

I say nothing. I'm obviously not going to tell him about sleeping with my stupid flatmate, or about the string of failed dates that have left me feeling much lonelier than I ever felt before I joined Tinder. I'm going to try and open up more, but that doesn't mean I have to tell my dad about casual, drunken sex with scoundrel flatmates. There are limits.

Instead I say, 'Thank you, Dad, I feel a lot better.'

'Love you, Lenny,' he says kindly.

'I love you too, Dad.'

Hanging up, I take a deep breath. I do feel a little better, but I'm not ready to call Sophie. Instead, I dash off a WhatsApp message to Jen.

How would you feel about me coming to the U.S.?

Her reply is instant:

Which part?

Your part, duh. Would you be up for me coming to visit sometime soon? Or – and don't freak out – what would you think about me actually moving there?

God, Ellie, I move a million miles away to escape you and now you want to follow me here? This is so typical of you.

She doesn't mean it.

I reply, feeling the sting of rejection again.

> Ha, OK, just a thought, I miss you and Milly though. I'd like to see you guys.

> You are so needy. Just get laid already.

I wince at how recently I did, in fact, get laid and put my phone down.

Whatever Jen thinks about me going there, I need to escape these last few days, weeks, months. I need to escape my life and see a friendly face (Milly's, not Jen's). I start Googling flights from London to L.A.X. I could leave this week. Have a total fresh start, piece everything back together, regroup.

After work, I hover uncertainly at my desk. I really don't want to go straight home to face the awkward music.

Speaking of awkward music, Elton John flashes through my head and I physically cringe into myself. I'll go sit out on the stairwell for a bit. That will kill some time.

Out on my favourite step, I find my loo twin Nick out there.

'Hello again!' he says cheerfully, but he's clearly been crying.

'Hi, Nick,' I say, matching his tone as I sit down next to him. 'I haven't seen you in the loo today, how are you?'

'Oh, I'm not too great,' he says, still cheerily, but his voice is cracking. 'My wife moved out. I told her I was ready to forgive her for the affair, but she said she doesn't love me any more. She said she would be willing to have an open marriage, but I can't do that. I can't cope with the idea of her continuing to sleep with Simon. I told her no way, so she's gone to stay at her mother's. She knows I won't dare follow her there, her mother is the scariest woman alive, Ellie. I think it might be really over this time, I can't believe it.'

'Jesus.' I'm silent for a second. 'Nick, I'm really sorry. But, er, maybe splitting up is the right thing for you guys. I bet it doesn't feel like it now, but I'm sure it'll work out OK for you.'

He nods a bit. 'I think you're probably right, but it's not easy.' He laughs, his voice shaking. 'I don't want to be alone; it scares the shit out of me. Do you think I'll be alone forever, Ellie?'

'Of course you won't, Nick,' I say, patting him kindly on the shoulder. 'You're a great guy, you'll meet someone. Someone who won't, er, sleep with your brother. That would be better, wouldn't it?'

He blows his nose. 'You're right as always. I should get on Tinder, shouldn't I? Jackie says you're on Tinder, is that right, Ellie? How's it going?'

I laugh. 'It's . . . '

I stop. Shit. I've forgotten I've got a date tonight. Shit. I look a total mess, but – I check the time – we're meant to be meeting in twenty minutes. I can't cancel now!

I take a deep breath. OK, at least this means I don't have to go home and see Josh.

'I'm sorry, Nick, I've got to run. You've just reminded me, I've got a date tonight, actually.'

'Good for you, Ellie! Never give up. You'll find someone eventually!'

I jump up, trying not to roll my eyes, and rush to the loos.

It's going to take all my best trowelling efforts to cover these puffy eyes.

As I totter towards the bar we're meeting in, I breathe a sigh of relief that I suggested somewhere so close. I'd never have made it if I had to travel across town. He's just texted saying he's there and what do I want to drink. But I'm here now, and I head in and up to the bar.

'Hello,' he says, kissing me on the cheek and smiling widely.

I smile back, it's nice to see him again.

'Hi, Nathan,' I say, shyly.

On my way to Dad's on Saturday, in a fit of pique at Sophie and Thomas and Josh and the world, I finally texted Nathan back. He replied straightaway, and then we ended up speaking on the phone for ages. He said sorry again for his tantrum text and we talked about everything. Silly stuff, serious stuff. He told me about his ex and how they'd been engaged, and how she ended it out of nowhere and moved out of the country. I told him about my mum and how tough that all was. He said sorry again about the way he'd acted at the end of our first date, and sorry again about his brush off text. He asked if I'd be willing to give him another shot at a date.

So here we are.

He's just as handsome and sweet as I remember, and as he hands me a wine, we quickly fall back into the easy back and forth rhythmic conversation we had on our first date.

But, fun and handsome as he is, I just can't focus. My mind keeps dragging me back to everything that's been going on lately, and I can hardly focus on what he's saying. I'm still too sad. As I try to fake some enthusiasm, I realise all my stupid, silly stories are about times I've shared with my friends. And when he asks me how Sophie is – the best friend I'd talked so much about on our last date – I feel myself well up.

Don't cry don't cry don't cry.

At least don't cry in front of a stranger, you unbelievable loser.

Don't cry don't cry don't cry don't cry don't cry.

Oh great, you're crying. I can't believe you're crying. This is so embarrassing.

Nathan looks horrified and a couple of other people nearby look at him accusingly as tears start rolling down my cheeks.

'Sorry, I'm sorry,' I say, starting to stand up. 'I can't be here tonight, I'm so sorry. I'm going to leave, please don't hate me.'

'No, don't leave!' he says, alarmed and standing up too. 'Or at least tell me if it's something I can help with? I'm so sorry I made you cry.'

'It's not you, it wasn't you,' I say, the tears still coming. I think there's snot too. Christ. 'I'm just having a really bad week and I need to go home. I'm really sorry, Nathan. You're lovely.'

'Of course,' he says, nodding kindly and helping me with my coat. 'Can I at least get you a taxi home? Let me order it for you now.'

I let him, knowing I've totally blown anything that could've been between us.

He gives me a hug as he puts me in a taxi and I watch him from the rear view mirror, watching me, as we drive away. I won't hear from him again. Or maybe – ha! – maybe I'll get another of his 'we're not compatible' texts. Which, I have to admit, would be fair enough. After all, I am leaving our second date in tears after only thirty minutes. I look at my messy, mascara-stained face in the mirror. What a catch.

The taxi drops me off and I pause on my front doorstep. The house seems quiet and empty inside, the windows are dark. But TS is always dark. Please, please, let Josh not be home. He's probably got a date, I think as I quietly let myself in, and feel a pang of something. Jealousy? Loss? Relief? I can't identify it. Everything is still and silent in the house as I move quietly up to my room. But as I turn my door handle, someone says 'Boo' and I scream my head off.

Fucking Josh.

He's just come out of the bathroom and he's grinning at me, naked apart from a towel, hair slicked back from the shower.

'Sorry,' he says, still grinning and very much not sorry. 'We have to stop meeting like this,' he adds, gesturing at his towel.

'You scared the shit out of me,' I say, breathing hard. I make careful eye contact with him, refusing to look down and knowing his abs are winking at me, daring me to objectify him.

'Where have you been these last few days? Have you been deliberately avoiding me?' he asks, in a wounded voice, leaning casually against the doorframe of the bathroom.

I shake my head. 'Er, no, of course not. Just . . . busy busy. You know how it is.'

'Yeah, I know,' he says, nodding. 'You career gals – always moving, right?'

He's teasing me again and I feel myself tense up.

'So . . . ' I say, casually, nodding at my door to indicate I'm going in.

'You want me to come in?' he says, innocently.

'No, no!' I say a little too quickly, and he looks faux-injured again. 'I just meant, I'll probably head into my room now. Leave you to get, um, dressed?'

'I'm not in any hurry,' he says, smirking and not moving. 'Shall we have a drink?'

'God no,' I say. 'I'm still hungover from Friday night. That was such a mistake . . . ' I trail off. I did mean the drinking, but the implication hangs in the air.

Disappointment darkens his face, and he stands up straighter, rallying.

'You don't want to do it again then?' he says, cheekily.

I force a laugh. 'Probably not! I wouldn't want all that . . . drinking to overcomplicate the situation here, with us living together.'

He nods, and bites his lip. I have a flashback of Friday. Him biting my lip.

I laugh awkwardly again and reach for my door, ready to say goodnight.

'Wait, Ellie.' He looks a little flushed. 'Look, don't go yet. Can we just talk a little bit more?'

What else is there to say? I hover, uncertainly. He takes a step towards me and I swallow hard. I'm very, very aware of the wet towel.

He touches my arm, and for a moment, he looks intensely vulnerable. 'Ellie, I . . . I like you. I know you think what happened the other night was just a drunken thing, but I've liked you for ages. I was so happy about all the sex – it was amazing – and I was so gutted when I woke up on Saturday and you were gone.'

WHERE THE FUCK IS THIS COMING FROM?

I'm frozen, watching his face move. He keeps talking, his words are coming faster and faster.

'I meant what I said on Friday, I liked you from the moment you turned up here. You're smart and funny and so easily annoyed. You challenge me. And you're, like, so beautiful. God, Ellie, I really like you. I want you to like me, and I know I've been an arsehole, parading girls around here, trying to make you jealous. Winding you up whenever I could. I didn't know how else to get you to notice me.'

He's closer now, and I can smell the toothpaste on his breath and the smell of Radox on his skin.

'Ellie, I want us to try—'

I interrupt him, pulling away and stepping back. 'Josh, I can't handle this right now,' I say, panicked. 'I didn't have any idea you felt like this. I had no clue. I don't know what to think. I thought Friday was . . . ' I trail off. I thought Friday was meaningless.

There's a pause. 'Do you at least like me a bit?' he says quietly.

'I don't know,' I say honestly.

'Is it Thomas?' he asks, his voice still low. 'Are you in love with him?'

'What? No!' I reply, and then I add, 'God, maybe. I don't know. How does anyone know these things? How is this stuff so easy for everyone else?'

He smiles at me. 'I want you to give me a chance,' he says, taking my hands again. 'I think you're amazing, and I really like you. I haven't felt like this in years.'

'Are you sure it's not just the oxytocin?' I say and he cocks his head at me, perplexed.

'Never mind,' I hastily add.

'Just think about it?' he says again, plaintively.

I nod dumbly, and we stand there looking at each other for a minute.

I'm so shocked. He's so beautiful. This beautiful man wants me, he likes me, he wants to be with me, and I can't think straight.

'Can I have a bit of time with this?' I finally say, breaking the silence.

He takes a deep breath, looking at me searchingly. 'Of course.' He reaches for my face and my breath gets short. He's going to kiss me he's going to kiss me he's going to kiss me he's going to –

He leaves.

I go into my room and lie on the floor. And then I get up and I start to paint.

14

12.27 p.m. Friday, 5 April in the U.K., or 4.27 a.m. Saturday, 6 April in L.A. – I guess we're somewhere in between that? Oh wait, now it's 12.28 p.m.
Location: A swanky BA flight, feeling a bit lost in time, but like a total badass with a tray table covered in BA-branded items. That includes an immaculately presented miniature portion of mackerel on a bed of elegantly presented salad, seven unnecessary napkins, two tiny, empty bottles of white wine, and a plastic cup with the letters 'BA' engraved on the bottom. So swish.

I'm halfway through *Ella Enchanted*. Have you seen this film? Goddamn, it's great. Why does everyone complain about Anne Hathaway? She's amazing! Look at her, under that spell, being completely adorable opposite the young Hugh Dancy. Life should be more like this. I should wear more dresses, have more adventures, cast more spells.

There's something about watching a film on a tiny plane screen, with your own personal freebie headphones, that feels extra special, don't you think? It's the same feeling as when you have a DVD you've seen five thousand times, but then it comes on telly and you cannot believe your luck. Or it's like the way food tastes so much better when someone else has cooked it. Or like that free latte from Pret that you only had to flirt with the barista every day for a month to get. Worth it.

I inhale the plane air deeply and feel the tension of the last few weeks ooze slowly out of me. I feel good for the first time in ages. Well, good-ish. And with every passing hour that takes me further and further away from the U.K., I feel more like myself. This was a great decision. Getting away from London, running away from my problems, spending a huge amount on my credit card for a flight leaving the next morning. And most of all, paying so much extra to fly with BA just because I knew it would make me feel cooler at the check-in desk, next to the sweaty, already-tired-looking EasyJetters. You've got to get your superiority buzzes wherever you can.

Glancing around, I make eye contact with the beautiful, immaculate air steward again and she rushes over to ask in a hushed voice if I need another tiny bottle of wine. Yes, of course I fucking do, lady. Look at them, they're so cute!

The last few days have remained DEFCON level utter shit. Still no word from Sophie or Thomas, and at home, Josh has been ignoring my request for time to think. Every evening after work, I've come home to him sitting on the sofa, studiously casual, definitely not waiting for me, not at all. There's been that crushing guilt when I've made immediate excuses to head to my room and he's looked at me like I'm stamping his penis under stiletto'd feet. Then yesterday I got back and found him standing by the door with flowers, wine and the karaoke waiting to go. As if he thinks recreating the circumstances of last week would make me realise how much I wanted to be in a relationship with him. In a relationship with a serial philanderer who has a set of dazzling abs that I could never be fully naked around. Like, even alone, I wouldn't be able to be naked, knowing my boyfriend looked like that under his clothes. I would genuinely have to start wearing Spanx in the shower.

And, Jesus, *flowers*? I understand people like flowers – they're pretty, I get it. But they are kind of literally everywhere in real life. Being given flowers is the present equivalent of saying, 'I have no clue what you like, but you're a girl, so you're bound to be pleased with some pretty roses I got from Interflora with a twenty-five per cent discount code.' You have to say thank you *so much*, then spend fifteen minutes of your hard-earned evening time cutting stems and arranging the flowers you didn't want in the first place into a pint glass because who owns vases? And then you spend the next few days watching them die. If you're really lucky, you'll forget about them altogether, and by the time you remember they exist two weeks later, they will smell really bad and you'll throw up coffee in your mouth, dispose of the water and have to go out to the big bins round the back to get rid of the rotting remains, wearing your slippers and you'll step in dog mess.

Tim used to buy me flowers a lot. Ugh.

Obviously I'm being a total bitch and I'm really sorry for it. But I'm angry. I'm angry about my life, and I'm angry that Josh won't leave me alone to think. And there's just too much stuff in my head right now to properly consider what he's offering.

The air steward comes back with two more wines and winks at me conspiratorially. The guy next to me grunts in his sleep 'Please Pam!' and we giggle a bit across him.

OK, I do like Josh. I will say those words. I know myself well enough to admit that. I like him, I fancy him. He challenges me, he makes me think, and he makes me laugh. He's probably riddled with STDs, but you can't have everything. And I could live with herpes, couldn't I? It's mostly dormant, right?

What exactly is the problem then? Why am I hesitating? I guess a small part of me worries that I would never feel totally secure and happy with him. I've seen him treat too many women like nothing to believe he could ever be fully mine.

But maybe that's just because I've come to know the wrong version of him. He said he'd been acting like that because he wanted me to notice him. It's not exactly a mature approach but maybe it's flattering? And this last week there's been a totally unknown, previously unheard of Josh. Lovely, sweet, considerate Josh. He even picked up all his almost empty Radox bottles out of the shower and threw them away. It nearly made me love him.

Oh, I just don't know.

Honestly, I need to work out what to do about Sophie and Thomas before I can figure out what to do about Josh. So, well, what *am* I going to do about them? I don't know why I haven't been in touch to say sorry. I don't know why they haven't.

Maybe it won't matter. Maybe this trip will be so amazing, I'll decide I have to move over there. I'll find new, tanned versions of my old friends.

On the tiny screen, Anne Hathaway adorably bites her lip and sweetly trips over. She giggles and everyone swoons.

I will never be cute like that.

Actually, yeah, that's why everyone hates her.

*

Several hours and several more tiny bottles of wine later, I arrive at the giant gates of Jen's, er – would we call it an estate? What constitutes an estate? It's pretty vast, and I can't see round the side of it. That's an estate in my book. As I buzz the intercom for entry, I wonder for a minute whether Jen will even let me in.

I didn't tell her I was coming until I landed a couple of hours ago. I told myself I wanted to surprise her, but maybe I also didn't want to give her a chance to tell me not to come. Because I had to come. Either way, the text I'd fired off, as I climbed into a cab, sweaty and overwhelmed by everyone's languid accent, had not been well received. Jen replied swiftly, and each of her well-chosen single-syllable words were annoyed. She said she was too busy to look after a fucking tourist; that the house was a mess; that Andrew would be angry about having an unexpected guest; that it wasn't OK for Milly to have her routine disrupted on my whims. She said I was selfish and that I could go find a 'sodding hostel' and come round one afternoon for tea, if I had to. I got back out of my cab, crestfallen, and almost ready to book an immediate flight back again. As I was debating my options, Jen texted again, more conciliatory, and relented about me coming to stay. Yes, fine, come, she'd said, but don't expect to be waited on, hand and foot. As if I ever pictured her doing that.

Her muffled voice crackles over the intercom now and the gates start to creak open. Jen's already waiting at the door, wearing her most-terribly-inconvenienced face. She looks angry, but it's more than that, she looks . . . bad. She is so thin, she's lost a lot of weight since I last saw her. They say the camera adds ten pounds, so a camera *phone* must clearly add at least a stone. I've never seen her this small before. It's all I can see – her thinness – and it makes her look so vulnerable. I study her drawn face; it is all angry features and lines in odd places – the bits missed by the *de rigeur* Botox.

'Hello,' she says coolly, opening the door a little wider and not offering to help with my bag.

'I'm so sorry about this,' I say again, awkwardly, as I lurch inside, heaving my bag over the threshold.

'Don't worry about it,' she says, avoiding my eyes.

'Please don't be angry with me,' I plead, setting it down and touching Jen's arm, gingerly. 'I was having a shit week. I just wanted to escape. I wanted to see you and Milly. I miss you. I used up the entire balance of my emergency credit card to get here! I'll be paying it off for the next seventeen years.'

She looks at me properly and reluctantly half smiles. I think my penalty is over.

'OK,' she says a bit more warmly, and gives me a hug. 'It's good to see you, little sister.' She pulls away and examines me critically. 'You look dreadful though.'

'Well, I have just been on a plane for eleven hours,' I say, relieved I seem to be out of danger. Thank God she doesn't hate me.

'Eleven hours couldn't have made that outfit any worse, Ellie. I think I've seen the local hobo in something very similar.'

'Then that hobo is likely very warm and comfortable,' I say, grinning.

She gestures at me to follow her into the kitchen and I abandon my bag by the front door.

I've never been here before, never even seen pictures, and I feel overwhelmed. It's impressive, mostly because of the size, but also because of the high ceilings and blinding light everywhere from the oversized windows. There's a lot of white. Lots of big, white space. Immaculate, but sparsely furnished. Very L.A.

'This place is amazing,' I say, my voice a little awed and Jen waves away my compliment.

'How was your flight?' she asks, more polite than I'm used to.

'Oh, er, it was fine,' I say. 'It's so great to see you, Jen. You look, gosh, well, you look . . . thin.'

'Thank you,' she says, pleased. I say nothing.

'ELLIE!' a familiar Milly voice shrieks as she comes running in, barrelling into me for a hug.

I laugh, pick her up, and then immediately put her down as my back groans in protest. She has grown a lot, lengthened in all directions. The changes really suit her. Her skin is glowing, her hair swishing bluntly around her shoulders, and she's wearing a T-shirt that declares her to be a Power Rangers fan. Power Rangers are still a thing? That is amazing.

'Wow, look at you, you're so tall!' I say, feeling like such a clichéd aunt.

'I'm taller than all the boys in my grade,' she says smugly with just a trace of an American accent. And then she adds – still smug – 'They all hate me.' She steps back from her hug and regards me with the same critical eye her mother always gives me. 'What are you doing here?' she says, curiously.

'I've come to see you!' I say, enthusiastically, feeling like a fraud. It's not the whole reason, but Milly *is* a huge part of why I've come. It's not just to escape my problems, it's to see the people I love. And looking at her now, I can't believe how much I've missed in the last year. She looks like a person now. Does that sound weird? The last time I saw Milly, I'm sure she wasn't really a *person* – she was a child. Now I can sort of see how she will look as a grown-up. It's bizarre.

'Stop staring at me, you creepo,' she says, and then takes my hand, leading me out of the kitchen and into the living room, where she is building a fort that she says is called 'Guantanamo Bay'. She even pronounces it right. I glance over my shoulder. Jen has turned away and is leaning against the sink, like she needs its support to stand.

When I wake up around nine the next morning, my first thought is surprise at being awake. Because being awake, means I've been asleep. I thought for sure the events of my recent shit-show of a life carousel-ing around my brain on a loop would result in all night, red-eyed ceiling analysis. But I've slept. Deeply. As I try to sit up, the disorientation hits me. I briefly wonder where I am and it crosses my mind that I am dead. That this is purgatory. A very white purgatory. And then it comes back to me – not dead, just in L.A. I look excitedly round the room at the daylight pouring in through the thin white curtains. It's a nice room I guess, but sparse, like the rest of the house. Just a chest of drawers and a forlorn-looking wicker chair in the corner. Oh, and my enormous, L.A.-sized bed, of course. I remember now, climbing in half asleep last night, and crawling for hours, desperately trying to find the middle.

Right. I throw the sheets off me. I need to start this American adventure.

As I pad softly downstairs, I spot Jen and Andrew in the kitchen. Andrew wasn't here when I arrived yesterday and no one mentioned him, so I didn't either. But there he is, looking the same as ever; grey from head to toe.

I realise immediately that I have walked into an argument. They are speaking in furiously loud stage whispers and Jen is using her seriously angry voice. As opposed to her day-to-day angry voice.

'I'm sick of it, Andrew,' Jen is hissing.

'What do you want me to do, then?' he hisses back.

'Anything!' she whisper-shrieks, 'Literally anything would be better than this. You need to tell Larry that you can't keep—'

I clear my throat.

They both look up at me, like squirrels caught stealing nuts.

Andrew clears his throat. 'Er, hello, Eleanor. How are you?'

'Good morning,' I say awkwardly. 'Sorry to drop in on you like this, Jen told me not to. I hope I haven't inconvenienced you . . . '

He shrugs, he is not interested.

'I'm going to work,' he barks, picking up his bag and nodding at me again as he stomps to the front door

I haven't seen him since the funeral, over a year ago.

'It's a Sunday, isn't it . . . ?' I say quietly to Jen as the door slams behind him.

She doesn't look at me as she moves around the kitchen, tidying breakfast things away and wiping surfaces.

'He works on Sundays,' she says, her voice shaking almost imperceptibly. 'He works every weekend.'

She stops for a second, her back to me, hunched. And then she straightens up and I see she is putting her defiant Jen mask back on.

'Milly's in there watching *The OC*, if you want to join her?' She nods behind me and then looks away again quickly. The room is thick with tension as I hop from one bare foot to another. Jen doesn't like to be asked if she's all right. She keeps gabbling. 'She says you recommended the series?'

'I did,' I say shortly, walking over to the sink and picking up my glass from last night to wash up.

'Don't do that,' she snaps at me, striding over and snatching it from my hand. 'I don't need your help.'

'OK,' I say, feeling stupid.

She puts it down, and starts talking again. 'Milly loves it. She says she's going to marry Seth Cohen. I told her he's like forty now but she called me a liar and stormed out. I'm not sure Summer is a very good influence on her.'

'No, I don't suppose she would be,' I agree.

'Right,' she says, turning back to me. 'Do you want breakfast? What shall we do today? Do you want to go shopping? You need sorting out.' She gestures with disgust at my outfit.

'These are my pyjamas,' I say defensively.

'You can't tell the difference,' she says as she barges past. I follow her into the living-room, where Milly is eating some kind of bowl full of chocolate blobs with chocolate milk in front of the TV. I say nothing but silently judge Jen's parenting skills.

'Clean yourself up, we're going shopping,' she informs her daughter, throwing a cloth in her direction and stomping out.

Not looking away from the screen, Milly dabs ineffectively at her Iron Man T-shirt.

I sit down next to her. 'Robert Downey Jr. is hot, isn't he?' I say conversationally. She looks up at me, brown cereal gunk leaking out of the corner of her mouth.

'What are you talking about?' she says, shaking her head, exasperated.

'Iron Man? He's hot?' I point at her shirt.

She gives me a withering look. 'His name,' she explains slowly, like I'm a moron, 'is Tony Stark. And it is irrelevant how warm he is because he's saving the world loads. Duh.'

'Gotcha,' I nod.

'Hey,' she says, thoughtfully, finally turning away from Seth's onscreen twitching. 'What do you think cat food tastes like?'

The day is pretty much more of that. We go to the famous Rodeo Drive, which is amazing and I ooh and aah over the posh brand names. I can afford nothing, obviously, and I'm disappointed to find none of the sales assistants try to *Pretty Woman* me. They just keep asking how I'm doing today and instructing me to have a nice day. I know the polite thing to do is just keep smiling, but I'm afraid to show them my un-whitened teeth in case they faint with horror. Maybe this is why Brits have an unfriendly reputation, because we come to this glossy place and feel too insecure to smile.

It's nice though. Hanging out with my girls. We bicker constantly and easily and Jen keeps threatening to turn the car around, even when we're not driving. But it's nice. I've missed them such a lot.

I never blamed Jen for moving away right after Mum died – I wanted to go, too – but it's been hard not having her and Milly around.

We stop for lunch and sit outside a bistro, eating bits of lettuce and admiring the waitress-cum-actresses who all look like Margot Robbie. I feel lighter than I have in weeks. There is nothing to make you feel that the world is a good place than the warmth of the sun on your face and knowing you don't have to be back at work for another week.

Maybe I really could live here, I think again. Maybe I could. I could get my teeth done, be a friendlier person who smiles at strangers, and spend my days in the sunshine, a million miles away from the gloom of England. It might be great. It might be the adventure I've been looking for. A square-shouldered bronzed man strolls by, smiling in our direction. There's another reason to stay.

On the drive home, Milly falls asleep in the back and I try to broach the subject of her father.

'Andrew seems busy,' I say carefully, watching Jen out of the corner of my eye. She revs the engine but says nothing, so I continue. 'Was everything . . . all right, this morning, when I came down?'

'Fine,' she snaps, hitting the steering wheel and muttering, 'Fucking traffic.'

We're sitting in a queue at a red light and I touch her arm, tentatively. It feels cheesy and forced so I stop. Looking straight ahead, I say, 'You know I'm here if you want to talk?'

She rolls her eyes. 'You people just love talking, don't you? Not everything needs analysing and dissecting, you know. I'm fine, we're fine, everyone's fine.'

I fall silent, but then the words in my mouth get the better of me and I ask the question: 'Jen, are you happy?'

She whips around, wide eyed and instantly angry. 'God, Ellie! What is this obsession you have with being happy? You know this is just life, don't you? Life is fucking shit and everyone just gets on with it. Why do you think you're so special? Why do you deserve to be happier than anyone else? No one is happy, that's not how life works. You get on with it and then you die in pain, just like Mum did. Being happy is a bullshit idea and you need to let go of it.'

Her face is red, and she looks like she might cry.

'That makes no sense,' I mutter. 'What's the point of anything if you're not happy? That's not how life should be, that's not something you should just accept. Life shouldn't make you cry in traffic.'

'Fuck off,' she snaps. 'I'm not crying, I'm just allergic to pricks. If you don't shut up, my face will probably start swelling up, and then my throat will close and I will die. Do you happen to have an epi pen on you? I don't carry one around with me because I don't usually encounter this much prick.'

'OK!' I surrender, checking Milly is still snoring obliviously in the back. Her mouth hangs open and I fight an impulse to throw something in there. 'Fine, I won't ask if you're happy ever again. But –' I chance one more sentence '– you know where I am if you do need to talk about anything.'

She pauses now, and turns to look at me, searchingly. I wait, wide eyed and hopeful. Here we go, maybe I got through to her. She speaks. 'Has anyone ever told you that you have a huge head? Like, a HUGE head? You're totally out of proportion.'

I roll my eyes and the lights turn green.

*

That night the jetlag finally catches up with me, and I lie staring at the unfamiliar ceiling of this strange empty room for hours. I think again about my sister. All this pressure on me to achieve what Jen has; a husband, a child – and I can't imagine anything more stifling and unhappy. But maybe she is happy. Maybe she likes the conflict. Maybe the argument this morning was just a one-off. She's made it clear she doesn't want my help or advice, and I can't do anything if she refuses to talk to me. I'm a guest here, a visitor who has popped my head round the door of her life very briefly and soon I'll be gone again.

I sigh dramatically and heave onto my side. I wish I had something to distract me. I brought my sketchbook but it's in my bag downstairs. I'm not sure I have the energy to climb for miles out of this bed to get it. I think about the painting I've just started, sitting in my room in TS, waiting for me to get back to it. My hands itch. It's good, I know it is. It's a face, but I don't know whose face just yet. It feels familiar, there's something in the eyes, but I can't tell just yet. I feel the rush of excitement in my stomach. It's that feeling I always used to get when I was painting something great. I've been sketching non-stop, too. If I do stay out here in L.A., I don't want to let go of that feeling. Rediscovering my art has been the one decent thing to come out of the last few disastrous weeks.

By 3 a.m. I've had enough and I get up to quietly explore this ridiculously huge place and find my sketchbook. I tiptoe out of my room feeling weird and like I'm in the Upside Down universe. It's exciting being awake in the middle of the night in a new house, but scary too. It's that sense of being in your school after hours.

Everything is silent and still, and I head for the kitchen for water. But as I reach for the tap, I stifle a scream when I spot a figure standing there in the dark.

It's Jen. She's standing unmoving by the window, staring out. Is she sleepwalking? I take a step towards her and she glances over.

Her face crumples when she sees me and suddenly she is properly crying. Jen, who does not cry. Jen, who I've never actually seen cry. Jen, who didn't even cry in front of me when Mum died. Jen. She's now sinking into a chair and sobbing as she collapses into herself, curling up like she's in physical pain.

I'm by her side in seconds, and I drop to my knees beside the chair, circling my arms around her. She leans into me and continues to cry.

I tighten my grip, realising how pathetically selfish I've been.

Bickering with friends? A few bad dates? How did I for even a second think those were real issues? I've been so self-involved that I didn't realise my sister was really suffering.

We sit there for a few minutes as Jen cries herself out. Every time I think she's about to stop, she starts again, and my arms are aching by the time she finally calms down. I still don't say anything, but I can tell she is almost ready to.

'I've been thinking, thinking about leaving him,' she says, her face still buried in my shoulder.

'It's just . . . this isn't the life I wanted. Andrew works all the time, I never see him. Milly barely knows who he is. They bumped into each other yesterday and she actually screamed in fear. I thought moving out here would make everything better, that we'd be able to spend more time together, but it's worse. I don't know anyone and I have nothing to do. I even tried to make friends with the cleaner but she said I was mean. I feel like I've settled for a life I didn't know I was signing up for. I don't know what to do. I think I need a break.'

I pause. Poor Jen. This is why she didn't want me to come, she didn't want me to see how sad she was. 'Then have a break,' I say quietly. 'You and Milly, come home with me. It can be a belated birthday surprise for Dad, you know he'd love it. Have some space for a couple of weeks and figure out what you want.'

She's looking down and I don't know what she's thinking.

I continue, 'I know you think life is meant to be a certain way, and follow a pattern, but it doesn't have to, Jen. You can be on your own. It's not bad like you think, I love it.'

She wipes her face and looks at me. 'I'm not making any decisions now. Don't start telling people I'm your sad sack single mum sister,' she says fiercely. I nod emphatically.

'I never would,' I say, even though I might a bit.

She goes on. 'But I think maybe you're right. Maybe a break is what I need. Milly's off school for the next couple of weeks anyway for Easter, so it would be a good time to come.' She sounds stronger, and then her voice cracks. 'I still love him though, Ellie.'

I pull my sister close and she starts quietly crying again.

This is probably the shortest holiday I've ever had. Barely three days after arriving in sunny L.A., it's time to go home.

After our middle of the night crying session, Jen came and slept in my bed, and when we woke up late, Milly was in with us too.

Lying there in the giant bed, we made arrangements for flights. Milly squealed excitedly about planes and seeing Grandpa's eyebrows in real life.

There's a fee to change my return journey, but it's uncomplicated enough, and I pack my things, feeling surprised at how ready I am to leave L.A. after such a short trip. Andrew had already left for work by the time we got up this morning, so Jen rang him at the office to break the news. It sounded pretty bad through the wall. I couldn't hear what was said, but the muffled shouts and Jen's red eyes were enough to know it didn't go down well. I feel so terrible that I haven't been here for her. Jen was going through this shitty time and I've been so wrapped up in my own dumb problems, I never even thought to probe her properly about Andrew. I am a bad sister. The guilt zigzags through my stomach.

Jen appears in the doorway, now, with her suitcase, and she's smiling. I realise I haven't seen her genuinely smile in ages. God, maybe not since before Mum got ill. And even with the swollen eyes and the giant under-eye bags, she looks beautiful.

'I've checked us in online,' Jen confirms, wandering in. She casually pulls a top I've already packed back out of my bag. 'You know, this isn't so ugly,' she says, almost kindly. She turns it round. 'Oh wait, no, it's hideous,' she adds, grinning and throwing it back on top of the pile. 'Hurry up, we're ready to go and the car's on its way.'

I zip up my barely unpacked suitcase. It's time to go. Time to stop being the idiot who runs away from every problem. I've done exactly what Sophie accused me of – the first sign of trouble and I've literally left the country. It's time to go home and get my life back together. No more running.

15

5.05 p.m. Tuesday, 9 April
Location: My dad's back garden, which I haven't been out in for at least a year because who goes outside for no reason? The sun is shining and Dad is pointing out flowers and naming them for us – 'sweet pea, peonies, tulips' – like any of us are listening or care. Jen is deliberately standing on a peony and Dad is trying subtly to get her to move without coming right out and asking.

You should've seen Dad's face when he opened the door. All his girls, standing there on his doorstep, smiling at him. He, completely predictably, burst into tears. And then Jen started crying, so I started crying, and then it was just Milly looking at each of us, completely bemused and trying to get in the doorway past Dad, shouting that she needed a coffee. Dad used his apron to dry his face and ushered us all in, whispering to Jen that Milly doesn't really drink coffee – does she?

Out in the garden now, I think about how much I could really do with some coffee myself. The flight back – especially so soon after my flight there – has really taken it out of me and I can barely keep my eyes open. I had planned to catch up with Jen properly on the journey, to see how she was feeling about the whole, y'know, getting some space from her marriage thing, but we all sat separately. I thought it was because it was a last minute booking, but when we got to the check-in counter, the attendant asked if we'd prefer to sit together – since it was a quiet flight – and Jen said an emphatic no. She said that she'd specifically requested seats apart so she didn't have to 'make small talk with her sister and daughter for eleven hours'. I could tell the lady on the counter thought we were all really terrific.

I ended up sitting next to a really nice older lady, around sixty or so, who wanted to talk a lot. She reminded me of Mum and for a while, with the forced intimacy of plane seats, it was kind of like having her back. Like all strangers do, she asked me straight off if I have a boyfriend, and I found that really funny for some reason. We ended up going over all my recent dating experiences and she laughed a lot about it, and it made me laugh again, too. It turned out the lady – Bella – has been single for most of her life. She'd had the odd love affair here and there, she told me, but it was her choice and destiny to stay on her own. She said she loved being selfish and not having to report in with anyone, or ask permission to make her own plans. She didn't like arguments or making concessions or having to worry about someone else's moods. She said she couldn't imagine having to make all that effort to make it work with one other person fulltime. I could see her point.

'I almost got married once,' she said, eyes twinkling. 'Back in the noughties. Paul was rather wonderful, a musician, you know. He begged me to marry him, promised not to bother me too much, but I called the whole thing off the week before the ceremony. I realised I just wanted to wear a nice dress and have a big party. I didn't mind the wedding but I didn't want to be married. He was nice about it, went off and married a woman called Heather, instead. Wrote a song called "The Lovers That Never Were" about me, I've got it on CD somewhere. So sweet, such a sweet man.'

I sat there for hours, entranced by Bella's stories and adventures all over the world. She'd lived and worked all over the place, meeting new people every day, having flings with men in every continent, including America, where she's been shagging a film star she wouldn't name, but it seemed a lot like it might be Bill Murray.

'When you're little,' she told me as we landed, 'you have all these ideas of how your life will turn out. As a girl, everyone assumes you will aspire to the only approved fairytale – marriage and babies. That you will be planning and dreaming of your wedding day from the age of five, but trust me, Ellie, there is so much more to life. And, for me, especially as a woman, there was always too much self-sacrifice associated with getting married. Self-sacrifice that I never wanted to make. I didn't want to give my life up to someone else. I wanted to be happy, and that meant being on my own. Go be happy, Ellie, choose your own path.'

It was almost the exact opposite speech Jen had given me in the car.

In the garden, we've started on the sherry and Dad's talking excitedly about extending the dining room table later on. Nothing gets him as excited as extending the table and he hasn't had much cause to do it lately. He's going to extend the hell out of that table and we are all going to sit round playing Boggle. It's a plan.

I'm half listening now as he regales Jen and Milly with his latest date. He launches into a story about a woman the other day who spent their dinner date bizarrely saying she liked drinking tea. Even half-listening, I realise the woman was trying to get Dad to 'teabag' her. Erk. I'm probably not going to explain that one to him.

Suddenly he stops talking and looks shy.

'Jenny, Lenny, Milly,' he says. 'Can I show you something?' He starts towards the end of the garden, and we follow him down past Mum's lady shed, where she would escape from Dad to listen to Britney albums. I gasp as we turn the corner. Back there is a totally beautiful mini garden. There's a bench, surrounded by green shrubs, twinkling white fairy lights everywhere, and so many bright, lovely flowers. It feels special and private, and I instantly know it's for Mum. It's a place she would've loved to sit.

'I made it for her,' Dad says a little bashfully as he looks anxiously from Jen's face to mine.

I swallow.

He goes on. 'The lilies aren't out yet, but I looked it up, and they're Britney's favourite flower, so I planted lots of them. I hope they grow OK.' He crouches down, knees creaking loudly as he absentmindedly strokes a leaf.

'It's nice!' Milly says loudly, approvingly. She jumps onto the bench and starts swinging her legs, oblivious to the sombre mood.

I glance at Jen, she's nodding, blinking hard. I think she's swallowing tears down too.

'Mum would've loved it,' I say at last, my voice cracking.

'Do you think?' Dad looks up at me, hopefully. 'I talked about the idea with my therapist Jacquetta during our last session a few weeks ago. I wanted to do something for your mum. Give her this place, so she knows this is still her home, wherever she is now. It's for me too. I come out here for a few minutes every day and I talk to her. I tell her about my day and about the people I've met. I don't know if she can hear me, but I still want to talk.'

'You haven't, you won't . . . forget about her then?' I say, trembling a bit. It's what I've been wanting to ask for months. The fear I've been holding on to since he first mentioned wanting to date again. I've been so scared of him letting go of my mum, replacing her, taking down the photos, not loving her any more.

He creaks back up to a standing position and takes my hands, looking at me, concerned.

'Lenny, I promise you, I never would. I never could.' He pauses and wipes his big red hand across his face. 'I know people throw the idea of soulmates and true love around – I don't know if it means anything any more – but I can sincerely tell you that every time I looked at your mum's face, I knew it. I knew she was mine with every little bit of me. She was the love of my life. She was the light in every day we spent together. Even after all those years and even in those awful last few months, I still looked at her and knew she was my everything.'

There's a silence and I step across the garden to sit next to Milly on the bench. Closing my eyes, I turn my face to the cold sun.

'I really miss her,' I say out loud. I haven't said it before. Not to the two people who would understand it most.

'Me too,' says Jen, in a low voice. 'All the time.' She's staring at the shed that shields this magic garden from the rest of the world. As kids, we used to come out to the bottom of the garden, giggling, looking for Mum. We would knock on her shed and then shriek and run away to hide. Mum would come bursting out, shouting 'FEE FI FO FUM, I SMELL SOME UNWASHED JENNIFER AND ELEANOR BUM!' We would scream melodramatically from our hiding place – which was always behind the same tree – and then furiously shush each other as Mum boomed past us, pretending to look. After a few seconds, I would invariably ruin the game by jumping out and shouting, 'Mum, we're here! We're over here,' and she would look surprised, while Jen scowled at me. Then we would all laugh, and Mum would take each of us by the hand, leading us inside for baths and cuddles.

We're all silent, lost in our own memories of her.

Eventually Jen clears her throat and offers casually, 'Hey, did Mum try and get anyone else to kill her?'

I burst out laughing. 'Yes, me,' I say, nodding. 'Especially in that last couple of months. She said she didn't want to ruin Christmas by still being around, and that it would save her getting anyone presents.' Then I add hastily, in case anyone is thinking it, 'I said no, obviously.'

Jen looks amused. 'I would've done it, but Dad wouldn't give me his Ocado login details. No way was I paying for all that Nurofen myself.'

Dad shakes his head. 'She asked me too, silly girl. As if I could.'

We're all silent again, and then I start laughing.

Dad joins in, looking at us. 'I can't tell you how happy I am to have you both here,' he says.

'Fine,' says Jen, clearing her throat and moving us away from the heavy mood. 'But enjoy us while you can, because I'm not sure how long we're staying. And I'm not watching fucking *Neighbours*.'

When we go back inside, we find Milly has pulled everything out of her suitcase to get to her season three *OC* box set. 'I can't get behind on this,' she says by way of explanation, like it's a major project at work that her boss is riding her about. She puts the disc into Dad's ancient DVD player and the two of us settle onto the sofa together. Dad and Jen wander out into the kitchen to make tea, talking about how much of a relief it is for Jen that she doesn't have to drink 'fucking hippy green tea' while she's out of L.A. I look around at my family, all together after so long, and think about tomorrow.

16

11.30 a.m. Wednesday, 10 April
Location: Outside the square, purpose-built office that is The Hales. It looks greyer than ever, as do the people hurrying by, gripping their Pret coffee. There's a man trapped in the glass revolving door – his suit jacket wedged in the gap behind him – and the front desk security are just sitting there, laughing at his awkward waving. Lesson learned: never ever use revolving doors.

OK, so there was another reason I didn't mind coming back early from L.A. I finally got an email back from Elizabeth. She apologised profusley for the radio silence and for my completely disastrous meeting with her and that idiot, Cameron Bourne.

She'd found a space at last and had scraped together enough investment to start work. Elizabeth said she could see my enthusiasm for the project and offered me the job of gallery assistant right there in the email.

And, she added as a P.S., 'Cameron Bourne's off the project'.

I went down there this morning, to the South Bank, to view the space with Elizabeth, and it was perfect; one large, white room with two smaller offices at the back. Elizabeth kept touching the walls and laughing, and then we both did a happy dance. We went for coffee afterwards, and started making plans. We talked about how we want this to work, possible launch dates, the party we'll have to celebrate its opening.

I still can't believe it's really happening.

There's a big, massive, gigantic to-do list. It's going to be a lot of hard work from here on out but it'll be worth it.

And who cares about that because NOW I GET TO GO QUIT MY JOB.

I pull open the side door of the building, waving cheerfully at the trapped man, who is looking increasingly panicked. I give the resignation letter in my hand a squeeze, a wave of excitement washing over me. God, I'm so ready for this. It's been a long time coming, but I can't believe it's finally happening. I feel so powerful. Even people who like their jobs love quitting, right? It's such a thrill. And honestly, I was probably going to get fired anyway. I gave them a whole day's notice before I took off for L.A. Obviously Derek didn't say anything when I told him I was going, but he started sweating profusely and stammering about responsibilities and half-finished projects. I went anyway, and I know Ursula stormed straight into that office to make an official complaint about me (another one).

As I walk into the office, a few astonished faces look over. I'm turning up in the middle of the day, when I'm meant to be in L.A. – this is what passes for shocking around here. I beam happily around the room, giving loo twin Nick the thumbs up, and stride over to my desk. I need to retrieve Mrs Beaver. Ursula scuttles over moments later.

'You're not meant to be back yet,' she says, accusatorily. 'We arranged to have you covered, at great expense, at the last minute, after you gave us no notice for your holiday. And now you stomp back in, expecting everyone to be happy to see you? Derek's going to have some serious words to say to you, young lady.'

She is waiting for an answer, an apology, and I smile serenely as I turn to face her.

'FUCK OFF, JACKIE,' I shout, as loudly as I can.

There's a shocked silence, and then a giggle; a smattering of applause.

Ursula gapes at me in astonishment as I wave in her face and head for Derek's office, my letter in one hand, and Mrs Beaver in the other.

Back at my dad's house, in the living-room, I think delightedly about my day. A dream job in the bag, and some retribution at last. Derek was really nice about me leaving in the end. He said he was sad to see me go but was proud of me for striving for something bigger. He got really choked up then, talking about how he's 'always known how talented I am'. And then he gave me a sweaty hug and I tried not to gag.

Beside me on the sofa, Milly taps my hand impatiently. 'Pay attention, you're missing the show,' she says, even though it's just the credits. 'Ryan and Marissa are having a really bad time at the moment,' she explains, and then adds, 'Did Mommy tell you? I'm going to marry Seth.'

'Cool,' I say. 'Me too.'

She looks sideways at me. 'Can we both marry him?' she asks curiously.

'Sure,' I shrug. 'Why not? You can do anything you like. Whatever makes you happy.'

She beams at me. 'Can I have some chocolate buttons then?'

I laugh and get up. 'You betcha. I'll have to go to the shops to get them though.'

She nods, already forgetting I'm there, instantly absorbed by Dad's 14-inch TV screen, where Ryan is either exasperated or jealous. I don't need to watch any of it to know he's always one or the other. But I do anyway, just for a minute. It's the episode just after Johnny's death and a flood of nostalgia hits me. Sophie and I were so furious about this storyline, we almost stopped watching the show in protest. We started a campaign at school to bring him back (somehow?) and wrote a lot of badly spelled letters to Fox TV demanding retribution. I start to replay in my head all the years of friendship this show inspired. How much we all shared.

Right. It's time.

I have to go see Soph.

Dad insists on driving me, and as we're about to leave, Jen and Milly come running out and climb in the back too.

'Why is everyone coming?' I say exasperatedly, but also relieved Jen isn't making me get out so she can sit in the front like she always did when we were kids.

'Because it's boring in there,' says Jen. 'What are we going to do, catch up on what we've missed of *Countdown* lately?'

'OK, well you'll all have to wait out here in the car when we get to Sophie's,' I say authoritatively, hastily changing the subject. 'I really have to talk to her on her own.'

Dad starts the engine and Jen opens her door.

'Hold on, Dad, Ellie and I are swapping seats.'

Dammit.

*

Outside Sophie's house, I take a deep, brave breath and fumble for the door handle.

And then I continue to sit there in the car.

'Aren't you going in?' says Milly from beside me, a little judgementally.

'I am,' I say, gripping the handle and still not moving.

'Do I have the child locks on?' says Dad, unbuckling. I can't let him get out, he'll start examining Sophie's front porch and talking about structural integrity even though he doesn't know anything about it.

'No, no, it's fine, I'm going, I'm out,' I say, inelegantly clambering out and looking up at Sophie's house. It's a house I've been to a thousand times, but now it looks so weirdly alien and cold.

I move slowly towards the front door. I don't even know if she's here, she might not be. I should've called or texted, but, I don't know, I thought this might be more dramatic. More like how it works in films and books, right? And a text seemed inadequate after so much silence.

I glance back at the car. Jen and Dad are bickering over the radio and Milly's face is pressed up against the window in the back seat. She gives me a thumbs up which should feel encouraging but I suspect is sarcastic.

I take another deep breath and ring the bell.

Nothing happens.

I ring again.

Still nothing. The house is dark. She's not in there.

Fucking shit bollocks cock.

I'm so disappointed. The disappointment rumbles in my stomach as I turn to go. I walk slowly, sadly back to the car and as I reach for the handle I hear:

'Ellie?'

I whip round, looking up. It's Sophie. She's leaning out of the upstairs window, blinking at me in astonishment.

'Ellie?' she says again, like she's not sure it's me. I stare up at her, mouth open. She disappears and a minute later the front door opens.

She looks pale and tired – worse than my last visit – and I can't tell from her face whether she's pleased to see me. I can't tell what she's thinking about me just turning up here like this. It's been nearly two weeks since we've spoken and it feels like so much longer. She silently opens the door wider and gestures for me to follow her to the living-room. The scene of the crime.

Everything looks the same, and I think about how much I hate how life and the world keeps going, even when things are bad.

We stand across from each other for a second and then Sophie crosses her arms defensively. I have to say something now or the moment will be lost and we'll be stuck forever with this giant chasm between us. Now. Start talking now. START TALKING, ELEANOR.

'I . . . ' I begin. And then I – like a stupid, idiotic child – just burst into tears. 'I'm so sorry, Sophie. I'm so *so* sorry. You don't know how sorry I am. I didn't mean any of those things I said. I'm so stupid and awful and you don't have to forgive me but actually forget that because you do have to forgive me. Please forgive me. I was just watching *The OC* with Milly and we can't let that go, Sophie, you could die in a car crash tomorrow, like Marissa, and I have to be allowed to come to your funeral. And I'm sorry I'm crying, I don't want you to think I'm crying to get sympathy. It's totally not that, it's just about being a pathetic wreck. I'm so sorry.'

My hands are over my face now, trying to hold in the tears, but I don't stop talking.

'Everything you said about me was right. I am a loser and you're right about me being afraid to try things. You're right about me running away too. I ran away to L.A., can you believe that? I totally maxed out my Barclaycard. But I'm back now and I don't want to run away from you because you're my best friend and you always have been and I can't believe I've ruined it. Please say I haven't ruined this? Please say you're still my best friend. I'll do anything, Soph. I'll do all your jobs, I'll clean this house right now. I'll clean this house from top to bottom every day for the next month. I will come down here every day after work and clean this fucking house. If you just say you forgive me, I'll do anything.'

I peek from between my fingers. Sophie looks annoyed.

'Are you saying my house isn't clean?' she says, tapping her foot. 'Do you think we should be cleaning it every day? I'll tell Ryan he better step up his dusting.' She smiles now, mischievously, and I snort some snot into my hands. She takes a step towards me and puts her arms around me.

'I'm the sorry one, Elle, you didn't deserve any of those things I said. It was so unfair and you know I think you're fantastic. I guess . . . I guess I just get lonely out here. Not all the time, but a lot of the time. It's just me and Ciara and it's lonely. Being a mum is amazing but it's so completely exhausting and one dimensional. You're never allowed to just *be* any more, just lie about all day at the weekend like we used to. I have to be on my feet every second. And everything is centred around guilt and worry and fear and sleep. I love Ciara so much, and I wouldn't change it, but you remind me of the freedom I had before. I've been redefined as a mother now. And when I'm not a mother, I'm a wife. And that's not necessarily a bad thing, it just feels like there's not a lot of room to be Sophie any more. I love my life, but it's a different one to the one I had before. I've been a bit lost trying to work out if I'm OK with that.'

I lean into her, holding on tightly and sniffling into her jumper.

She keeps going. 'I accused you of being left behind because I'm afraid it's what is happening to me. I feel left behind by you. I forced you into dating so you would settle down and maybe join me out here. But even your dating made me feel left out. I miss our old life together. This new life is wonderful in all kinds of ways, but I'm sad it meant leaving our old one behind. I'm so sorry I put all that on you. And I'm so sorry I forced you onto Tinder. It sounds awful, please quit.'

I laugh, that is good to hear. 'I get it,' I say, shaking my head. 'I really get it, and I'm so sorry if I haven't been there for you enough. I want to be. And I want to be a part of this soccer mom life of yours.' I smile, she smiles, we laugh again.

'You know my life isn't beige?' she hiccups and gestures at the walls around us. 'It's eggshell white.'

Someone behind us clears his throat.

'Room for me?' says Thomas, who's just emerged from the direction of the kitchen.

'Thomas!' I shriek and he climbs into the group hug.

We stand there for a couple of minutes, holding on to each other, remembering how it feels to be together, smelling each other, hugging away the crappy feelings of the last two weeks.

I'm the first to pull away, narrowing my eyes at Thomas. 'What are you doing here?' I ask, remembering my visions of him and Sophie still being friends without me. My fear of them making new memories as a duo.

'Well,' he says, squeezing my arm. 'I couldn't take any of this silence any more, so I called in sick at work and went over to your place this morning. I was looking for you. I wanted to clear the air and then drag you down here to sort things out with Soph. You weren't there, obviously, but I met Josh. Er, nice guy.'

Shit.

'He said you'd gone to L.A.?' Thomas adds, eyebrows raised. 'And he told me I was a, er, "lucky man".'

Shit.

'I don't exactly know what that meant,' [Sophie pinches me] 'but I didn't ask. He tried to make me drink a beer with him, said he wanted to talk. I had to pretend I'd left my car unlocked just to get out of there.'

Thomas pauses again.

'Plus, it was like ten in the morning. The guy seems like he's a bit of a wreck.'

Shit shit shit.

'I'm so sorry, Thomas,' I say sincerely. 'For everything that happened, and also that you had to endure The Shithole.'

'I'm sorry too, Ellie,' he says, patting me gently.

Sophie looks from Thomas to me. 'Were you really in L.A.?'

'Yep,' I nod. 'I went to see my sister, we got back yesterday. She and Milly have come back with me for a bit – things aren't great with Andrew. She's in the car outside right now, with my dad and Milly.'

Sophie glances in the direction of the window. 'Invite

them in?' she says half-heartedly. She and Jen never really got on very well, and I know she fears Milly's terrible influence on her own daughter.

'Nah, leave them be, let's just all hug some more,' I say, drawing them both in again. 'And agree never to fight again?' I say, hopefully.

Sophie steps away from the group, looking worried. 'Actually, there is one more thing I have to confess,' she says hesitantly, sitting down on the sofa. 'Please don't be cross with me, but you know that art competition your company was involved in?'

Oh fuck.

'I know you said you didn't want to enter –' (I didn't say that) '– but I thought it sounded amazing, so I . . . ' She looks so uncomfortable. 'I entered it for you. I entered the painting you did of me last year. The one you gave me for my birthday that usually hangs in my room. So anyway, you won't believe this, but I got a call this morning, and it made the top twenty! Can you believe that, Ellie? Out of thousands of entries, you're in the top twenty. You're one of the winners!'

She waits, nervously, looking at me intently. Thomas is watching me too.

I don't say anything so she goes on. 'You'll be part of the exhibition next month.' She looks excited. 'Your painting will be touring the country. Isn't that amazing? It might be the start of something huge for you.'

She waits again, and I think about how to say what I need to say.

'Are you angry with me?' she says, her voice shaking. 'I just wanted to do something for you. Give you that push. You're so talented and—'

I cut her off.

'Actually.' I take a deep breath. 'I didn't come top twenty, I came first.'

Sophie looks confused. 'No, you—'

I interrupt her again. 'I'm not angry, Soph, I promise. Thank you for doing that. But you're wrong, I wasn't scared to enter, I was just scared to tell anyone I'd entered. The truth is, I was one of the first to send in my entry.' Thomas and Sophie are gawping at me, so I go on. 'Remember Elizabeth at The Hales' party? She was talking about the "new Banksy" people were getting excited about? Well . . . that was my entry. I got a call today, same as you. I won the competition.'

Both their faces have gone slack. They're looking at me with absolute astonishment.

Thomas is first to speak. 'But, but, your work is nothing like Banksy. You're all about bright colours and intricate faces . . . ' I'm touched that he has paid so much attention to my work.

'I think they just meant like Banksy, in the anonymous sense,' I explain, embarrassed. 'I left my name off the entry. Because – like Sophie says – I'm a chicken.'

'You won?' Sophie says at last. 'You fucking WON?' she shouts the last part and starts jumping up and down, screaming and hugging me. Thomas joins in and they both start whooping and shouting over each other.

Thomas pauses, mid-jump, eyes big and round. 'But the prize was huge, wasn't it? Like, a huge pile of money?'

'It's a big grant, yes,' I say carefully. 'It's to put towards my – what was the wanky phrase they used? – my "artistic endeavours".'

'Holy shit,' says Sophie quietly. 'This is amazing.'

'I already know what I'm going to do with it,' I say, grinning. 'I'm going to invest in Elizabeth's new gallery. I went to see it this morning. She'd already offered me a job as her assistant when it opens, and now I also get to be an investor! I got the call from the NAH organisers while I was with her this morning so I made the offer then and there. I'm going to help Elizabeth run it and then keep painting in my spare time. Can you believe it? This is my dream job. I'm going to be one of those smug twats who love their work.'

'Fuck,' Thomas says admiringly, and we all look at each other for a bit.

When I finally leave the house, a very pissed off Jen shouts at me about being 'no better than a dog left in a hot car' and threatens to call the RSPCA, but she can't bring my mood down. A huge weight has lifted. My friends are my friends again, and my career is about to take a huge step in the right direction. I can't believe it's finally coming together.

There's just one other person I know I need to say sorry to.

'Ellie?'

At the sound of his voice, all kinds of weird feelings pool in my stomach.

'Hi Tim,' I say, awkwardly. 'How are you?'

'I'm fine, Ellie, what about you?'

We haven't spoken in about five months. I've never apologised for the way I treated him, never said sorry for the way things ended or the way I cut him off. We were everything to each other, and then we were suddenly nothing. It was awful. We exchanged a few emails about when he would sell our flat, but even that was put on hold for so long, I'd given up hope of it happening. And now, here I am, hiding in my dad's room while the others play Boggle on the extended table downstairs. Here I am, *speaking to Tim on the phone.*

I swallow. 'I'm fine. Sorry to ring you like this, out of the blue.'

'That's OK, it's nice to hear your voice,' he says kindly. 'Is everything OK? Is it about the flat? Because I actually—'

'No, no,' I say hurriedly. 'I wanted to speak to you. It's long overdue. I need to say sorry to you, Tim.'

There's silence on the line for a second, and I wonder if he's still there.

Then he speaks. 'No, you don't,' he says quietly. And it's in such a nice, kind voice that I want to start crying again.

I really need to get this crying under control. I'm getting to be as bad as Dad.

'I do,' I say hurriedly, I need to get this out. 'I behaved so, so horribly to you. I . . . '

How much do I tell him?

I falter and there's silence again.

He says quietly, 'You cheated on me. Yeah, Ellie, I know.'

He does know. There. I feel a wave of crushing guilt and start to say sorry again, over and over.

'Stop it, Ellie,' he interrupts. 'Look, it wasn't a particularly great situation, but I've thought about it a lot over the last year, and it's fine. I understand what you were going through. Neither of us handled it very well.'

'You did, you were wonderful—' I start to say and he cuts across me.

'I wasn't. Maybe you don't remember. Your mum was ill and I kept making everything about me. You needed space to breathe – you kept asking for it – and I wouldn't leave you alone. You couldn't even nap without me insisting on lying there with you. I was so afraid of you leaving me, so afraid of you pulling away. I turned into an insecure, needy wreck, when it should've been you that got to hog all the emotion. You were pulling away and my behaviour just pushed you away even more. I'm so sorry.'

Is that really how it happened? I don't remember.

'I still shouldn't have behaved the way I did,' I say slowly. 'I should have talked to you, I never should've cheated.'

'No,' he agrees. 'But it happens.'

'So you don't hate me?' I ask quietly.

'Of course I don't hate you,' he sighs. 'Look, Ellie, we had a lovely relationship for a long time. But ultimately, it wasn't right for us. I will always care about you and be there for you if you need me. I want you to be happy. Are you happy?'

There's that question again. I smile into the receiver. 'I'm getting there actually,' I say. 'How about you, Tim?'

'I am,' he says, and I can tell he's smiling too. 'I met someone. It's pretty new, but she's great, we're great.'

'That's really nice,' I say, and I mean it. I want Tim to have a nice life. There are exes I only wish death and destruction for, but Tim is not one of them. I'm so glad I haven't hurt him too badly. I'm so relieved he doesn't hate me or blame me.

We talk a bit more about our lives and what's been happening. He cheers when I tell him about the art competition and I cheer when he tells me about being promoted at work. It's so lovely to catch up, and I feel light headed that the guilt I've carried around with me this past year has lifted. I can get on with my life, I haven't destroyed his.

I spot the wall clock and realise I will be in trouble for missing the Boggle tournament.

‘I have to go, Tim,’ I say reluctantly. ‘This has been so great, thank you.’

‘Oh, before you go?’ he says. ‘I’m sorry this has taken so long, but, Ellie, the flat has finally sold.’

17

1.34 p.m. Saturday, 13 April
Location: Back at Dad's to celebrate my birthday. Intriguingly, he seems to have used the same yellow balloons I had out for his 60th. God knows how they've survived this long, and several are severely deflated, but they're here, and it's good to see them. Sophie, Thomas, Jen, Milly and Dad are all here too, standing awkwardly around the balloons, listening to Milly explain why she's glad Marissa Cooper is dead.

It's my birthday. Thirty.

I don't mind turning thirty. I totally don't mind.

Actually, I genuinely don't. Everything's looking pretty bloody rosy right now. Jen and Milly are here with me and Dad, exactly where they should be. I don't know what's going to happen with her and Andrew, they've been talking on the phone a lot and he's promised to cut down on his work – be a better husband and father – but Jen doesn't seem convinced. I don't know if things are going to work out between them, but she seems happier somehow. Marriage is complicated but so's life, I guess. My friendship with Sophie and Thomas is back to being as brilliant as ever, and everything's moving forward with work and the gallery. My latest meeting with Elizabeth on Monday was amazing. We are totally on the same page (art pun!) about how we see everything working and what we want to achieve. We've got a business plan and everything.

So yes, thirty is looking pretty damn great. The only thing I'm a little bit sad about is that, with everything that's been going on, I never got round to organising anything. When Jen heard this last night, she took it upon herself to post on my Facebook wall that since I was such a 'sad loser' we would be heading down to Dad's favourite cocktail place, All Bar One, from six, should anyone wish to join us.

Which is not humiliating *at all*. And it's also not humiliating that seven whole people 'liked' it. Seven people including my dad, Jen – who makes it a policy to always 'like' her own posts on Facebook – and Milly, who's just joined social media but don't tell Grandpa, because she doesn't want him to add her.

So today and tonight are set to be fairly tame and family-based, but I don't really mind. All the people I love most are going to be out with me; Dad, Jen, Sophie, Thomas. Although, not Milly, because duh, Alan the bouncer would have to draw the line somewhere. He can let the odd tube of Pringles through the net, but a six-going-on-seven-year-old is probably a bit much. She's going to pop over to Candice and Peter's for the night.

But that's OK too, because she's here now, and she's waited until last to proudly present me with a birthday card she's made. It's another pencil drawing she's done. This time it's of the two of us, sitting in Mum's magic garden. There's so much detail – even the peonies make an appearance – and I give my niece a little thank you squeeze. She's really talented.

Maybe I'll do a whole exhibition of Milly's drawings at my gallery. Or maybe I'll just put it on my fridge.

I turn back to Sophie, who's explaining in detail the plan to redecorate her house again this autumn. She hasn't once today mentioned my love life, and I am forever grateful. But it's also slightly annoying timing that she finally climbed off my back about dating, just as I could actually really do with her advice on Josh.

I've not been back to TS yet to face him. He thought I was in L.A. for the whole week so I figured I'd stay at Dad's and mull things over. He's the last leftover confrontation I need to have, but I still don't know what I want to say. I need Sophie's advice.

'Hey, I need to talk to you about something,' I say, cutting her off and checking around for any eavesdroppers. Thomas is chatting to Dad and Jen is watching the TV with Milly.

I clear my throat. 'I accidentally slept with Josh a couple of weeks ago and now he kind of says he likes me and wants us to go out together.'

'WHAT?' she says, exploding. 'How could you not tell me this already? What is wrong with you? Cunt Josh? What did you say? When did you have sex? Was it good sex? He's so hot, what was it like? Did you have sex to the left, like you always do? Are you going to say yes?'

'Shush, shush, shush, *shush*,' I say, panicked, but Jen has already stood up to join us.

'What's going on?' she demands, aggressively.

'Ellie's flatmate is in love with her and wants to be her boyfriend!' says Sophie, a little too enthusiastically. Dad looks over, a worried look on his face. Thomas looks away.

'Is he good-looking?' says Jen, turning on me. 'Do you

love him? Is he The One? And do you really always have sex to the left?'

'Those questions, seconded,' says Sophie, pointing at Jen's face. Finally they agree on something.

'There's no such thing as The One,' I say mildly. 'And I don't know what I'm going to say yet. I don't even know if I like him as a person, never mind as a potential boyfriend.' I look at Sophie. 'When did you know New Ryan was the guy for you?'

Sophie looks thoughtful, and I add seriously, 'Was it when you saw his big house?'

She giggles, nodding. 'Yes, it was when I first saw Pemberley. Actually, no, it was when we started dating, and I felt OK about pooing at his house almost immediately.'

'That is very romantic,' I say.

'I know it is.' She giggles again. 'I've never been able to do that at a boy's place before, but New Ryan made me feel so comfortable and safe, straightaway. Like I could always be myself and he would never judge me. I knew then.'

Next to us, Jen rolls her eyes. 'Oh whatever. I pooed at the dentist's yesterday. What's the big deal?'

Sophie and I applaud.

On the other side of the room, Dad clears his throat. This means he has a speech to make. He looks very nice today, in a smart new checked shirt and dark jeans. Jen and him went into London yesterday, where he says she made him buy lots of things from 'The Topmens'.

'Lenny, Jenny,' he starts.

Why is Jenny included in this? I think sulkily, it's my birthday.

'You know I love you both very much.'

Here we go. Jen and I glance at each other.

'And I'm very proud of you.'

I resist the urge to roll my eyes.

'And I know you've been wondering why you haven't had any of the latest instalments of *75 Hues of Tony* to read lately.'

Jen and I exchange another look. We'd forgotten it existed. To be honest, I've stopped checking my Gmail so much lately in protest over HungryHouse's constant shaming emails asking how my recent massive takeaway was.

Dad goes on. 'Well, the reason for that is, well, how do I say this? I'm in love.'

He beams at us. I gape back at him, while Jen grimaces.

'Old people love,' she shrieks. 'Disgusting.'

Dad is looking at me, expectantly.

'Er,' I try, 'Dad, that's wonderful. Um, who is the lucky lady? Can we meet her? It's not the teabagging woman, is it? You can do better than that.'

'No, no,' he says waving a hand. 'Actually, well, it's . . . Candice from next door.'

WHAT. Candice? CANDICE?

But what about Peter?

BUT WHAT ABOUT PETER?

'But,' I say aghast, 'what about Peter??'

'Peter?' Dad says, looking perplexed.

'Er, Candice's husband?' I say, my brow furrowed. Please tell me my lovely dad isn't having an affair. Imagine the scandal in the town. 'Are they getting divorced?'

'Peter?' he says again, and then his face clears. 'Oh, oh no. No, no, Ellie. Peter is Candice's *dog*. Peter is a dachschund.' Sophie and Thomas burst out laughing.

'What?' I am totally thrown. 'No, no, he can't be. You say they're a married couple all the time, don't you?'

Dad shakes his head. 'I don't think I'd do that, darling. He's a dog.'

I scan back in my head through all the times he's talked about visiting Candice and Peter, about Candice and Peter coming over for dinner, about going out for walks with Candice and Peter.

'Wait,' I say. 'What about when you kept going on about how affectionate Peter is with her?'

'Well.' Dad rubs his eyes, glancing at Sophie and Thomas who are leaning on each other and gasping for air. 'He *is* very affectionate with her. He's always cuddling up on Candice's lap and licking her. He does it with me now too.' He pauses. 'What did you think I meant this morning when I said Peter keeps licking my face?'

Oh right, yeah, I did think that was weird.

'OK, so there's really no husband?' I say feebly.

Dad laughs, kindly. 'No, darling, there's no husband. She was married a long time ago, but she's been divorced for about four years now. And I . . . ' he smiles coyly around the room again ' . . . have fallen completely in love with her.'

He looks into the distance in the direction of her house, like he's trying to see her through the walls. When he speaks again, his voice is dreamy. 'She's so sweet and loving. And so thoughtful. She makes me laugh, and she knows all about the internet. It's really very impressive, she taught me about attaching things to emails, and colour printing.'

'Well, that's me sold,' says Jen, standing up. 'Does she know? Have you told her how you feel?'

Dad's face turns red. 'No, not yet. I want to, I really want to, I'm just . . . I wanted to tell you two first – see what you thought – and then speak to her.'

Jen strides towards the door. 'No time like the present,

Dad. Let's go over there right now and get this locked down. I want to meet this Steve Jobs-type internet overlord.'

I'm still sitting on the sofa, shell-shocked, and Dad looks at me anxiously. 'Are you OK with this, Ellie?'

Am I OK with this? I prod myself. Actually . . . yeah I really bloody am. I haven't seen Dad so happy and excited about anything in so long. So she bakes really terrible cakes, I've had worse things in my mouth (see: my night with Josh). And so what if she seems really obsessed with colour printing everything? Dad obviously likes all that. He deserves all the happiness in the world, and if he's met someone who gives him that – well then, yeah, I'm bloody well OK with this!

I stand up. 'Too right I am.' I grin at him. 'You have to go tell her, right now!'

He quivers a bit and then straightens up, nodding determinedly.

'Let's do it!' He follows Jen to the front door, matching her confident stride. He glances back into the room. 'Come on, Lenny and Milly. And you, Sophie and Thomas, you come too! You're all family, and I want you there.' We cheer happily and follow him to the door, ready to watch my dad tell the woman he loves how he feels.

Is this weird? It's probably weird, but who cares, right?

The entourage files out the front door, chatting excitedly, and march their way down the front path and up to Candice's. We're all buzzing – I can't remember the last time I felt so excited and scared. Please let her say she loves him, too. Please, please. I glance at Dad. He looks thrilled by all this. He thinks he's in an episode of *Neighbours*. I'm the only one who seems nervous.

We reach the door and Jen – who's always first to arrive

anywhere – thumps aggressively, three times. Thomas nudges my dad up to the front of the group and we all gather round him, expectantly.

As the door opens, we all hold our breath.

The lady standing framed in the doorway is like a mirror image of my dad. Small, round, about the same age, with a lovely face – they could be a lesbian couple, or lesbian twins even.

I shake my head to erase the Pornhub search term (banked for later), focusing on the adorable confusion on her Angela Lansbury-esque face.

'Alan?' she says, nervously, and a dog – Peter, presumably, God I'm an idiot – joins her at the door, tail wagging and nose sniffing the air.

'Hello, Candice,' Dad says, suddenly looking awfully pale. I hope he's not going to faint. 'And hello to you too, Peter,' he says, bending down to pat the dog, who licks him affectionately and then buries his face in Dad's crotch. 'Sorry to barge in on you like this,' says Dad, anxiously glancing round at all of us who are watching him expectantly. Dad is, no doubt, suddenly realising that bringing a gang of people to watch this moment might not have been ideal.

He swallows and turns back to Candice. 'I wanted you to meet my family.'

She smiles, and it is the absolute loveliest. Dad's right, I can see already that she's one of those people who radiates warmth.

'Oh my goodness, how lovely,' she exclaims. 'Please come in, everyone!'

But we don't move and Dad is frozen to the spot. 'Before we come in . . . ' He clears his throat again, and we all fall silent, glancing furtively at each other. 'Candice, there is something I have to tell you.'

She looks alarmed and I suppress a giggle.

We all collectively inhale. Here it comes. Will he do it? Come on, Dad!

'I love you, Candice,' he blurts out, and I clutch my chest, my heart singing. 'I love you very, very much. And I don't know if you feel the same, or could ever feel the same, but I had to tell you. I've wanted to tell you for quite a while now, because you are the kindest, nicest woman in the world, Candice. I—'

Candice steps out onto the mat beside him in one smooth motion, and reaches up with her finger to shush him. She smiles now, shyly, as she whispers, 'Alan, I love you too. I think you're completely wonderful.'

Then they kiss.

And it is gross. Sorry to ruin the romance, but it is *really* gross.

Jen loudly dry retches, Milly shrieks and I turn away, pretending to check my phone. Sophie covers her eyes and Thomas snorts.

But they keep kissing, really badly. It's like they've forgotten we're even here.

After a couple of minutes, they finally stop, and a very red-faced Candice beckons to all of us to follow her into an extraordinarily orange living-room. We make ourselves at home – Jen and Milly immediately start picking up and examining the various dog-themed knick-knacks lining every surface. Candice kisses each of us warmly and even manages not to look too baffled when Dad introduces 'Lenny's friends, Sophie and Thomas, who also wanted to meet you.'

'Can I get anyone a cup of tea?' she offers, and Dad jumps up to help. They look at each other like love sick puppies and Candice offers her hand for him to hold. He takes it.

They don't come back for fifteen minutes, by which point we're all too sickened by what they might've been doing to drink the tea.

Back at Dad's with Candice in tow, we're starting to get drunk when Jen takes me away and up to her room. There, she presents me with a dress.

'It's your birthday present – to wear tonight,' she says. I pick it up, admiring the soft fabric. It's beautiful. Midnight dark blue, knee length, it's cut perfectly to fit my shape. And when I try it on and twirl in front of the mirror, I feel like Ella Enchanted. I look completely amazing. Behind me in the mirror Jen fiddles with my hair. 'And you should wear your hair up, like this. I'll do it for you if you like?' she says, and I smile at her, nodding. I am so relieved to see her back to herself. It's like she was holding her breath for a year and has finally let it go. That tan is starting to fade, but the pink is returning to her cheeks. And I think maybe she's already put on a bit of weight (although I will not be telling her that). She looks much better on a diet of Dad's carb-heavy food and Candice's baking (interestingly, Jen says she actually likes the weird cakes).

It's hard to tell if this change in her is because things are back on track with Andrew, or because she's away from him. I'm not even sure she knows. She's going back to L.A. in a few days, so I guess we'll find out.

'Thanks so much, Jen, I love it,' I say, holding her hand.

She squeezes it back, 'Thank you, Ellie,' she replies quietly.

*

Alan the Giant spots us immediately as we arrive at the bar a few hours later, and shouts for us to come straight in. The teenagers in the queue tut at the strange group, consisting of me, Jen, Dad, Sophie, Thomas – and the last minute addition, at my insistence, Dad's new girlfriend (Aunt Susie got lumbered with Milly at home) – all filing past them and straight into the bar. I think about the last time I was here, with just Dad on my arm, and how much has changed.

Inside, an overexcited Liza hands us Cosmopolitans and directs us to a booth where several familiar faces are waiting. Oh my God, I hadn't expected this.

Maddie's here with her new boyfriend, Zack. He's tall, with a lovely open face, and he doesn't let go of Maddie's hand even once as she introduces us.

'It's so great to meet you,' he says enthusiastically. 'If it wasn't for you getting Maddie on that dating app, we'd never have met and fallen in love.' He looks down at Madds, who is gazing up at him, wide-eyed. 'Thank you so much,' he adds, warmly.

'Look who else came,' says Maddie, nodding behind me. I turn around.

Ugh, Rich? Rich is here? He waves happily from across the booth, and shouts, 'Happy birthday, Ellie, haha!'

At least we brought Pringles. That should keep him occupied for most of the night. And holy fuck – is that my loo twin Nick here too? Is he . . . is he slow dancing with URSULA? Oh Jesus. I have to delete Facebook.

Two more people come over to say hi. It's Lois and Zoe from our last visit to this place. 'We saw your sister's post on Facebook,' says Lois. 'We were in the neighbourhood, so we thought we'd pop along. Is that OK?'

'Of course it is,' I say, hugging each of them.

Lois holds up her right hand. 'We made it official!' she says, wiggling the big silver band and squeezing Zoe, who smiles and rolls her eyes lovingly.

'I gave in,' she says, by way of explanation.

And there's Josh.

Josh is here.

We make eye contact across the group and he raises a jam jar cocktail at me, smiling.

I should go speak to him, I've left him waiting for long enough.

But then suddenly someone else is hugging me. Some weird, random girl is clinging on to me – what the hell? 'Oh my God, Ellie, happy birthday my gorgeous darling girl,' she squeals affectionately. Who is this? Why is she pretending to know me? She's still hugging me, pinning my arms to my sides as she whispers emotionally in my ear how happy she is to be here with me. 'I got the night off specially,' she adds.

Josh wanders over.

'All the flatmates here together at last,' he says smiling at us both.

Flatmates?

'*Gemma?*' I say out loud, gaping at this total stranger.

'Yes, sweetie?' she says, letting me go, but looping her arm through mine, familiarly. This is our third flatmate, Gemma. The one I've only seen once from the back. The one I wasn't even sure really existed. So she definitely exists, because she's here. Wow.

'Er, just really happy you made it,' I say to her, grinning at Josh, who is trying not to laugh.

I clear my throat and look at him. 'Can I talk to you for a minute, Josh?'

A shadow crosses his face, but he keeps smiling.

'Sure. Gemma? Can we have two minutes?'

'Oh my goodness, of course!' she squeals, waving her arms. 'Don't you two worry about me! I'll go see how Sophie and Thomas are. Oh, and I'm so thrilled Alan could make it too, Ellie. He looks so cute with Candice, I'm so glad that all worked out.'

She wanders off in the direction of my dad, shouting, 'Alan? Alan, how are you, sweetie?'

Josh and I look at each other and burst out laughing.

'Strange world,' I say, and he nods, scratching his head. 'So, Josh,' I start, 'I know this is a bit out of nowhere, but I'm going to be moving out soon.'

'What?' he looks shocked.

'My old place has sold at last,' I explain. 'The money's coming through in the next couple of months, so I'll be looking for somewhere else as soon as possible. I'm giving you a month's notice to find someone else, I hope that's OK?'

'But it'll take you ages to find somewhere – especially if you're buying,' he says, panicked.

'Yeah, but I'm going to stay with my dad for a couple of months. He's met someone, so it looks like I'll mostly have the place to myself.'

He nods, flummoxed.

'And what about you and me?' he asks at last. 'If we're not living together any more, it won't be such a complicated situation. Have you decided if you're willing to give me – this – a shot?'

The question hangs in the air and for a minute I just look at his face, searching for something. He's so sincere and vulnerable looking. So ridiculously pretty.

But I know it's not what I want.

'I'm really sorry, Josh,' I say. 'I can't. It's not the right thing for me, I just don't feel that way about you.'

He sighs, defeated, but he's already nodding. He knew this was coming. I reach for him and we hug for a bit.

'I am sorry, Josh,' I say again. 'You know you're so ridiculously hot.'

'Oh don't you worry about me, babe,' he says, pulling away. 'It was just meant to be a pity bang when you were upset, after all. I will be fine, got loads of chicks knocking down my door.'

I snort at his bravado. Typical.

'Sure, sure, I know,' I say nodding. 'I know what you mean, being single is the best. I love it.'

It's his turn to snort. 'Yeah, right,' he says. 'We both know you're going to immediately start dating your friend Thomas. It's so obvious. This couldn't have worked out better for you guys. He's a great bloke, you've been friends for ever. It's always how these things pan out.'

I laugh. Oh my God, no. Hearing it out loud like that, I realise how much I *so* do not love Thomas White. I mean, OF COURSE I DON'T. Yuck! He's my best friend, I love him as a friend, but absolutely nothing more. Not at all.

I think all this pressure I've had from everyone to find a boyfriend made me temporarily think maybe I *should* fancy him, but I really, really don't. I shudder at the very idea of kissing him. It's almost as disgusting as watching Dad and Candice go at it. Which, yep, they are doing again right now on the dance floor.

'Actually, Josh,' I shake my head. 'That's not true. I don't feel that way about Thomas at all.'

'Of course you do,' says Josh scornfully. 'You've left him

hanging on, waiting for you to say the word for years. If you really didn't love him, you would've told him ages ago that it wasn't going to happen.'

Shit, he's right. I mean, he's wrong about my feelings – I know now for sure me and Thomas will never happen – but he is right that I've left him hanging on. I've been really selfish. I was scared Thomas might not want to be my friend if I confronted the situation. What if he's only part of the trio because he thinks I might love him back one day?

I have to tell him.

'OK, Josh,' I say with determination. 'I'll go speak to him now. Tell him we'll never be a thing.'

Josh smirks. 'Best of luck. I'm off to get off with that pair of tits over there.' He pats me on the head and stalks off in the direction of a blonde girl by the bar. Good old Cunt Josh.

Scanning the room, I spot Thomas in a booth on his own, checking his phone. Here we go. This one is going to be tough. I know Josh will bounce back – oh, look at that, he's bouncing right into that girl already – but Thomas has always loved me. Like *always*. This is going to be brutal. I don't want to lose him, but it's time to be a grown-up. If he's ever going to meet someone else and fall in love with someone who will reciprocate that feeling, he needs to know that I'm not a possibility. He needs to let go of this.

'Thomas White, my old friend, can I sit?' I ask pointing at the pile of coats next to him.

He looks up, surprised. 'Hey, birthday girl! Saw you getting cosy with Josh over there, how's that going?' he says, moving the coats out of the way and avoiding my eye.

'Oh!' I say. 'God no, that's one hundred per cent not

happening. We're just friends. I told him I'm not interested. He's fine about it.' I glance over at Josh and the girl he took three whole minutes to be fine with.

I take a deep breath. 'Listen, Thomas, as you know – as you've pointed out to me – I've never been too great at expressing my feelings or talking things through. But I'm trying to change that.'

Thomas looks bemused. 'Right, I'm glad, Ellie. But don't change too much though, eh? You're great as you are.'

Erk. I bob my head awkwardly and go on. 'So I want us to talk about the . . . feelings here . . . ' I gesture at the space between us and Thomas turns pale.

Shit. He looks terrified. He wasn't expecting me to bring this up here and now. Why *am* I bringing it up? Fifteen years later? Why now? Oh God. Well, too late to go back now.

I cough. 'So, er, I wanted to clear the air, so that we could all move on and know where we stand. Give us both the chance to be happy.'

He nods, resigned. I think he knows what I've come over to say. I think he knows in his heart that I don't feel the same way about him.

We look at each other for a second. 'I guess you're right, we should talk about it,' he says, looking pained. Oh, this is miserable. He takes a deep breath and goes on, 'I know you've loved me for a long time, Ellie, and I—'

'Wait, what?' I interrupt. '*I've* loved *you*?'

Thomas sighs again, and puts his hand on my arm, comfortingly. 'I know, Ellie. You don't need to say it. And I'm so sorry, I've tried to be careful with your feelings. I never wanted to hurt you. I've tried to return those feelings too, I've tried so hard over the years to love you back like that, but I just can't. I've never been able to think of you that way.

You're like a sister to me. I love you, Ellie, but I never have and never could love you in any romantic sense.'

My head is spinning. What is happening here?

'No wait, Thomas, wait,' I say impatiently. 'You've got this wrong. I don't love you – you love me. You've always loved me.'

He snorts. 'I have not!' he says. 'You've always loved *me*. You're always looking at me all sad eyes whenever stuff about your love life or dating comes up.'

'Yes,' I explode. 'Because I was worried you'd be upset because YOU LOVE ME.'

'No I don't!' he says again, looking bemused. 'In fact, I've wanted to talk to you about this situation for a few weeks now, because I've been going out with someone for a month or so, and it's getting serious. I didn't want you to find out from someone else and be upset.'

WHAT THE FUCK IS HAPPENING HERE. My whole world view tilts. Thomas has never been in love with me? But, but, but . . . what?

'You've never been in love with me?' I say again slowly.

'That is very correct,' he confirms. 'Not even close.'

'And I've never been in love with you,' I say. 'So neither of us has ever been in love with the other?'

We look at each other for another second and then both burst out laughing.

'We're so stupid,' Thomas says in between fits of giggles.

'We probably should've had this chat a while ago,' I say, wiping my eyes. 'Of course the trio has never been anything more than mates.'

'Hmm,' he says mischievously. 'Since we're being totally honest, I did have quite the crush on Soph for a while, when we were teenagers.'

I whack him with my handbag and we start laughing again.

When we finally stop laughing, we hug and I ask, 'So who is this girl you've been dating? Get her down here tonight! I want to meet her!'

He pauses. 'Actually, Ellie, you kind of know her.'

I what? I glance round the room. Most of the people I know are here.

'Oh my God, Thomas,' I say. 'Are you seeing Ursula?'

His turn to whack me. 'No, but if you meant it, I will invite her down here now. I was just texting her.'

'But who is she?' I say again, mystified.

'Her name is Cassie,' he says, searching my face.

Cassie? Cassie? Who is . . .

Oh my God!

That date!

That Valentine's Day date! The lovely, lovely barmaid who'd just been dumped. Was that really only a couple of months ago?

'CASSIE!' I shriek.

Thomas laughs. 'Yep. I had to see the gold-plated moose head for myself, so I went in that bar one night with some work mates. I recognised Cassie from your description and we got talking. She's pretty great. I really, really like her.' He smiles bashfully.

'This is the best news ever!' I say happily. 'I can totally take credit for this relationship. I practically introduced you. I will make a speech at your wedding.'

Thomas grins and we hug again.

'I'm so excited for you,' I say. 'And I'm so glad you're not in love with me.'

'I'm so glad you're not in love with me either,' he laughs again.

'Phew! Right, I'm going to get another drink,' I say, standing up. 'Cassie is brilliant, Thomas, I thoroughly approve. Get her down here right now! Tell her to bring Nutella and plastic forks.'

I dance away, floating on happiness. I LOVE being thirty! Everyone is right, thirty is the new twenty. I finally feel like I'm getting my shit together, and I'm adult (sort of) enough to appreciate it.

As the night ticks on, I look round the room at the contented, drunk group around me. Dad and Candice are snogging again, which is still the grossest thing you can imagine, but it's also lovely, I suppose. Psychic Sharon turned up about an hour ago, claiming not to have seen the Facebook post and insisting she simply 'sensed' that All Bar One was where she should be tonight. She bullied Alan the Giant into letting her in, and now she's in the loos, ostensibly doing her make-up, but really, persuading drunk girls to let her read their palms. For money. She and Jen nearly came to blows earlier over Psychic Sharon's reading for her, and Psychic Sharon then predicted that Jen is a 'cow', but if they stay out of each other's way for the rest of the night, it should be fine. Over in the corner, Josh is already over me, and also over the earlier blonde tits too by the looks of things. He's now directing his weaponised testosterone towards the lovely barmaid, Liza. Cassie has just arrived, and after much reunion hugging, her and Thomas are goo-goo-eyeing each other in the booth. Even loo-twin Nick seems to be having a good time, trying fruitlessly to seduce Ursula.

Everyone is happy. But – I realise – no one more than me. A

few minutes ago, I finally deleted Tinder, and I can't tell you how good it felt. The truth is, I'm genuinely, really, honestly, deliriously happy being single. It's taken me a while to understand that, but I am. I love it. Having a boyfriend feels like wearing a coat all the time. Like a big oppressive coat. Sometimes you're cold and it's nice to have it on – especially in the winter – but mostly I just feel sweaty and claustrophobic in it. And, as my mum always said, keeping your coat on all the time means I won't feel the benefit when I go outside.

I think my mum would want me to wear lots of different slaggy coats at lots of different times.

Being single means I can just be me. I want to be selfish and have adventures and be just like plane lady Bella. I want to work hard and challenge myself with my painting. It might not be the path most people would choose for themselves – or even the path most people would choose *for me* – but being on my own is what I need. In the same way as I don't feel ready to give over my whole self to a child, I don't feel ready to give myself to a man either. I'm happy to give bits of myself to many different men (winky face), but just one all the time is too much for me. Maybe one day that will change, but for now, these people here around me tonight are all I need to be violently happy. Fuck relationships, I think, as I go join Jen on the dance floor.

From: Alan Knight <Alanknightinshiningarmour@BTInternet.co.uk>
To: Eleanor.knight@gmail.com, Jennifer.seevy@hotmail.com

21 April

Alan Knight
106 Castle Rise

Judfield
East Sussex
TN22 5UN

Dear Eleanor and Jennifer,

I hope you are both well.

Sorry again for the delay, as explained, I have been rather "caught up" with my new romance! L.O.L. But you will be pleased to hear I have finally finished my "novel". Although Candice says it's probably not a "novel" exactly, more of a "short story", which is quite exciting. Maybe it will become a TV series? Just to warn you, I'm afraid I've had to change my character's name from Tony Braxton. Candice's ex-husband was called "Tony" and I realised I don't like that name at all. So we had a "brainstorm" and I'm renaming my "hero" Duncan James. Candice said it had a "nice ring" to it. What do you think?

Jenny – I hope you are all settled back in L.A. I miss you already. I've been recording all the episodes of "Neighbours" you've missed and will post them to you on VHS once a week, so you don't "miss out".

Lenny – thank you again from me and Candice for inviting us to your party last week. We had such a nice time and cannot believe how late we stayed up! We both said it was really good fun, although we weren't too sure about your friend "Rich". He ate all our Pringles and was a bit "annoying".

Love you both so much and we're very proud of you.

Best wishes,
Dad and Candice

---

75 HUES OF DUNCAN

A short story, by Alan Bernard Knight

Duncan James has barely slept in days. He cannot stop thinking about Svetlana and the offer she had made him just after their very arousing kissing at B&Q the other day. The contract Lana had mentioned arrived very efficiently by recorded delivery the day after the arousing kissing at B&Q, as well as his new private jet which he had nowhere to park so it's currently on his front lawn but none of the neighbours seem to mind.

For the most part, the contract Lana wants him to sign is a very standard-issue contract. He had his BT customers sign something very similar back in his BT days, but there were far fewer sex clauses. Duncan understands contracts very, very well and Lana's contract says that Duncan will belong to Svetlana forever and ever and ever. It says he must tell everyone at the Book Club that she is Duncan's girlfriend and that he has really a lot of really excellent intercourse with her which he knows he could do really very easily because he's had a lot of compliments on his intercourse. But here is the most shocking part of the contract: it says that he must never see his neighbour Wanda again!!

Duncan cannot deny he is upset by this part of the contract because Wanda is his very good friend, and in the very long time since Anita left last Tuesday, she has become a very supportive ally and is helpful with dinners, especially nut roast and chicken. Could he really sacrifice that friendship for Svetlana?? On the other hand, Svetlana is so very, very good-looking and that is very alluring.

It is an almost impossible decision to make for Duncan James which is why he has barely slept in days as previously mentioned. Svetlana has also been calling a lot to ask when Duncan might make up his mind which is very difficult with so much going on and she has just this second put a deadline on the contract signing for TOMORROW which has really worried Duncan because he still doesn't know what to do. He decides to ask his new live-in butler, Cartwright, for advice. Cartwright is another gift that Svetlana sent him the other day, which is an extra thing Duncan has to worry about because he's never had a butler before, having been incredibly self-sufficient right from the moment he was born.

'Cartwright?' says Duncan impressively. 'Do you think I should sign the sex contract with Svetlana?'

Cartwright looks a bit surprised to be consulted on such an important matter when it is clear that Duncan can solve any problem himself, but he is really professional and says, 'Well, sir, it sounds like it might be fun for you. Svetlana is a pretty lady and you are a very attractive man. I don't see why not. You seem like a man who could handle a sex contract because you are so strong and manly.'

Duncan suspects Cartwright has a crush on him. He has caught him looking at his calves a number of times.

Logistically, Duncan can see the appeal of signing this contract. He would have a beautiful, rich girlfriend who would give him lots and lots of things, including maybe a place to store his private jet because it's really getting in the way out on the front lawn even though his front lawn is massive. But there is something stopping him from signing it.

Duncan decides to go and see Wanda next door – possibly for the very final time!! – to ask her advice because really Cartwright just said nonsense and wasn't very helpful at all and Duncan thinks maybe Cartwright was distracted by lust.

Wanda is very pleased to see Duncan and compliments him on his calves.

'Your calves are very nice today,' she says. Duncan realises Svetlana has never even mentioned his calves. Does she really care about him at all?

'Hello Wanda,' says Duncan sensually. 'How are you?'

'I'm very well thank you,' says Wanda, clearly turned on. And then suddenly they are kissing!! Duncan cannot believe this because it definitely wasn't what he came over for. He just wanted the tea and three Custard Creams that Wanda always gives him.

The kissing is really lovely and Duncan is excellent at it. It might be the best kiss Wanda has ever had, and even though it doesn't have the B&Q fire that he had with Svetlana, Duncan realises it is a really lovely kiss for him too. He realises that Svetlana was right to be suspicious of Wanda because there IS something between them. After they've had their kiss and a cup of PG Tips tea and those three Custard Creams, Duncan explains about the sex contract and Wanda nods really sympathetically because she understands this kind of thing must happen to Duncan all the time.

And then she tells him, 'Duncan, I understand this must happen to you all the time, but know that I am in love with you as well as Svetlana. I have been in love with you for a really long time, ever since Anita left you last Tuesday. I know I cannot offer you the B&Q fire that Svetlana does but I am a nice person, and I will cook nut roast and chicken for you in the way you specifically like on nut roast and chicken night. I also won't make you sign a contract.'

It is a compelling offer and they start snogging again. When they've finished, Duncan tells Wanda he needs to think and he goes home again to think and this time he doesn't ask Cartwright for advice, he just goes straight to bed.

He has a lot to think about.

Yes, Svetlana can offer him everything and he has never felt such sexual tension that could fill a whole village hall but he suspects very insightfully that she is also a bit mad. Wanda is not as exciting but she is really nice and she isn't a bit mad. It's such an impossible choice, he thinks as he finally drifts off to sleep.

The next day Duncan is awoken by a loud whirring noise and a helicopter landing next to his private jet on the front lawn. It is a really big front lawn so they both fit.

O.M.G.!!! Svetlana is here!!!

Duncan hops out of bed and luckily he looks really good when he's just woken up despite what Anita always said about his eye bogeys. He throws on his sexiest tracksuit – his red one this time – and hurries downstairs, telling Cartwright to make tea, please, for the visitor and maybe prepare his bath for afterwards.

The doorbell rings and he goes to let Svetlana in, only to find Wanda on the doorstep, TOO! As he looks from one to the other, Duncan realises he loves them both. But he knows he cannot have them both and even though he loves them both he knows he must choose one of them right now. And he thinks he knows which one he is going to choose right now.

'Have you decided to sign my contract yet, Duncan?' says Svetlana, looking more good-looking than she ever has before in a really new-looking pink top and pink skirt.

Duncan shakes his head sadly. 'I am sorry, Lana, but I have decided that even though I love you and really, really fancy you, I cannot sign your contract. It is too scary and weird and also, I love Wanda. And so I choose Wanda. She might not have an enormous house or a helicopter in my garden, but she is really nice. What we have is solid and lovely and you don't risk getting your head chopped off when you climb into her Prius.'

Svetlana is DEVASTATED. She cannot believe her ears and tries to kiss Duncan again right there on the doorstep. Duncan is afraid for a moment that he will succumb to her dark allure, but Wanda gets in the way and Wanda is a lot bigger and stronger than Svetlana. For a moment it looks like they might have a fight, and Duncan cannot believe they would fight over him, even though women have fought over him a million times before. But at the last second, Svetlana glares at them both and then storms off into the garden where the helicopter awaits.

Wanda and Duncan cannot believe it and they look at each other for a really long time. And then they snog for a really long time in the hallway of Duncan's house, while Cartwright stands really close by, feeling so proud of his master but worrying that the tea and the bath are going to get cold.

When they stop snogging for half a second, Wanda says, 'Duncan, thank you for choosing me. I'm glad you love me. And

I have a secret to reveal now. I am secretly rich too, Duncan! I didn't want to tell you because I wanted you to love me and choose me for me, but now you have, I can reveal that I too have a massive house on the edge of town, with helicopters and butlers. I only bought this house next door to you to be close to you and cook nut roast for you very easily. So you can still keep your private jet and Lamborghini Veneno and there's even a spare wing for Cartwright to live in at my house so you don't have to sack him!'

It is really good news for everyone except maybe Cartwright who is clearly a bit jealous, and Wanda and Duncan snog a bit more and all the neighbours who've gathered round while all this was going on, all give a big cheer because they've always really liked Wanda and Duncan and have been rooting for them to get together ever since Anita left last Tuesday. It is a really happy ending.

But across the garden, as Svetlana climbs back into her helicopter, she turns back and catches Duncan's eye. 'I'll be back,' she mouths really sexily at him, and Duncan shivers . . .

THE END.

END SCENE

Epilogue

12.45 a.m. Wednesday, 1 January
Location: Maddie's New Year's Eve wedding. It's a huge do – turns out her dad is super wealthy – and there are about 250 guests in attendance, including my dad, Candice, Sophie, New Ryan, Thomas, Cassie, and a bunch of old work colleagues. I was assigned to the singles' table with Maddie's cousin and a bunch of twenty-year-old boys who keep calling me a cougar and trying to get off with me. Best wedding ever.

God, everyone's so drunk. Look at all of them. If I have to watch my dad putting his tongue down his fiancée's throat one more time I will actually start campaigning for euthanasia (euthanasia for old people who are in love, at least). I've been hanging out on the in-laws table for the past hour, sucking up to Maddie's parents to the point where they now definitely love me more than they love their daughter. They keep telling me I have to go over for Sunday dinner next weekend. I can't wait to tell Madds I'm taking her place in the will.

I glance over at the bride now. She's drunkenly slow dancing with Zack, even though the song playing is nineties banger 'Horny' by Mousse T. Everyone around them is jumping up and down and screaming, but they're totally, adorably oblivious.

It's been such a nice day. Maddie looked so incredible in

a silvery silk Ghost dress and long veil. And I, as is right and proper, looked dreadful in my pink shiny bridesmaid dress. The service was lovely, the food was delicious, the booze is free and the speeches went on too long. Oh, apart from Zack's speech, which was only four minutes because every three words, he would break down sobbing. Eventually Maddie made him sit down, wiping his snot with her veil as she did so. It was dead romantic.

I say goodbye to Madd's family and head over to join New Ryan, Sophie and Cassie on the dance floor. Across the room I spot Maddie's ex, Ben, and his new boyfriend, Dan, and I give them a wave. It's nice that Ben and Maddie are finally on good terms again. That custody battle over Alfred got really ugly for a while there, but this every-other-week deal seems to be working out OK so far. Sophie and Cassie WOO at me as I join them. They're dancing frantically moving just their hands in that way drunk people do. You know, when it's like their hands are the bus and Keanu Reeves will get blown up if they slow down for even a second. It's great fun and I start doing the small boxes and screaming all the words to yet another nineties classic; 'I'm A Bitch'. This wedding playlist is the best.

'Hey, where's Ciara tonight?' I ask New Ryan.

Sophie interrupts. 'She's with his bitch mother.'

'I can hear you!' New Ryan moans, looking pained.

Sophie blinks at him. 'I know you can?' She turns back to me. 'Yesterday that woman let herself in to our house and re-washed and re-ironed the load of laundry I'd just done. I got back with Ciara from nursery just as she was finishing and she just stared me out until I actually choked out a thank you. She's such a bitch. Never have a mother-in-law, they're the worst. Yet another reason to stay single.'

New Ryan shrugs, and I giggle. 'At least they're handy babysitters?' I try and New Ryan nods. Sophie's dancing gets more frantic.

It's been an interesting eight months. My gallery finally opened in November and it's doing pretty well. It's early days, obviously, but we've already featured some fantastic new artists and the reviews have been really kind. The job is everything I ever wanted. I work flexible hours, spend my days surrounded by beautiful things. My colleagues (employees!) are smart and cool, and I feel so stupidly inspired all the time. It's all I can do not to paint on the walls. In fact, this week Elizabeth suggested we turn one of the back stockrooms into a mini studio for me, which will be amazing. I asked if we could have a mini fridge for the Nutella and she said that was OK.

I've also been flat hunting like a maniac for the last few months. I wasn't having much success finding anything not-horrible in my price range, until this week, when I found a lovely little one-bed in west London. It's in a new building and I can't tell you how much the prospect of living with clean surfaces appeals to me. Everything is brand new, and there's no mould or Radox bottles in the bathroom. There's even a dishwasher – can you imagine? A DISHWASHER. I've put in an offer and am just waiting to hear, but I've got all my fingers crossed. As lovely as it's been living with Dad again, I realised over Christmas that I can't stick it out much longer. Jen and Milly came to stay for the week – no sign of Andrew again – and it all got very claustrophobic. I tried to talk to Jen a few times about her marriage, but she told me to mind my own business. She knows where I am if she does want to talk. And if she ever wants to leave him for real.

*

On the dance floor Cassie woos at me again and I woo back. This girl has fit into the group unbelievably well – it's like she was here all along. Sophie and I love her and we've informed Thomas that if he ever dares dump her, Cassie will retain full custody of us. She's just wonderful – always taking our side in arguments with him, and never once making any complaints about us spending so much time with her boyfriend. Actually, she and Thomas shared some big news with us a few minutes ago. They're planning on moving in together next month, and they're looking at flats near my new place! I'm totally thrilled (Sophie's obviously really jealous, her passive aggression came out so bad).

Still, I can't wait. It'll be exactly like *Friends* but with less ugly naked guy. I'm hoping for lots of hot naked guys.

Oh, and defying all known cat lady conventions, I got a dog at Christmas. Her name is Ryder and she comes everywhere with me. She and Peter are getting a bit too friendly though, which Jen said is proof that I am literally the only person who can't find a boy to have sex with me. What she doesn't know is that I've been having plenty of sex in the last few months. Remember Tinder Nathan? Yep, turns out I didn't scare him away by crying all over him that night. He texted me a few weeks later and we had a couple of dates. I quickly realised he was waaaaaay too messed up about his ex to be a real contender for Project Happiness, but he has a genuinely lovely penis, so we've stayed in touch. Stayed in touch genitally, I mean. We don't see that much of each other – it's super casual – but it's a very nice arrangement. And we have a great system worked out where, every time he mentions his ex in my presence, I sit on his face. That's how we ended up having sex in Warner's Park recently. That place is so defiled.

Someone taps me on the shoulder and I turn to find – ugh – Rich from the old office. I haven't seen him since I left The Hales in a blaze of glory, but I hear he's officially the deputy manager now and loving it. He's doing all the confrontational stuff that Derek can't handle but Maddie says he's just as bad at it. The only difference is that he sweats less. In fact, he had to be the one to sack my loo-twin Nick recently. I still can't believe all that – it was so dramatic. So, yeah, after their weird smooch-y dancing at my thirtieth last April, Ursula and Nick started having this major embarrassing office affair. My last few weeks at The Hales were spent watching them duck in and out of the loos, while Maddie and I messaged each other about wet patches on their clothes. It was hilarious and awful and not subtle in any way. Nick and I even stopped going to the bathroom at the same time, because he was in the disabled loo at least a couple of times a day doing it with Ursula. It carried on for months after I left. Derek and Rich kept pretending they didn't know anything, so they wouldn't have to deal with it, but when Ursula ended up leaving her husband for Nick, and then going back to her husband, and then back to Nick, I think they realised they couldn't ignore it any more. Nick and Ursula were hauled in and Rich informed them that the disabled loo was for the exclusive use of the one disabled guy The Hales has on its payroll, even though he's been working from home since 2008. Anyway, it got even more dramatic a couple of weeks ago when Nick turned up at the office on a Monday morning looking like he hadn't slept in three days. He announced to the whole room that Ursula had left him again, and he couldn't live without her. He flipped a desk!! Maddie put it all on Facebook Live and I watched as Nick was escorted out by security. It was pretty exciting for everyone. Poor Nick got sacked, obviously, but apparently Ursula has now left her husband once and for all, and she and Nick have shacked up together with her teenagers in St. Albans. I'm happy for them.

'Ellie!' Rich exclaims, happily. I wince.

'Yeah,' I say resentfully. I'm too drunk to be enthusiastic about small talk with people I hate. 'Hi, Rich. How are you?'

'I'm excellent, thanks, haha! What a wonderful day. Haha. Zack is a lucky guy, right? Haha. I had to miss the service earlier because I volunteer at an animal shelter on Saturday mornings, but I hear it was beautiful.'

Monster.

'It was lovely,' I confirm, looking around for help and making note to plan revenge on Cassie and Sophie who are both now deliberately dancing away and avoiding eye contact.

'So how is life?' he goes on, settling in for a big chat. 'I hear your gallery is doing really well, that is fantastic. I'm so pleased for you, Ellie.'

I roll my eyes, not very discreetly.

'Yeah, it's great,' I sigh. 'And congrats on the deputy manager position, Rich.' I so want to ask him about Nick and Ursula – that would send him scuttling away – but I resist the urge.

'Thank you!' He looks so pleased. 'So what else is new with you, Ellie? Have you finally trapped yourself a boyfriend? I'm sorry I'm not in the loop on the latest happenings . . .' (*latest happenings*? Ugh) 'I'm currently on a major internet and social media cleanse.' (Internet and social media cleanse? Ugh.) 'My life coach says –' (life coach? Ugh) '– it's super important for me to have the break, but, er, it means I haven't heard from any of my friends for weeks.'

Yeah, sure, *that's* the reason no one wants to talk to you.

'Sounds really great, Rich. And nope, I'm still very happily single.'

'Oh, I'm sorry, Ellie.'

I laugh. I can't help it.

'There is no need for apologies, Rich. Believe it or not, I like being single. I choose to be single. I'm happy.'

'You are such a trooper,' he says, doing the head tilt. 'Don't worry, I just *know* you'll get your Disney ending someday. You're a total catch, Eleanor Knight! Haha! Anyway, it's been so great talking to you, Ellie. I'm going to get a drink. BRB, haha!'

Cassie dances back over. 'Did that prick just say BRB out loud? As in, be right back? He said that *out loud*?'

'He's the worst,' Sophie confirms, shaking her head.

I laugh and we get back to our hand dancing.

I guess I know I'm always going to hear shit like that. The sympathy. The fake reassurances I don't need. It's part of being single. But I care so much less than I did a year ago. I have stopped feeling like I have to pretend to be looking for someone. Probably because my life is so totally brilliant. We can blame Disney all we like for this idea of a princess who needs rescuing by a prince/husband, but if you think about it; actually most of those Disney chicks wanted to escape those conventions as much as I do. Belle didn't want to marry the hot-as-fuck Gaston, she wanted an 'adventure in the great wide somewhere'. She wanted to escape her life and all those villagers who thought she was smart literally just because she was a female who could read (EVEN THOUGH SHE WAS TOTALLY CLEARLY READING CHILDREN'S BOOKS). Princess Jasmine didn't want to be forced to marry either. She tried so hard to escape the palace and her life as a princess – bro, she got *a tiger to eat all the princes who came to visit*! She couldn't have tried much harder to stay single.

(Hmm, mental note: look into buying tiger.)

Princess Ariel just wanted to go off and explore the human world and add to her thingymabob collection. Elsa wanted to literally chill in an ice palace. And who knows what Sleeping Beauty really wanted because she got cursed by a spinning wheel when she was just a kid, and then, while she was trying to sleep it off, she got sexually assaulted by a passing prince.

I could write a thesis on the subject. Maybe I will. I can do anything I want.

My point is, I can still have my 'Disney ending', thank you, Rich – thank you everyone. But a fairytale ending doesn't have to mean a prince riding in on his white horse to save me. It means adventures and fun and talking candlesticks – all of which I currently have (talking candlesticks TBC). I want my life to be exciting forever and full of possibility, not spent worrying about someone else's moods and bad day at work. I have love in my life in the form of friends and family. Being a third wheel works just fine – Delboy and Rodney had a three-wheeler and they ended up as millionaires. And, OK, maybe there will be a shining white knight eventually, but the point is I don't *need* him. I've never needed him. It took me a while, but I'm there, I know that now. I know what I'm capable of. I'm Ellie Knight, and I don't need a boyfriend. I might not be perfect, but I'm a hot mess who's getting her shit together, and I've bloody well rescued myself.

From: Alan Knight <Alanknightinshiningarmour@BTInternet.co.uk>
To: Eleanor.knight@gmail.com, Jennifer.seevy@hotmail.com

12th January

Alan Knight
106 Castle Rise
Judfield
East Sussex
TN22 5UN

Dear Eleanor and Jennifer,

I hope you are both very well. I am very happy because Candice has been encouraging me to watch "Hollyoaks" and I am really enjoying it!!! As you know, I was always afraid of "Hollyoaks" because of all the young people shouting. But it turns out that is not so very different to middle-aged people shouting, like on "Coronation Street" and "Eastenders". Candice has been such a "blessing" in my life and opened my eyes to lots of new things.

I'm so glad you enjoyed my third "short story" so much. Candice says she very much enjoyed the "rollercoaster ride" of this latest one, but said I probably should not have posted them all on "Twitter" because now I won't be able to sell them to a big "publishing house".

I think she's probably right, but I have now got 174,898 "followers" – is that good? Lots of them are "Twittering" me asking me to do more "short stories", so I have decided to continue with a whole "series" about Duncan James and his erotic tales with Svetlana and Wanda.

Of course, I will keep sending them to you, although you can also "follow" me if you like!!! L.O.L. Although, do either of you know why people keep "Twittering" me about "Blue" and writing things like "One Love" and "All Rise"? I am getting that a lot.

Anyway, Lenny, see you on Saturday for "house viewing". Candice and I are very much looking forward to seeing your new flat and we hope the sale "completes" quickly. Please do not think that means we are eager to get rid of you though. This will always be your home and you can stay as long as you would like.

I know I say this a lot, and I hope it doesn't lose its meaning because of that, but I love you both very much. You are both brave and clever and you inspire me to try and be those things every day. Your mum would be so very proud of you, I know I am. I'm bursting with it.

All our love,
Dad and Candice

From: Jennifer.seevy@hotmail.com
To: Eleanor.knight@gmail.com
Cc: Alan Knight <Alanknightinshiningarmour@BTInternet.co.uk>

He means me. You're still single and fat.

Acknowledgements

Before I begin, imagine me crying like Gwyneth Paltrow accepting her Oscar, but much redder and wearing Winnie the Pooh pyjamas.

There we go. Scene set.

When I was little I used to hide in the loo for hours reading every book I could find, and now here I am, with my own book I can read when I'm hiding in the loo. It's still completely surreal, and I am incredibly grateful to so many people. Firstly, to Katie Seaman at Orion, who made this entire thing happen and believed in me the whole time (even when I didn't). Thank you so much. Thanks also to Elaine, Laura, Sarah, Loulou, Mark and everyone else at Orion for working so hard on the book. You've been wonderful. Thanks to my amazingly cool agent Diana Beaumont at Marjacq, who has been all things; agent, crisis manager, friend, wine provider.

Enormous thank you to my entire huge, amazing family for being so brilliant and supportive. Mum, Nigel, Dale, Lisa, Carey, Nick, Phil, Dad, Liz, Frankie, Charlotte, Ali, Flo, Sam, Leon, Charlie, other Mum Ros and especially to my twin sister, Becky, who was the only civilian I let read the draft, and was so fucking lovely about the whole thing. Also thanks to her three little ones, Boo, Tizz, Lollipop (who requested a co-author credit but seriously, your suggestions were all rubbish).

Thanks to all my amazing friends, who've been such

cheerleaders too. Cookie, Fred, McHefferDoris, JD, Shell, Neil, The Legends; ClairBelle, Abi, Bell, and the other GFSC members; Ushman, Kate, Horse. Brilliant friends Daisy/Lucy, Wills, Ledge, Zoe, Rhi, Issy, Lynn, and the Paw Walkers. And just because I know it will freak him out, thanks also to my old A-Level English teacher, Mr Andrews.

And finally, thank you to all the fuckboys and all the nice boys I've met over the years, who helped inspire me. But, obviously, everything in this book is fiction, and if you spot yourself in here, you are an arrogant piece of shit and this is why I dumped you.

In summary: I REALLY, REALLY HOPE YOU DIDN'T HATE THIS BOOK.

Thanks.

Enjoyed

We'd love to hear from you

Leave a review online

Tweet @Lecv and @orionbooks with #HotMess

Follow Lucy on Twitter to stay up to date
with all her latest news, including details of
her new book coming in 2018